OVER YOUR
SHOULDER

CJ Carver

Praise For Over Your Shoulder

Praise for CJ Carver

"One of the best thriller writers working today"
Tom Harper, former CWA Chairman

"A terrific page-turner"
Harlan Coben

"Draws you in and keeps you on tenterhooks all the way to the end"
Waterstones Bookseller

"A gripping thriller, perfect for fans of Lee Child and Mason Cross"
The Guardian

"A top-notch thriller writer. Carver is one of the best.'
Simon Kernick

"A page-turning thrill"
Mick Herron

"Don't expect to sleep, because this is unputdownable"
Frost Magazine

Chapter one

We were on the sofa as usual at 10pm, watching the news. Susie lay curled next to me, her head resting against my chest, my arm around her. The BBC's political editor was discussing the Brexit narrative – nothing new that I could tell – and I was looking at the wood burner and thinking about nothing more than putting on another log, when Susie went quite still.

Whenever she did that – not that often to be honest – I was reminded of a wild animal. A rabbit who'd just sighted a fox. Or a wolf sizing up their prey. It depended on the situation. I quickly checked for spiders (Susie hates spiders, they are the only thing that seems to freak her out) and since we appeared to be spider-free, I followed her gaze to the TV, unable to see what had triggered her sudden tension.

The reporter was talking about a terror attack in London that happened earlier that day. Susie worked in London. That was weird, because she hadn't mentioned anything. I glanced down at her but she was immersed in the TV, where the BBC reporter was pointing across a large pedestrian area strewn with police cars and news vans.

Apparently, a masked gunman had entered a restaurant and opened fire while yelling *Allāhu Akbar!* Four people had died and eight had been injured but it could have been much worse except for one of the diners who had taken the gunman on. Incredibly, the man had launched himself at the terrorist and either through luck or excellent timing hadn't been shot. The second he'd brought the gunman down, three other men had joined in, disarming the attacker before sitting on him until the police arrived.

'He's been called a superhero,' the journalist was saying. 'And like a superhero he's vanished. As soon as police officers arrived and arrested the gunman, our unidentified hero disappeared. All we have is CCTV footage.'

As the screen changed to a grainy black and white image, Susie yawned. Stretched a little before settling back in my arms.

I watched as a man in a balaclava, dressed in dark jeans and fleece, charged into the restaurant, firing his weapon. A man to one side launched himself from his table, diving for the gunman with no seeming concern for his safety, laying the gunman flat. I watched him deliver a full-fisted punch into the face – followed by a powerful blow to the throat – and wrestle the gun free. At that moment other men piled in too, but there was something about the first man – the hero everyone was talking about – that had me riveted. Was it his unreserved heroism? The way he hadn't hesitated? Or was it the efficiency of his blows? As he sat astride the gunman's chest, he looked up, straight into the camera's lens. My heart stopped. My ears rang.

He was older, but then he would be. Twelve years had passed since we'd last seen one another. His hair was longer, curling at the nape, but appeared just as untidy. His face had always been boyish, but now it looked leaner, more mature. His gaze was direct, his eyes blazing from the adrenaline rush – a look I could remember all too well from when we competed against each other. My heart gave a gigantic thump when I saw the scar I'd given him when he was three still marred his chin.

I heard the reporter asking viewers to help identify the superhero but the voice faded into the background as the years poured away.

I was no longer in our cottage with my wife in my arms. I was standing on a wind-blasted beach staring at the debris of an eighteen-foot skiff shattered by one of the worst storms to hit the south coast in a decade. I was listening to the policeman telling me this was all there was, that they'd found no flotation devices, no body.

I was looking at the pieces of wreckage and hearing Mum sob.

I was shivering with grief as I laid a wreath on his grave.

I stared at the TV, straight into the eyes of my brother, Rob, who'd supposedly drowned at sea. He was still alive.

Chapter two

No sooner had my brother's face disappeared from the TV screen when our phone rang. I should say phones, because not only did our landline ring but my mobile and Susie's too. I didn't move. I didn't want to speak to anyone. I wanted to sit by the fire and pretend I hadn't seen my brother. I wanted to pretend he was dead and that he hadn't let me bury him, grieve over him and miss him with a gut-wrenching loss that could still catch me unawares. Above all, I didn't want to face the fact the brother I loved, had looked out for since he was born, had betrayed me. Had *lied* to me all this time.

'Nick?' Susie had twisted round and was staring at me. 'Was that who I thought it was?'

Our phones continued to ring but neither of us moved to answer them. I felt numb, my emotions oddly suspended.

'Nick.' She gripped my hands in hers. My skin felt icy against her warmth. Shock, I suppose.

'Was it Rob?' she insisted. *'Was it him?'*

I didn't want to speak. Instead I gave a nod.

'Fuck.'

'Fucksake. Where the fuck…?' She closed her eyes briefly. 'I can't…' She exhaled. 'Fuck.'

Nausea washed through me. I needed to breathe. I got to my feet. Walked to the front door. Opened it. A rush of cold air laced with the smell of seaweed and salt steadied me a little. I felt Susie come to stand at my shoulder.

'You okay?' she asked.

I didn't respond. Just stared out into the blackness of the harbour.

'You want me to come with you?'

I shook my head.

She offered me my sailing jacket but I stepped outside without taking it even though it was close to freezing. For some reason, I needed the cold. There was no moon and the sky was a brilliant black scattered with stars.

Bosham – pronounced Bozz-um, another of those bizarre English names that don't sound like they're spelled – was a heartbreakingly pretty village with a harbour in its centre. I loved high tide when the sea came right into the village, flooding the lower road and several car parking spaces. There were warning signs everywhere but visitors still got caught out when they returned from a look around the church, or a pint in The Anchor Bleu, to find their car practically floating out to sea.

We lived in a quaint cottage whose official name was Sea Breeze but which Susie called the Mouse House. I bought it because it had a studio on the second floor, along with French windows and a tiny balcony. From my desk, if I leaned out and craned my neck slightly, I could see the sea. It has one bedroom, one bathroom and the ground floor's one large room combining a kitchen and sitting room with a worktop in between. There's a small garden, but I'm not a gardener by any stretch of the imagination so I employed my aunt's gardener, Mrs Downing, to keep it in shape. She planted flowers I never know the name of along with a variety of herbs, and created a really nice space that I use all the time in summer. I thought the cottage would be too small for two, but luckily Susie fell in love with it.

'It's the perfect weekend getaway,' she told me, beaming. She had her own flat in London, a large modern white and chrome space with bleached wooden floors in the heart of Chelsea. I never asked how she could afford it and assumed her parents must have had a hand in its purchase because as far as I knew, she had no mortgage and owned it outright. Lucky me, marrying into money. I pay for the upkeep of the cottage, while Susie takes care of her flat. She stays there four nights a week: Monday to Friday.

Sometimes she works from home but not that often. Besides, I think she likes her space and for me, absence makes my heart grow fonder and our weekends are usually fantastic reunions. We've talked about selling both our places and buying somewhere bigger closer to London, but that's all it's been. Talk. I'm not sure if living away from the water would necessarily be easy for me, but I'd give anything a go for Susie. She's the love of my life, and I'd pretty much do anything to make her happy.

I turned the corner and paused, looking at the breadth of harbour, the outlines of a handful of skiffs bobbing gently on the water and lights from the village shimmering in the black. This was where Rob and I had learned to sail. This was where I'd taught Susie to sail. We'd met at Rob's memorial and now he wasn't dead after all.

I stood quite still, staring at the view. I was perfectly aware I was keeping my thoughts light. I felt as though if I let my true emotions out, actually looked at what Rob had done to us – to me – I might lose it. So I kept my thoughts skimming across the surface of my emotions. Skim-skim, like a shiny grey stone gleaming above the water and never sinking into the depths below.

I could picture Rob as a toddler in my skiff, clutching the side and shrieking every time the wind caught the sail and tipped us towards the water. I could picture Susie as clearly, her narrow intelligent face topped by a frown of concentration, her deep brown eyes intent on the job in hand. I loved watching her at the tiller, her silky hair snapping in the breeze, her slender body taut as wire, her hands quick and capable. She'd look up and our eyes would meet and I'd feel a kick in my stomach, a punch in my heart, and she'd grin, safe in her feminine confidence and power – she knew I adored every inch of her.

How much do you love me? she'd tease.

To Betelgeuse and back. With no beginning, no end. I love you without knowing how, or when, or from where. I will love you until I die, and if there's an afterlife, I'll love you then.

Susie and Rob. The two people I loved most in the world

It may sound odd, but I'd always thanked Rob for getting Susie and me together. If he hadn't died, she'd never have come to Bosham to pay her respects and we would have had a whole other life apart from one another. Whenever I think how it could have been, I feel a chill in my heart because I've never loved any woman like Susie. She's a one-off, the only woman I've met who loves sailing and rollercoasters as much as I do. I wondered whether Rob knew we'd married. What he thought about it.

Susie had met Rob through someone at work, apparently. Yup, that's right. My feckless kid brother, who we despaired about because he couldn't hold down a job – he'd get bored, get restless, itching for something more exciting, more fun – had actually been hanging out with grown-ups at the civil service. She'd met him several times at social events and liked him enough to join a couple of Rob's work colleagues and come to his memorial service.

Had Rob's skiff *Kingfisher* got into trouble and he'd taken the opportunity to vanish? Maybe he'd suffered memory loss? Or had he orchestrated the entire scenario? If so, *why?* I suddenly wanted to talk to Susie. She may not have known him well, but she might know someone who did. Maybe she could give me another insight.

Time to head home.

Chapter three

No sooner had Nick vanished into the darkness of the harbour than his family turned up. His mum, dad, Aunt Julia and Nick's sister Kate and her husband Simon crammed into the kitchen area, all talking at once. Susie hastily poured them all drinks. Whisky for her father-in-law, white wine for everyone else except Simon, who only drank red. Susie stuck to water. She may have felt like downing a treble vodka and tonic – actually snapping open a bottle and necking it down neat would be more appropriate – but she wanted to keep a clear head.

Now she'd got over the initial shock, her nerves had steadied. She had to be honest, she couldn't help admiring Rob for faking his own death. Because that was what he'd done, wasn't it? She remembered the column on the second page of *The Guardian*.

The boat builder and international sailor's body was never found despite an extensive air, sea and coast search after debris from his yacht was found washed ashore.

Clever, huh? She'd fallen for it along with everyone else, and his ruse had kept him safe. But for how long?

Susie poured everyone another round of drinks, letting their panicky talk wash over her: *Where's he been? What's he been doing? Is it really him? It's been twelve years. Why did he take Kingfisher out when he knew there was a storm brewing? Why did he sail into danger? How did he survive the storm? Why hasn't he rung? Susie, did Nick know he was alive? What about you?*

Susie shook her head and excused herself to move into the living area, where she called Rob's wife, Clara, who everyone seemed to have forgotten. Luckily, Clara hadn't seen the news and Susie took advantage of the fact to ask a few questions before telling her what had happened. When she hung up, poor Clara sounded as though she'd been rabbit-punched in the gut.

Next, Susie rang the office but they already had a team checking the CCTV to see if they could get a bead on Rob. Not for the first time, she wondered if she'd made a mistake not telling Nick what her real job was. What her relationship had been with Rob before he'd supposedly drowned. She was naturally secretive – hence being drawn to a secretive world – but it was more than that. She wanted to protect him. Not have him worry about her, or be put on the spot when talking about her work. Then there was the small problem that he was a terrible liar. He wouldn't give her away on purpose, but he'd still give her away. Plus, he'd probably want to tell his family, and she didn't want that. What she did was her business, not theirs.

She was aware that she might have to tell him at some point, but if she thought about it for too long she got a panicky sensation in her lungs because she knew he'd take it badly. The time she should have told him was well past. All she could hope for was that if… or *when* she told him, he'd understand her reasons, and forgive her. Because life without Nick – her entire world, her *raison d'être* – life would be untenable.

Chapter four

I hadn't been gone long, fifteen minutes max, but by the time I returned the family had descended. That's the trouble when you don't move from the village where you've spent your childhood. Everyone lives seconds away, and everyone, it seemed, had been watching the ten o'clock news.

Susie topped up Dad's whisky before grabbing a fresh one and pouring one for me, but I didn't take it. I didn't want alcohol to blur my senses. I was surrounded by my family, all talking over one another, their voices rising into a hysterical pitch.

I held up both hands in the faint hope they might calm down. 'I know as much as you do. I saw him on TV tonight. That's it. That's all I know.'

'You'll find him, darling,' Mum said. 'Won't you.'

It was a statement, not a request.

'And bring him back,' my sister added, 'so I c-can…' She started to break down but with a huge effort, she swallowed, adding firmly, 'So I can sodding well kill him.'

Mum put her arm around Kate and they held each other, crying. Although Mum was in her mid-sixties, the resemblance between them was strong. Soft curly brown hair, wide brown eyes and open features that made people like and trust them instantly. Rob took after them. I looked more like our father. Taller, darker, lots more angles.

'Ditto that,' Dad growled.

Simon took a slug of wine. 'We should contact the journalists,' he said. 'The BBC. I mean Rob's a *hero*. They'll track him down for us.'

'No.' The word was said very flat.

Everyone turned to look at Susie.

'We need to find him first.'

Simon opened and closed his mouth. 'But it could take us twice as long. They've got resources we haven't.'

'There's a reason why he disappeared,' Susie continued. 'What if he was in danger? What if, by finding him, we bring that danger to him again?'

Everyone looked blank but I could see the sense in what she said, *if* Rob had been in danger, that was. But what in the hell could it have been? Why hadn't I known about it?

'I think Susie might be right,' I said cautiously. She sent me a swift smile of encouragement so I added, 'We should be asking ourselves why he vanished, and why he's pretended he's been dead for the past twelve years.'

Silence.

'Perhaps he got hit on the head,' Kate offered, 'and he's got memory loss.'

More silence.

'What if he hasn't got memory loss?' Susie suggested gently.

I drew in a deep breath. 'He didn't hang around waiting for the accolades today, did he. As soon as the police turned up, he disappeared. He's the *unknown hero*. It's my guess he doesn't want anyone to know it was him.'

They were all staring at me as if I was talking Swahili, but after another look of reassurance from Susie, I ploughed on. 'I think we should give him the opportunity to explain himself to us first, and before we drag in any journalists.'

'What sort of danger?' Mum was looking baffled. 'I don't understand.'

'Are you saying he set up his skiff's wreck?' Kate's eyes rounded. 'That he *planned* it?'

'But how did he get ashore?' Simon was shaking his head from side to side like a baffled buffalo. 'That couple saw him way out in the Channel. I know he was a strong swimmer, but it was crazy out there…'

Everyone was talking at once and through the bedlam, Susie's phone rang. She checked the display and, to my surprise, handed it to me. My heart faltered when I saw who it was. Rob's wife, Clara. The wife who – twelve years earlier – had buried her husband with two toddlers at her side.

I took the phone to the studio.

'Is it true?' she asked. Her voice trembled. 'Susie rang me. She didn't want it to come as a shock in case I heard it elsewhere.'

'Yes,' I agreed, feeling like the worst brother-in-law in the world. I hadn't even thought of Clara. Thank God for Susie.

'Is it him?' she pressed.

'I think so. I mean, he's older, but he hasn't changed much. He still has that scar I gave him on his chin.'

'Oh, God.'

I let a silence fall. I couldn't begin to think what she was going through. I remembered the Coroner stating that Robert Ashdown, twenty-five, most likely died by drowning when he went missing on Saturday August twenty-fourth. *I feel strongly this is not a suicide. I want to be perfectly clear that is not the situation here.* After the inquest, Clara said that although the ruling put legal closure to her husband's disappearance, no one would ever know what had happened, or why Rob had uncharacteristically taken his eighteen-foot skiff out when a storm was blowing up.

'Does this mean my marriage is null and void?' Clara asked. She was breathing hard. 'That it doesn't exist?'

She was talking about her current marriage, obviously. After Rob's death, Clara didn't date for years. Not until the kids were ten and eight. Rob and Clara had lived in Bosham and even though Rob had eventually got full time work in London, they'd never discussed moving closer to the city. Like Susie, he'd commuted.

After he died, Clara stayed in Bosham where we all helped out. I babysat sometimes, and when the kids grew up – Finn was fifteen, Honey fourteen – I taught them how to sail. Clara met her second husband John at the sailing club – where else? – and they got married within the year. What John was going through right now was anyone's guess, but having your wife's dead husband suddenly pop up on the TV had to be one of the world's least pleasant experiences.

'I don't know,' I said, 'but I can't imagine anyone's going to come after you guys for infidelity.'

She started to cry. My heart twisted. She and Rob had been childhood sweethearts and although they were having a rocky period when Rob vanished – a house filled with nappies and squalling never helped anybody's mood – I'd never had any doubt about their love for one another. He'd sold his car – a third-hand Ford Fiesta – in order to buy Clara an engagement ring. I'd rolled my eyes at what I perceived to be an act of romantic folly – I couldn't live without my car – but Clara had adored him for it. As usual, he'd landed on his feet when Aunt Julia told a friend of hers about Rob's grand gesture and the friend sold him her little Vauxhall for a song. He always came out on top, Rob, no matter what he got up to. At least that's what I'd thought, until today.

I heard voices clamouring in the background. Finn and Honey. My heart twisted a second time. How could Rob have done this to them?

'Do you want to come over?' I asked Clara. 'Everyone's here.'

She didn't hesitate. 'We're on our way.'

Chapter five

It was three o'clock in the morning when everyone finally went home. Susie and I sat on stools at the kitchen worktop. I did some more staring at the fire.

'Thanks,' I said after a while. I leaned over and gave her arm an I-love-you squeeze. 'I don't know what I'd do without you. You're a trouper.'

'They're my family too.' She sighed. 'I'd do anything for them, you know.' She slid me a cautious look. 'Are they serious about you finding him?'

Being the eldest, it nearly always fell on me to be the responsible one and look out for the others, and today it was no different. When my family left that night, they kissed and hugged me and told me they were so glad I was going to find Rob, and to let them know what I wanted them to do and they'd do it. I'd been elected Vice Admiral of the Family Fleet a while ago (Dad was still the admiral though) and right now I felt a bit like my sister, happy to find my baby brother so I could kill him for putting us through this.

'Yes.'

'How are you going to go about it?' She was frowning.

'I don't know.' I suddenly felt exhausted. 'I'll think about it tomorrow.'

Susie spooned me in bed that night, pressing her lithe form against my spine and kissing the skin between my shoulder blades. I fell asleep to the sound of her soft breathing.

As usual, Susie left for work the next morning to catch the 0618 train to Victoria. I felt the bed dip as she came to kiss me goodbye.

'Hmmm.' I hooked an arm around her and pulled her close. I was about to slip my hand beneath her jacket to the silk shirt below to stroke the small of her back with my fingertips when I suddenly remembered.

Rob. My brother was alive.

Abruptly I opened my eyes.

The room was dark. A slim strip of orange outlined the curtains from the streetlight outside.

'Hope Clara's all right,' Susie murmured. 'Let me know what she says.'

During the mayhem the previous night, Susie had gleaned from Clara that the day before Rob vanished – a Saturday – he'd had three men visit him at home. It was the first I'd heard of it, but then we hadn't been analysing anything at the time because we thought we knew where he was – sailing his woefully small skiff into the English Channel. He'd been *seen* going out by the Quay Master, along with a couple in a motorboat who were returning into Chichester Harbour. They'd apparently passed him going out as they were motoring past Eastoke Point.

Susie pressed a kiss against my lips. 'Love you.'

'Hmm. Me too. Look…' I pushed up onto an elbow. 'You don't have to come back tonight. It's a horrible commute.'

'I'll be on the nineteen thirty-two,' she said firmly.

Which got into Bosham at eleven minutes past nine. I'd make sure I'd have something hot for her to eat when she got in. It wouldn't have to be anything special. Susie wasn't a great foodie and saw food more as fuel than something to be savoured, so a big bowl of pasta or chilli con carne would be fine.

I lay in bed and listened to her leave. I didn't think I'd fall asleep again but the next thing I knew it was light and next door's dog was barking to be let in for its breakfast. Which meant it was just before eight o'clock. The precise time I woke up every day. Nice to know my body clock wasn't affected by my brother's sudden reappearance.

As I climbed out of bed, I wondered who else might have recognised him. His old school friends maybe? The Ashdown family might not have been the only ones who'd got a shock watching the TV the previous night.

Before I showered, I texted Clara and told her I'd come over to her place later. Then I checked the BBC news website. Rob was fourth under the Most Popular column: ***Unknown hero tackles armed killer.***

An unknown man brought down an armed killer who opened fire in a popular Italian restaurant yesterday in central London, killing four people and injuring another eight. Dramatic video footage shows the fearless bystander leap onto the murderer as he strafed the restaurant.

My chest hollowed as I studied the photographs. There were quite a few thanks to people's mobile phones snapping him as he sat atop the gunman. My mind buzzed with what felt like a million trapped bees, but one thought sat quietly in the centre: It was my brother.

No doubt about it.

He wore black jeans and a leather jacket over a T-shirt. A pair of suede Chelsea boots. He looked casual but stylish. I'd always envied his effortless flair with clothes. We could wear the same outfit – shorts, sailing fleece and deck shoes – but where he'd look cool, I merely looked workmanlike. Same went for everything really. Rob had the golden touch, the effortless charm, the *joie de vivre* that most people found irresistible. I was the stodgy elder brother, the sensible one, and yes, okay, people liked me – just not as much as Rob.

As I pictured him the last time I saw him, standing at The Anchor Bleu bar, his hair tousled and salt-whipped, his cheeks as round and red as a pair of billiard balls, his head thrown back as he laughed his infectious laugh, I felt a pain tear through me like a chainsaw.

I bent double and wrapped my arms around my middle.

I heard a weird groaning sound, like a horse in agony, and with a shock, I realised it was me.

I couldn't get Rob's image out of my head. He'd been drinking with Etienne, a sailing buddy of his. The pub's landlord had just posed a question from his crossword – a double entendre – and they were ribbing one another. When Rob had seen me, he'd beckoned me over, hooked an arm around my shoulders and bought me a pint. My brother, who I liked enormously, loved deeply and trusted absolutely, had betrayed me.

Something inside me, an innate instinct, knew that nothing would be the same again.

Where had he been?

The pain inside me twisted. Feelings rioted through me. I'd *trusted* Rob. Why hadn't he told me the truth? If he'd been in danger, why hadn't he come to me?

I remembered him being bullied at primary school, two boys taking his pocket money as well as his sweets, and although he'd begged me not to do anything – he was convinced my intervention would make things worse – I'd lain in wait for the two toerags and jumped them when they weren't expecting it. I'd grabbed one and punched him straight on the nose. I can still see his face, filled with a combination of surprise and horror. The other boy legged it, but neither of them bothered Rob again.

I tried to think why he'd lied. Allowed us to think he was dead. I thought about the coastguard's search for him. The police and their kindness in alerting us each time a fresh piece of debris from *Kingfisher* was found ashore. I considered the pain we'd gone through.

Gradually, anger seeped past the other emotions and took root. It rose from my belly and into my heart, snaking through me as hot as fire. It burned all my other emotions clean.

I wanted answers, and I wanted them from him.

Chapter six

I made a coffee – Susie had bought us a Nespresso machine the week she'd moved in – and sipped it looking out over the garden. Being February, it was looking particularly drab. No flowers, not even a snowdrop. Leafless shrubs surrounded a muddy lawn that the blackbird had ripped up searching for worms.

Who had Rob been meeting at the restaurant? Susie had managed to see on the TV that although it looked as though he'd been on his own, two glasses of wine were on the table. She's got the eyes of a sharpshooter that girl.

Who had he been meeting?

I looked up the restaurant's phone number and called, but unsurprisingly, nobody was answering. It was no doubt full of investigators and forensic experts bagging every bullet, photographing every drop of blood spilled. I looked at the BBC report again. I couldn't explain it, but I had an increasing urge to go there. See the spot where Rob had launched himself at the gunman. See the table where he'd sat. And if I was lucky, talk to people who'd seen him.

I'd just put on my coat, when the phone rang. Susie's dad. Victor Fleming. For a moment I dithered, but then I realised I'd have to speak to him at some point.

'Hi, Victor.'

'Susie sent me an email. I've checked out the news your end about the man who stopped that terrorist in London. She says it's your brother. Is that right?'

'Yes.' I sighed.

'They don't have his name yet. The media, I mean.'

'No.'

'I won't ring up *The Sun*, if you're worried.' Victor tried to make light of it. 'How are you bearing up? What about your mum and dad?'

'We're all a bit shocked.'

'I can imagine.'

'But we're okay.'

Short pause.

'Where,' he asked, 'do you think he's been?'

'No idea.'

'He saved those people in the restaurant. He's a hero.'

'Yes.'

Another pause.

'Look,' he said. 'Tell Susie I rang. And I know we're not exactly around the corner but if we can do anything, let us know.'

Talk about a British understatement. Just after Susie had graduated from uni, Victor and Marjory had retired to New Zealand, the furthest country from the UK. Living the outdoor life – hiking endless scenic trails, trout fishing – along with owning a winery and building their own luxury ocean-view home – had been a dream of theirs for years. Thankfully for me, it hadn't been Susie's dream. She'd had nothing but a career in London in mind. *The centre of the universe,* was how she'd put it. *Why would I go to a backwater like New Zealand?*

'Will do,' I said, although I doubted we'd call upon them. 'Thanks, Victor.'

'Love to you both.'

I hung up. Got in the car. Drove to the office. I may have had a studio at home, but I hadn't made the move to start my own business yet. Susie nagged me, saying I could do a lot better being self-employed, but I liked having the guarantee of a wage every month. It allowed me to sleep every night without panicking about how to pay the electricity bill, or my mooring fees. One day, I'd do it. But not quite yet. Maybe next year.

Ronja was already at her drawing board when I arrived. She's Swedish and spectacularly tall with a mane of blonde hair that turns every male head wherever she goes. She'd set up UrStudio with her English boyfriend over ten years earlier. The boyfriend is now long gone, but she's still here, along with the rest of us – half a dozen designers housed in an airy building overlooking Eastgate Square in the centre of Chichester, not so much a square as a broad area with four roads conjoining.

We do branding, logo and graphic, website and digital design with motion graphics, video, infographic. Big agency vision, Ronja always said, with the personal touch of a Chichester boutique. Our clients range from a dental practice to a bespoke jeweller and a countywide recycling company. Ronja had landed our biggest client just before Christmas, HAPS, and given them to me to develop their brand nationwide as well as their presence online. On the one hand I was delighted to have such a big company to take on but on the other struggled with finding much creative joy in heating and plumbing services let alone things like angled bypass valves and saddle clips. Still, it brought in the money so I couldn't complain.

'Hey,' Ronja greeted me.

'Hey.' I looked around. The others were still settling in, making coffee, chatting. 'Could I have a word? Um… just us two?'

She looked surprised, but nodded and got to her feet. I followed her into the meeting room, closed the door behind me.

'Thanks.' I ran a hand over my head, gathering my thoughts. Then I told her about Rob.

'Good God,' she said when I finished. Her blue eyes were wide, her mouth parted. 'That's incredible.'

'Yes,' I agreed.

Before I could ask about taking some time off, she said, 'You must go and find him. Find out what's going on. Take the time you need. I'll look after HAPS for the moment. Are you okay with that?'

'Of course.'

'Can I do anything else to help?'

'Giving me time off is fantastic. Thank you.'

'Seriously, Nick.' She came and stood close to me, and put her hand on my arm, expression sincere. 'Call me if I can help in any way. I mean it. We've known each other a long time. We're friends. I'd like to help.'

Before I could thank her again, someone knocked on the door and without waiting for our response, one of the designers opened it. 'Sorry,' he said, 'but there's someone here to see Nick.'

He stepped back as a man walked inside. Thirties, flat brown hair cut short. Chunky build. He was wearing a big navy overcoat over dark trousers and jacket. 'Nick Ashdown?' he asked.

'Yes?' I said.

'DI Gilder.'

Even as I felt my lungs compress and my heartbeat accelerate, I somehow managed to keep my composure. He brought out a wallet, flashing a warrant card, too fast for me to see. I asked him to show it again, making a point of reading it properly and ignoring the way his mouth pursed. *Metropolitan Police. Detective Inspector Barry Gilder.* For no reason other than bloody-mindedness, I made a mental note of his six-digit warrant number.

'You're a long way from home,' I remarked, glad my voice was calm, my attitude nonchalant.

DI Gilder sent Ronja a pointed look. 'If you wouldn't mind…'

'You've found my brother?' I asked.

Gilder was still looking at Ronja, waiting for her to leave.

'If you need anything…' she said, looking at me, not the policeman.

I gave her a nod. She closed the door behind her with a little click.

'So,' Gilder said. 'You know he's not dead.'

'Yes. I saw him on TV last night, along with however many millions of others. Have you found him?'

DI Gilder shook his head. 'I was hoping you might have.'

'Me?'

'I thought if he contacted anyone, it would be you.'

For a moment I was speechless. 'But he let me think he'd drowned. I organised his memorial. Why the hell would he contact me? So I could punch his lights out?'

Gilder's eyes narrowed. 'Are you saying he hasn't been in touch?'

Caution rose in me as I remembered Susie's warning that Rob might not want to be found. 'Why do you want to know?'

Gilder held my gaze. He seemed to be considering how to answer. Then he said, 'He might need help.'

'What sort of help?'

'My kind.'

I stared.

Gilder spread his hands peaceably. 'I can understand you're feeling angry, probably confused. But I'm sure he disappeared for a good reason. I just want to make certain he's all right, and in a safe place.'

'In a safe place?' I repeated. 'What does that mean? And what exactly was the "good" reason that made him disappear?'

Silence.

I took a breath. 'You said *he disappeared for a good reason*. You can't just drop that into the conversation as if you're talking about the weather. What reason?' My voice rose.

More silence.

'Come ON,' I said. 'You have to tell me. I'm his *brother*.'

'It's complicated,' Gilder said. 'Do you have *any* idea where he might be? Any idea at all?'

My lips tightened. 'No.'

He studied me at length. 'Don't think you can protect him.'

'How can I do that if I don't know where he is?' Belligerence laced my voice. I could feel rage building. 'Or why he vanished in the first place? Why does he need protecting? Come on, tell me.' I took a step forward.

He didn't like that. 'Careful, Nick.'

He'd used my first name. I didn't like that much either.

'If you hear from him, call me.' He put a hand in his breast pocket and withdrew a card. Passed it across. Without dropping my gaze from his, I snatched it from him and shoved it in my jeans pocket.

'Don't leave,' I said. 'Until you tell me what's going on. How do you know Rob?'

He didn't respond. His face turned perfectly bland.

'What made him disappear?' Emotions spilled as hot as molten lava, nearly choking me.

'Just call me,' Gilder said.

'No, wait. You're from the Met. You knew my brother in London, right?'

He turned to leave. I put out a hand, wanting to stop him.

'Don't touch me,' he said.

His voice was like ice.

I snatched my hand back.

Without looking at me, he opened the door and stepped outside.

Chapter seven

I followed DI Gilder out of the office but my surveillance skills were obviously zero because within ten minutes, I had lost him. Had he known I was there? Or was I just useless at this game? Probably a combination of the two. That said, I hadn't given up easily, scouring the area fast, widening my search until I ended up at the station. Since I was there, I bought a ticket for London, Victoria, and headed to the Italian restaurant in South Kensington where Rob had jumped on the terrorist.

When I exited the tube it was to a phalanx of white vans with enormous satellite dishes on their roofs, bunches of paparazzi and journalists swarming for sound bites. Police officials were everywhere. The whole area was bound with blue and white police tape. Members of the public crowded the pavement, gawking and taking snaps on their mobiles.

I stepped as close as I dared to see the chaos that had exploded inside the restaurant. Two floor-to-ceiling glass windows were shattered. Tables and chairs inside were turned over, cutlery and tableware scattered across the floor. In the deli section, bottles of wine and olive oil lay smashed. It was a large restaurant, seating around a hundred people. If Rob hadn't intervened, many more would have died. No wonder he'd been labelled a hero.

'Move on, would you, sir.' A policewoman was looking at me, her eyes hard.

'I'm sorry,' I said. 'It's just that a friend of mine said they were going to lunch here yesterday. Who should I speak to about finding out whether they're okay or not?'

The policewoman gave me another stony stare. 'Me, if you like.'

I didn't like, particularly, but I ploughed on. 'Thanks.'

'What's their name?'

'Bethany Champs.' God knows how I came up with that one. I didn't know any Bethany's, let alone Champs.

The policewoman turned away slightly and spoke into the radio clipped to the webbing on her shoulder. She turned back to me. 'We don't have a record of anyone by that name being here yesterday.'

'She might have hidden in the toilets when the gunman opened fire then run away afterwards.'

The policewoman stood there and stared at me. I struggled to hold her gaze.

'I suggest you move on, sir,' she said, proving she was better at weeding out fraudsters than I was at lying.

I walked away. When she was out of sight, blocked by another plain white van, I peered again at the restaurant. Where had he sat? Where were the CCTV cameras? I craned my head, trying to imagine where his table had been positioned. I pictured him sitting there, calm as can be, and then the gunman striding inside and opening fire...

Someone coughed behind me.

'You know someone who was in there?'

I turned to see a round-faced woman in a puffer jacket.

Wary, I shrugged, not saying anything.

She stepped forward and lowered her voice. I had to bend to hear her clearly which, I supposed, was what she wanted.

'They didn't get everyone's name,' she told me. 'Three or four people disappeared before the police arrived. People who shouldn't have been there because they should have been at home sick, or at work, or maybe they were here with someone they shouldn't be with and didn't want to get caught out.'

She looked up at me, her eyes asking the question, bright with curiosity.

I tried to work out if a journalist could help me and decided not to open that particular door. What was I doing here anyway? I looked around, feeling at a loss and oddly emotional.

'He was meeting a woman,' she said softly.

My eyes snapped back to hers. 'I'm sorry?'

'The superhero. He'd brought a small bouquet with him apparently. The waitress remembered.'

I stared at her, my mind filled with a rush of images. Rob aged four, clutching a bunch of wild flowers he'd picked for Mum. Rob pinning a corsage on Clara's dress at his junior prom. Rob giving Clara a single red rose every Valentine's Day. I felt a pain deep in my heart for Clara and the children, and also for Rob who'd loved his family so much.

'Where is he?' she went on, her voice gentle. 'Do you know?'

I blinked.

'Tell me, how does it feel to have a superhero as your brother?' She put her head on one side. 'He is your brother, isn't he?'

For a second, I thought I'd misheard her, but then it hit me. Someone who knew Rob must have rung the media, no doubt wanting to sell their story. The media obviously had photographs and biographies of the entire family at their fingertips. My God, they moved fast.

I walked away.

She followed, calling after me. 'Ted Scott told me Rob must have faked his own death. How do you feel about that?'

I would happily wring Ted's neck when I next saw him. He ran the tea shop in Bosham and probably saw this as his great opportunity to put his tea shop on the national map and make him a millionaire overnight. I increased my pace.

'Nick, wait a moment.'

I heard her pattering after me. I broke into a jog.

'Hey, wait… we can give you an exclusive. Put your side of the story across.'

I lengthened my stride. Raced into the tube station's entrance and galloped down the steps. I flashed my Oyster card over the card reader and ran down the escalator. Jumped on the first train I came to, which happened to be a Piccadilly line train for Cockfosters. Wrong train.

Nerves hopping, I checked the passengers but couldn't see the journalist or anyone taking an overt interest in me. I changed at Green Park and one stop later, I was at Victoria Station.

My train didn't leave for twenty minutes, which I spent in Costa Coffee anxiously keeping an eye out for anyone who might start to approach me. I brought up the BBC News website. Read a quote that was attributed to the waitress who had served Rob.

He'd brought a bouquet of flowers with him. I asked if he was celebrating an anniversary but he didn't reply. He just smiled. He seemed like a nice guy.

Apparently, she'd given him a menu which he'd taken before ordering a jug of tap water. He was going to wait until his companion arrived before he ordered any wine.

The next quote was from Ted.

He was always in the thick of things as a kid. Bold as brass. Cheeky too. Everyone liked him. The whole village was devastated when he died, but now we know he's alive we should celebrate.

I wondered if he'd supply the champagne at his tea shop or if we'd have to bring our own.

I trawled more newspapers to find more quotes from school friends, teachers, sailing friends, and friends of friends who pretended to know him when they didn't. Not really. *The Mail* had a headline: **Superman Where Are You?** The opening paragraph detailed his vanishing act twelve years earlier, speculating he may have done something similar before. Some expert in missing people stated he could be a "ghosting", a form of identity theft, whereby he'd taken on the identity of a deceased person.

Theories abounded, and for the first time I stepped outside and saw what an extraordinary story it was. Little wonder the media was going crazy. They'd sell the story worldwide with no problem, with book and movie rights attached no doubt.

Feeling unsteady and off balance, I walked to get the correct train, wondering if our family should offer one of the media outlets our exclusive story. It might be the only way we could keep other journalists from bugging us. I'd talk it over with Susie that night and then Mum and Dad and the gang before deciding what to do. Meantime, I wanted to know more about DI Gilder.

I googled *Gilder, police* but it wasn't Barry's face that popped up on my screen. An older man with pouches beneath his eyes and a deeply pockmarked face gazed gravely at me. DCI David Gilder was Assistant Commissioner with the Met and had, apparently, retired six months earlier. Barry Gilder's father maybe?

I scanned his biography to find he was married to Elaine and had two children: Barry and Alisha. I pulled out Barry Gilder's business card. Toyed with ringing him, but what would I say? I've just seen a photo of your dad on the Internet? I put the card back in my pocket. Then I brought it out again and put his details into my phone.

I spent the journey gazing outside, wondering where the hell my brother was, and why he hadn't contacted us yet.

Chapter eight

It was raining by the time I arrived home, but it hadn't put off a couple of journalists who were hovering on my doorstep. As soon as I saw them, I turned around and headed for Clara's, texting her as I went. She told me to come through her neighbour's garden around the back.

Feeling like a burglar, I slipped over the wall between them and rapped on Clara's conservatory door.

She arrived in a flurry of sheepskin booties and curly blonde hair, bangles jingling. Her eyes were bruised, indicating she hadn't slept much, but otherwise she appeared to be bearing up okay.

'Dear Nick.' She kissed my cheek and pulled me inside. 'What can I get you? Coffee? Or would a brandy be better?'

'Coffee would be great. I can always add the brandy.'

We settled in the kitchen, the warmest room of the house with a wood-burning stove in the hearth. The kids were at school, John at work. I took a deep breath. Sipped my coffee. 'I'm sorry,' I said. It was all I could think of to say.

'It's crazy,' she said.

'I know.'

We talked for a while. I didn't mention the flowers Rob had apparently brought with him to the restaurant. We didn't speculate much. I think we were too disorientated. She told me none of the family had given any interviews yet. We agreed we should come up with a plan to cover us all and implement it as soon as we could. I told her about DI Gilder's visit. Then I asked about the men who'd visited the day before Rob had vanished.

'I'd forgotten about them,' she admitted, 'until Susie asked me to remember if anything out of the ordinary had happened around the time he vanished. It wasn't really unusual though because people dropped by all the time. I only remembered it because they were fairly big guys and it was a bit of a squeeze, especially with the toys and stuff.' She gave a smile. 'One of them played with Finn, he seemed really nice. They wanted to take Rob out for a beer.'

'Had you met them before?'

She shook her head.

'Anything bother you about them?'

Another shake. 'No. Rob's friends came around all the time, remember? He didn't even have to be here, they'd simply walk in and help themselves to whatever.'

It used to drive her mad, I recalled, Rob's open-house philosophy. They'd had a huge row after one of Rob's sailing buddies – who'd just sailed in from the Netherlands – had used the key tucked in the drainpipe above the back door. The friend had helped himself to a pack of beer and food from the fridge before falling asleep in front of the TV, which is where Clara found him when she got home. When she'd asked Rob to stop giving his friends *carte blanche* to their house, he called her miserly. She called him irresponsible.

'Were they anything to do with his work?'

She brushed a curl back from her forehead. 'Could have been, I suppose.'

'You didn't know anyone from his London job?'

'Just Susie.'

I racked my brains as to who Susie had been with at Rob's memorial. She said she'd come with a couple of his work colleagues but I couldn't remember them. I could remember Susie though. She'd been wearing a sundress of strawberries and cream, a pair of strappy sandals, pearls at her ears. When she shook my hand, I thought I could smell wild flowers.

She said, 'I'm so sorry for your loss.'

'Thank you.' Even through the fog of grief, I couldn't help but notice her. She was striking, with a shock of dark hair and deep brown eyes behind long eyelashes. 'How did you know him?'

'Through work. At the Home Office.'

It still came as a surprise to hear my wastrel brother had taken on, at least in the last year of his life, a real-life responsible job. Communications strategist, apparently, which in retrospect would have suited him, being a well-liked people person.

'I only saw him at a handful of social events. He's working with a colleague of mine...' She closed her eyes briefly, took a breath. 'Sorry. I mean he *was* working... I didn't know him well but he seemed like a really nice guy.'

'I still can't believe he got an office job.' I could feel my mouth twist wryly.

'I didn't think he could either.' Her brow cleared. 'He showed us photographs of boats and trips he'd done. He was a bit of a risk-taker, wasn't he?'

Now, I wondered if he'd taken a risk at work that had backfired for some reason.

'Did he have any enemies?' I asked Clara.

'Enemies?' She looked incredulous for a moment, but then gave my question serious consideration. Eventually she shook her head. 'Do you know, Nick, I can't really remember. Honey was a toddler and into everything, and Finn five years old – you couldn't keep him still. I was permanently knackered and all I cared about was when he could come home and take Finn off me.' She grimaced. 'Sorry. It makes me sound really awful, doesn't it, but it's true.'

I racked my brains, trying to think back to what Rob had said about his work, but I couldn't recall any details. All I could remember was his gloating about delivering fabulous boats around the world, usually twelve-metre-plus sailing boats with all the bangs and whistles. He'd delivered boats from Alicante to Auckland, New York to Martinique, all expenses paid and flights thrown in. He'd helped sail a super yacht to the Mediterranean once, a monster vessel with a swimming pool and helipad.

'The men who visited just before he vanished... were they from the yachting world maybe?'

She frowned. 'I couldn't say. They weren't wearing oilskins and sailing wellies if that's what you mean. Do you think they had something to do with his disappearance?'

'No idea. But I'd like to talk to them since they could be some of the last people to see him. Were they English?'

'Oh, yes. Very much so.' She was still frowning, trying to remember. 'They all drank tea and sat around, waiting. They weren't in any hurry or anything. No stress. I just kept on with what I was doing, I can't remember what. Making more mini shepherd's pies probably.'

For some reason, their quiet patience gave me the creeps.

Chapter nine

I looked outside, at a robin sitting on a branch, its feathers puffed out and turning it into a brown and red ball. 'How were you doing for money then?' I asked.

She opened her mouth to answer, but then paused. 'Do you know, I was going to say crap, but actually we were doing pretty well when he... I was going to say *died*. Jesus Christ.' She pressed her fingers against her eyes. 'I can still barely believe he's alive. What the hell, Nick... When he went, it was the end of my world. It was like having my emotions stripped out of me, my veins filled with cement. Nothing meant anything. I had to drag myself out of bed. Sometimes I couldn't even get up. I just wanted to disappear. But Finn wouldn't let me. Nor would your mum and dad.'

I'd forgotten how grief had prostrated Clara, laid her flat. How she'd stopped eating and turned into a ghost almost overnight. How we'd all stopped smiling. How sorrow had strangled my usual good nature and joy of life. How every day seemed grey, even when the sun was shining.

'If it hadn't been for the kids I don't think I could have gone on. It was awful, trying to move past the pain. Trying to forget. Trying not to miss him *every day*.' She wiped her eyes with the back of her fingers. 'How could he, Nick? He *lied* to me. How could he put me through such a terrible thing?'

I took her hand and gave it a squeeze. 'That's what I want to find out. Can we talk a bit more about his work? Would you mind?'

'Of course not.' She brought out a tissue and blew her nose. 'But I'm not sure if I can tell you anything new. All he cared about was paying for his sailing habit. You know how obsessed he was, how much the water meant to him.'

'But it doesn't come cheap.'

'Tell me about it.' Her smile was rueful. 'The amount of times I made spag bol, I can't tell you.'

Cheap food, but in the hands of a decent cook like Clara, delicious and nutritious.

'But yes, things had changed,' she added. 'We could afford things we couldn't before. Like the occasional babysitter. Being up to date with the mortgage – that was such a relief I can't tell you – and he started bringing takeaways home. Really nice ones, not rubbishy pizzas or anything. One time he came back with a bag from Harrods Food Hall. My God, it cost a fortune but it was as good as any restaurant. Beef Wellington, stuff like that.'

'Wow.'

'Yes.' She was looking past me, at the memories in her mind. 'For the first time, I really thought we were on the up. He talked about getting a bigger house. Buying a boat of his own, a cruiser we could all sleep on, maybe sail to France and Spain, and keep the skiff for the kids.'

'What was the last big sailing job he did?' I asked. I didn't think it relevant, but you never knew.

She put her head on one side. 'Do you know, I wish I could remember but I haven't a clue. You'd be better off asking Etienne. You know how they were thick as thieves.'

Etienne was French, the same age as Rob, and Finn's godfather. Etienne and Rob had met crewing a boat from Gibraltar to the Canaries. I remembered the trip because I'd been green with envy that while he was sailing into the tropics, having an adventure, I was slaving away at my graphic design degree. I also remembered Mum telling me to stop being so grouchy about it. She'd been quite snippy, saying I could be doing the same thing if I wanted, but deep down I knew that lifestyle wasn't for me. I loved sailing, but I wasn't a wanderer. I liked my life more ordered, more secure.

'Do you have a contact number for Etienne?' I asked.

As she went and fetched her phone, I realised darkness had fallen, which meant it was after 5pm and I hadn't done any shopping for supper yet. I'd grab something from the Co-op on my way back. I checked my phone to find a message from Susie.

Hope you're ok. Am on earlier train, bringing a bit of Arabia with me.

I smiled. No need for me to go to the Co-op after all. She was bringing a takeaway home, much as Rob had done for Clara all those years earlier. I texted her back.

Now I know why I love you. I'm at Clara's, home at 6. Any baklava, perchance?

Of course. x

I stuck another log on the wood burner then checked my emails. I heard a door close somewhere and glanced up, expecting Clara, but all was quiet. My phone pinged, alerting me to an incoming email and I answered one from Ronja about HAPS and another from a toy shop client before I realised how much time had passed.

'Clara?' I called. 'It's time for me to make a move.'

I rose, put my phone in my pocket. Walked into the corridor. Although I could see a crack of light coming from the sitting room, it was dark, and as I reached for the light switch above the hall table, I saw a shape moving towards me, not slowing, and before I could raise my hands it had grabbed my hair and slammed my head against the wall with such force that I heard the *crack* echo down the corridor and my vision exploded into stars.

I couldn't help it – my legs collapsed. I thought he hit me again but I wasn't sure because a roaring started in my head and grew louder and louder until it seemed as though I was falling head first into a tunnel filled with the roaring of a million trains.

Chapter ten

Susie put away her phone, relieved Nick seemed okay. She could always tell his mood by his appetite, which was prodigious. She'd never known him to go off his food except when he had flu, and the only other time had been when his father had been rushed to hospital with a suspected heart attack. The fact he'd mentioned *baklava* in his text – he loved the syrup-drenched pastries – meant he was coping pretty well.

She alighted from the train, briefcase in one hand, a vivid yellow Selfridges Food bag in the other. Her neighbour in the train had spent a full five minutes studying her, obviously trying to work out what she did ever since he'd taken in her Prada reading glasses and burgundy leather briefcase with her initials embedded in silver just below *Aspinal of London*. He'd surreptitiously tried to read her laptop screen, but since she never worked on anything sensitive in public all he gleaned was that she might be a lawyer, or a high-powered exec of some sort, which suited her fine.

Susie liked being looked at. But only on her own terms. She could vanish in a street in a second, slip on a wig and a pair of trainers and turn into the plainest of plain Janes where nobody gave her a second's glance, so she revelled in the attention when it came.

She loved labels, showing off her wealth, her power. Thanks to Victor – she still struggled with calling him Daddy, she was an adult for Chrissakes – she had a generous trust fund which gave her an annual income a family of four could live off comfortably. Rob was utterly unaware of this. He knew she came from money – how could he not, when she had a wardrobe full of designer clothes and an apartment worth over two million pounds – but he didn't know *how much* money.

She'd considered telling him, even offering to sub him so he didn't have to keep working with the dreadful Ronja, but Susie was smarter than that because although some men would have jumped at such a chance, Nick wasn't one of them. He might think he'd like being a kept man – he joked about it from time to time – but deep down she knew he'd hate it. Nick was a traditional sort who wanted to be able to provide and protect his family, not become some kind of lapdog to his wife.

So Susie kept her wealth quiet and everything trickled along just fine.

Beeping open her car – a nice anonymous Audi but with a beefed-up turbocharged petrol engine and fortified wheels – she put the shopping in the footwell, her briefcase behind the driver's seat. Then she climbed inside, brushing droplets of rain that clung to her shoulders and hair.

She switched on the wipers, then flicked the heater to demist, and pulled out of the car park, checking her rear-view mirror and side mirrors, the pedestrians, the people on the opposite side of the road waiting for a bus – always checking her surroundings, always vigilant, always alert. It wasn't a conscious thing, her preternatural awareness. It had simply grown like a soft carapace over the years and most of the time she didn't even know she was conducting light surveillance.

Luckily, Nick had never noticed, although on one of their early dates he'd baulked at sitting in the back row of the cinema, her preferred spot because she had a clear view of everything and everyone, with easy access to the door.

The cottage was dark when she arrived. Although Nick was usually prompt about timings, he'd obviously got caught up with Clara. Not surprising given the shock of Rob's arrival into their lives. She still found it hard to believe, and had run and rerun the news clip dozens of times at work, but each time she looked into Rob's eyes, she felt a punch in her gut that told her again and again that against all the odds, it was him.

Susie let herself into the cottage, already warm thanks to the central heating, timed to kick in at five thirty in readiness for Rob's homecoming after work. Kicking off her shoes, she padded into the kitchen and poured herself a glass of wine. She felt like she needed it. Looking for Nick's brother on top of her current workload wasn't the best of situations, but she had to admit that it wasn't unusual to have an extra case file shoved on her desk.

Where was Rob?

She let her mind continue to chew over this question as she sipped her wine and unpacked the Selfridges bag. There had been nothing after that first sighting. Not a whiff of him on any CCTV cameras, and nothing on the ground. He'd vanished like a pro and when she got her hands on him, she'd kill him very slowly for putting her and the team, as well as Nick and his family, through this.

Where was he? Which hole had he crawled back into? Or had he decided to do something else? Like plan his resurrection? Nick's family wouldn't just kill the fatted calf when he returned, but the whole damned herd. They'd be eating meat for years, oblivious of the prodigal son's infamous stupidity.

She leaned against the worktop, sipping her wine and wondering where Rob would be sleeping that night – whether he was sleeping rough, or tucked up with a friend or a lover – some poor sap who didn't know what a monumental pain in the arse he was.

Her mind suddenly gave a shiver.

Had Rob contacted his family? Was he in Bosham? Had he contacted Clara? Was that why Nick was delayed?

No. She took another sip of wine, shaking her head. Rob would never come home. Not just because of the shame he'd bring with him, but because he'd do anything to protect his family. That was why he'd disappeared. Wasn't it?

Chapter eleven

I came round to find myself sitting on a kitchen chair, my hands tied behind me.

Clara sat opposite.

Her arms were also tied to a chair. A gag covered her mouth. She was chalk-white, tears pouring down her cheeks, but she didn't appear to be injured.

'You okay?' I choked.

She nodded.

I looked up as a man stepped between us. He was tall, well over six feet. Late fifties or so, with thick white hair. He wore a beautifully tailored herringbone overcoat with a black velvet collar. Nice shoes. Black leather gloves. A long face like a chisel. Expressionless. He reeked of wealth and menace.

He said, 'So, you're Robert Ashdown's brother.'

He looked me up and down.

'You don't look much alike.'

'Who are you?' I asked. My voice was remarkably calm considering my pulse was through the roof.

He frowned.

'I'm known as The Saint.'

When I didn't react, a spasm of irritation twitched his lips. He didn't like not being recognised.

'I gained my nickname,' he added, his ego obviously getting the better of him, 'from The Saint of Killers in the book series *Preacher*.'

I licked my lips. 'You read comic books?'

His eyes held mine. Hard, grey and shiny, like wet quartz. 'You have a problem with that?'

'Not at all,' I said. 'I'm actually doing some work for Top Dog Comics at the moment.'

He stared at me. Although his facial muscles hadn't moved a millimetre, I got the feeling I'd surprised him.

'What kind of work?' he asked.

'I'm an artist,' I added.

Long silence while he continued to survey me. I guessed whatever was on his mind was something that he hadn't bargained for, so I decided to press what could be an advantage. Don't they say that when you're kidnapped you should make friends with your abductor?

'I'll look out for *Preacher*,' I told him. 'Do you think I'd like it?'

A flash of amusement crossed his face. 'If you like comics full of profanity and graphic violence,' he said, 'along with death and redemption packed alongside sex, booze, blood and bullets. Oh, and angels, demons, God, vampires and deviants of all types.'

'Sounds like it packs a punch,' I said agreeably.

'It's gripping,' he said. 'The graphics aren't as sophisticated as some comics but they're attention-grabbing, lots of energy. What's your style?'

'Kind of similar,' I said. 'I've got some panels on my phone. Would you like to see?'

Interest flared in his eyes but then he glanced back at Clara and then at his watch, and I knew I was losing him.

'My phone's in my back pocket,' I said.

'No, it isn't.' He reached inside his coat and withdrew my phone. Brought it over and held it in front of me so the face recognition kicked in. I didn't protest. I thought keeping him on side more important right now. I talked him through my files. Finally, he had the set of panels I'd done to introduce Colossal, a character one of Top Dog's writers was working on.

His eyebrows rose. 'These are really good.'

'Thanks.'

'Why don't you do this full time?'

I shrugged.

'Money,' he said, nodding as though he knew all about my business, bank balances and paltry pension plans, which maybe he did.

'Money,' I echoed, unable to think of anything else to say. Plus of course, it was true. If I had a million pounds in the bank I would love to spend my days in my studio being a comic book artist.

He looked at the pictures some more then turned and put the phone on the kitchen worktop. When he turned back, any semblance of friendliness had gone.

'Where's your brother?'

'I don't know,' I said. 'And I'm not just saying that. I *really* don't know. I swear it.'

He raised his hand slightly and another man stepped into view. He was built like a wrestler. Lots of muscle as well as fat. Thick arms, wrists and neck. I recoiled slightly: I hadn't realised there were two of them.

'Now,' said the Saint. 'I'd rather not ask Tommo here to get physical with you. Normally I wouldn't hesitate, but with you being of a profession I admire greatly, I think we can make an exception. I shall ask again: where is your brother?'

I held his gaze with all the self-composure I could muster against the terror sitting in my stomach. 'W-why do you want him?'

He paused. He was looking at me but I had no clue what he saw. Anger? Fear? Determination? He looked at Tommo the muscle man, then back at me. 'You have no idea, do you?'

Not knowing what he was referring to, I just stared at him.

His eyes went to the ceiling. I saw him take a long breath. He began tapping the sole of his leather shoe lightly against the stone floor.

Tap-tap-tap.

What was he thinking? Whether to set Tommo on me? Smash me into a pulp? The tension in me rose to fever pitch and when the tapping stopped, I couldn't help my flinch. He looked straight at me once more.

'Where is he?'

'I don't know!'

To my horror, he put his glove back on and pulled out a knife. Then he stepped to Clara and grabbed her hair in his fist and twisted it, forcing her head back. His other hand encircled her exposed throat.

'Don't hurt her,' I pleaded.

'Where is he?'

He forced her head back further. Pressed the knife against her neck. A tiny drop of blood bloomed where the tip broke her skin.

Clara made a strangled sound. Her eyes were on mine, desperate, pleading.

'Please,' I begged. 'If I knew I'd tell you, I promise.'

He raised his eyes to the ceiling and shook his head, making a tsk-tsk sound, like a teacher disappointed with one of their pupils. 'You're beginning to sound like a stuck record. WHERE THE FUCK IS HE?'

He bent Clara's head back a fraction further. Behind her gag, she began mewling like a distressed cat.

I'd have to give him something, I realised. Make something up. I let a silence drag out as though I was coming to a difficult decision. I was opening my mouth to tell him Rob was in Yeovil, Edinburgh, anywhere but here, when at that exact moment, the doorbell rang.

His head switched round, his whole body stiffening and becoming as alert as a hunting dog.

My phone gave a *ting* as a text came through. The Saint had a quick look. Came and stood in front of me.

'Nice to meet you, artist,' he said.

And with that, he and his goon were gone.

Chapter twelve

Susie released us fast. It had been Susie who'd rang the doorbell, and who'd sent the text that the Saint had read, saying she was outside. When we didn't answer the door, Susie used the front door key magnetised to the underside of one of the windowsills, something Clara insisted upon since her kids were continually forgetting or losing their keys.

Calm as the proverbial cucumber, Susie called the police. Then she rang Clara's husband John who came straight home. While John comforted Clara, Susie and I went around the house, checking the windows and doors were locked. After that, we stepped outside to check the perimeter of the house.

'How did they get in?' Susie asked Clara when we returned.

'The conservatory.' Clara hung her head. 'I didn't lock it behind Nick when he got here.'

The conservatory was at the opposite end of the house to the sitting room which was why I hadn't heard them. Plus, I'm sure they could be as quiet as cats if they wanted. Both men had that air about them.

Before the police arrived, Susie sat me down and asked me questions. I told her about my head cracking against the wall and regaining consciousness in the kitchen and she came and checked my head – a small swelling the size and shape of a gull egg had formed – and then my pupils.

'You'll live,' she pronounced without much sympathy. She wasn't the nursing type I already knew, but even so, it would have been nice to have had a bit more commiseration.

'Thanks to a thick skull, no doubt,' I said a touch sourly.

She looked at me. Then she rose and came over and pressed a kiss against the top of my head and stroked it gently. 'Poor Nick,' she murmured. 'Poor hurt Nick.' She pulled back. 'Is that better?'

I couldn't help shaking my head ruefully at her, which made her smile and kiss me again. 'So,' she said, 'what happened next?'

'I asked him who he was.'

She raised her eyebrows in expectation.

'He said his name was the Saint.'

She didn't blink, didn't move, but that strange stillness dropped over her, alerting me something was wrong.

'He's named after a–'

'Comic book character,' she interrupted. 'From *Preacher*.'

Astonishment and disbelief flooded me. 'You know him?'

'Not personally.' Her voice turned distant as she looked at something in her mind's eye. 'But…' She brought out her phone and opened Safari. Tapped briefly then passed it to me.

The picture showed the front page of an online newspaper. The headline read: **POLICE SAY GANGLAND MONSTER IS UNTOUCHABLE.**

Below was a photograph of the Saint and beneath that, I read:

For the last two decades, George Abbott has revelled in his reputation as the untouchable boss of an organised criminal gang.

This supposedly respectable "businessman" enforces his will with acts of extreme violence, which makes sure no one stands up to him. Even the police fear that this villain, who makes his money through human and drug trafficking, fraud, prostitution and money laundering, is simply "too big" to bring down.

Abbott, or The Saint, as he is known in gangland circles, has evaded justice for years despite brutal attacks on his enemies. He has led groups of assassins to rid him of unwanted competition, hunting down and murdering anyone in his way. Claims have also been made that Abbott has infiltrated key parts of the criminal justice system from the police to the Crown Prosecution Service to the prisons, ensuring he has never been convicted.

'Holy shit.' Something inside me quailed at the knowledge I'd faced what sounded like the country's most notorious gangster. I quailed even further when I thought of DI Barry Gilder. Was he one of the officers on the Saint's payroll?

I stared at the gangster's picture. 'What does someone like him want with Rob?' I asked out loud.

'He didn't say?'

'No,' I said, but it certainly made Rob's disappearance understandable. If I had Abbott hunting me, I'd do a vanishing act too. I rose and went next door, to Clara. She had wept when John arrived and wrapped her in his arms, big deep sobs borne out of fear and relief, but she seemed to have regained some of her composure and was sitting with John on the sofa drinking tea.

'Fancy a cup?' John offered with a tense smile. 'Or would alcohol be a better option?'

'In a sec,' I said. 'Clara, love, did you recognise either of those two men?'

'What do you mean?'

'I was wondering if they could have been the ones who wanted to take Rob out for a beer the day before he disappeared.'

Her hands went to her mouth. 'You think they were?'

'No idea, because it wasn't me who saw them all those years ago. But you did. Can you think back to that time? Try to remember.'

She closed her eyes. Opened them and shook her head. 'Honestly, Nick. I don't know. I just remember three big men struggling to fit into our tiny cottage.'

It had been worth a shot but even without Clara's confirmation, instinct told me it could well have been Abbott and a couple of henchmen who'd visited that Saturday twelve years earlier, but why? What had Rob done? What had he got himself involved in?

I turned round as Susie spoke. 'The police are here.' She closed the door behind her and came and knelt before Clara, her gaze flicking from me to Clara and then to John. 'But before you see them, I think it's fair to say it would be wise not to mention the Saint's name.'

Clara and John looked about to object until Susie showed them the online newspaper article.

'Christ,' said John. His skin lost some colour.

Clara's lips wobbled but she made a Herculean effort not to cry again.

'We'll tell the police in due course,' Susie added. 'But right now, I think we're better off keeping quiet until we have more information about what he wants with Rob. Mention his name to the police and the roof will fall in. You'll have all sorts of authorities here wanting you to take Abbott to court, pressuring you into giving evidence against him so they can get him for something, *anything*, and I'm not sure if that's a good idea. Agreed?'

Although I knew it made sense, I felt a flash of outrage that Abbott's reputation was dictating our response to his attack. He hadn't even told us not to say anything, and I supposed he either guessed we'd keep quiet for the reasons Susie had given, or he was confident that he had enough people in the right places in his pocket to be able to undermine anything we said. Really nasty stuff, when you thought about it.

I looked at Clara. 'What do you think?'

'I don't want to ever see him again,' she said, suddenly turning fierce. 'Keep him away from us. I don't care how you do it.'

I looked at Susie. 'Okay. No names.'

Susie went and fetched the police. I faced them with a fair bit of equanimity because at last I had an idea why my brother had faked his own death.

To keep him, and his family, safe.

Chapter thirteen

After the police had interviewed Clara and me, Susie took me home. As promised, she'd brought a takeaway, and when I saw the dishes of Lebanese food – baba ganoush, sumac-roasted chicken wings and skewered lamb, salads slathered in molasses and tahini – my appetite kicked in. I opened a bottle of Lebanese red I'd been hoarding for such an occasion and devoured my food and drink as though I hadn't eaten in a month.

We were clearing up in the kitchen when she leaned her hips against the worktop and said, 'Nick. I have something to tell you.'

An odd note in her voice made me put down the glass I was drying and turn to face her. She was staring at me with an intensity that sent a chill through me.

'What is it?'

'It's…' She took a breath. 'Something I should have told you a long time ago. But I didn't.' She glanced away. 'I had my reasons. I just hope… you'll understand.'

She ran a hand through her hair, took a step towards me, then back. When she twisted her wedding ring around and around, I knew this was serious. She only did that under immense duress, like when my mother had accused her of caring more for her job than her family. Susie hadn't argued. She'd fallen silent, turning inward and twisting that ring around and around.

'I haven't been entirely honest with you, Nick.' When she swallowed, her throat made a little click. 'God.' She gave a laugh but it held no humour. 'I never thought this would be so difficult.'

With a shock, I realised she was scared. Really scared.

'Suze,' I started, but she held up a hand, stopping me.

'Let me just say it, okay? And I'll let the cards lie where they will.'

My imagination went wild. She'd been having an affair. She spent so much time in London, away from me, how could she not? She worked late a lot, spent days, occasionally weeks away at a time. How could I have been so stupid not to have thought of it before? *Because I trusted her.*

'You know I told you I worked in IT at the Home Office?'

'Yeees,' I said cautiously.

'I work for the Home Office, but not in IT.'

What? I struggled to rein in my imaginings of her lithe form lying in another man's arms and concentrate on what she was saying.

'I'm an officer for MI5. Military Intelligence, Section 5. The UK's domestic counter-intelligence and security agency.' Her words came out like bullet points. 'I work in G Branch. We deal with international counter-terrorism.'

I reached out a hand to the wall, steadying myself.

'You work for *who?*'

'I'm a case officer. I'm a trained specialist in the management of agents – sources – and agent networks. I manage human agents, and human intelligence networks. I spot potential agents, recruit them, and train them in tradecraft, especially how to avoid detection by people who would harm them if they knew what they were doing.'

I felt as though the air had left my lungs. I listened to her run on, more from nerves than any intention to give me her CV, thinking: *My wife is a spy?*

'I can't tell you what we work on specifically because as you can appreciate it's classified…'

My next thought came crashing through: *It suits you.*

And then I wondered how on earth I could have believed she was happy doing something bland in the IT department of the civil service. She was so much more. Secretive, clever, self-reliant, composed, ice calm under pressure… She could have been born to it. How could I not have seen it before?

'You were vetted by the security services when we got together…'

'I passed, I take it?' My voice surprised me. It had a sarcastic edge I was unaccustomed to, and from her response, Susie heard it too.

'Flying colours,' she mumbled. She hung her head. She looked so unlike the Susie I knew, the calm one, who's unremittingly self-possessed, that my heart clenched.

'Why didn't you tell me sooner?'

She waffled on about wanting to protect me, but we'd been married eleven years, I knew when my wife waffled.

'Suze,' I interrupted. 'Just tell me the truth.'

She raised her head and met my eyes. 'You won't like it.'

'I haven't liked hearing that you've lied to me since we first met,' I shot back, 'so another axe in my heart won't hurt, I'm sure.'

Tears sprang to her eyes. 'I'm sorry.'

'Just say it.'

She spread her hands helplessly. 'You can't lie.'

'And you can,' I snapped. 'Clever you.'

She looked stricken, her face pale. 'It's to keep us safe. Not just me, but you too. If anyone suspects I'm not who I am, or if we meet a mark or source by accident, it could put us both in real danger.'

'You didn't trust me not to lie well enough?' My tone was disbelieving.

She twisted her wedding ring around again. 'I guess so.'

'Shit.' It was my turn to run a hand through my hair. I knew I was a crap liar but I hadn't thought it would be the reason why my wife withheld her real job from me.

'I'm sorry,' she said again. 'I wish I'd told you ages ago, but the longer I left it the harder it got.' Her whole body drooped in misery.

I looked at the woman I loved with all my heart. My god, I thought I married Superwoman. I really had.

'Do you have a gun?' I asked, suddenly curious.

She blinked. 'I don't own one, if that's what you mean. But yes, I am fully trained and I do have access. But before you get excited, Nick, MI5 agents are more office workers and observers than guys running around with guns stopping terror plots. It's not all *Spooks* you know.'

Through my confusion of shock and disbelief came a rush of pride. This woman was amazing, incredible, and I was going to spend the rest of my life with her.

'Oh,' I said, feigning disappointment. 'I hoped you might show me your gun. Isn't it nestled inside your stocking?' I moved towards her, my love all-consuming. 'Or perhaps you have a pea shooter tucked in your bra?' I added hopefully.

Relief and happiness flooded her face. 'You don't mind?'

'Yes.' I was honest. 'Very much. Intellectually I can understand your reticence, but emotionally… it hurts like hell that you didn't tell me before.'

'I can understand that.' She came close and touched my face. 'I love you so much. I was terrified I'd lose you.'

I put my hands on her waist. 'You'll have to do more than confess you're Mata Hari to get rid of me, you know.'

She wound her arms around my neck and raised her face to mine. 'Thank God,' she breathed.

Chapter fourteen

When we awoke, it was past eight and next door's dog was barking. Susie wriggled out of bed, grabbed my dressing gown, and padded downstairs, returning with two cups of tea, which we drank in bed, looking out of the window.

She'd taken the day off so I could settle into my new-found knowledge of her, and her career.

'I want you to ask me anything that comes to you,' she'd told me the previous night. 'Anything at all.'

My questions ranged from how much she got paid to how she got the job. 'It was a friend of Dad's who gave me the old-school spook's tap on the shoulder when I was at uni.'

Susie had gone to Oxford, no less. Where so many spooks came from, including the notorious Philby and Blunt. I could feel my mind bending with the knowledge she was as bright and as talented as these men (but hopefully not a traitor).

She told me she was well placed to rise to head of section in G branch in a couple of years. She was pretty ambitious, my Susie, and she went on to confess she'd been fast-tracked from the start.

'My line manager tells me I'm a rising star,' she said proudly.

I finished my tea and kissed the rising star roundly before asking if I could talk to her dad. Caution rose in her eyes. 'Of course. But why, in particular?'

'I'd like to know how he lies. How he keeps you safe.'

'Living in New Zealand helps,' she said drily.

'You know what I mean.'

Susie messaged her parents and arranged for us to Skype later. We didn't do this often, just at Christmas and on birthdays, which

I found sad at first, but when I learned the reason why, it made sense.

Years ago, before she joined MI5, before she'd met me, Susie had been attacked in London and mugged really badly. She'd ended up in hospital with serious head injuries, brain damage, a broken nose and fractured eye socket and cheekbone. The bruising had left her almost unrecognisable apparently, but more serious was the drastic alterations in her mood, memory function, and also personality.

At first, she seemed to have bounced back fast, returning home within weeks instead of the year-long recovery that doctors predicted. But this seemingly miraculous recovery was nowhere as straightforward as everyone hoped. While the brain swelling subsided, her emotions, memory and other functions suffered more lasting damage.

'My brain had to rewire itself,' she told me on our third date. She'd wanted me to know her medical history in case I changed my mind about continuing to see her. 'That's all. I'm fine now. Just a little different to how I used to be, or so my parents say, but I wouldn't know. I'm just me. The way I am. Today.'

'I think you're wonderful,' I told her. 'The way you are. Today.'

The smile she'd given me lit up the sky. She liked that about us, immensely. That I loved the woman she was, and not the woman she used to be before the attack.

Her parents had flown over as soon as they'd heard she'd been mugged.

'They only saw me a few times,' she confessed to me one day, 'because I couldn't bear them visiting. They kept comparing the old me with the new me. I hated it. I hated the girl I used to be. She sounds so *wet*.'

It had been Susie's doctor who'd gently suggested her parents return home, to New Zealand.

'He could see how stressful it was, for all of us. They wanted their compliant docile daughter back but I couldn't do it. Having them drip all over me wasn't doing my recovery any good. It was awful, but it was such a relief when they left…'

Her mother, gamine like Susie, with a thick shock of short black hair, seemed to agree. 'We wanted to help, but all we seemed to do was make things worse,' she acknowledged once, in a rare moment of honesty. 'She got terribly angry with us. The doctor told us this was normal, but I found it really difficult. The old Susie was much gentler. She's quite impulsive now, and less able to control her temper. She says it makes her better at work. More edgy.'

That would be right.

Her father said, 'The doctor said they think the frontal lobe was compromised. Which is why she didn't behave like herself anymore. She thought she was fine, that nothing had changed, but we could see this was absolutely not the case.'

'And now?' I asked him.

'She's pretty much back to normal. She wouldn't be able to do the job she does, if she wasn't.' Victor smiled, but it was sad. 'I miss my little girl though.'

Susie never talked about the attack but I knew it still haunted her. Out of nowhere she'd turn moody, antagonistic and difficult, and if I didn't know it was because of the bastard who'd beaten her up, I would have really struggled because she's pretty unbearable at those times. Luckily, they don't last, maybe two days max, and then she's back on track. I'm sure she lashes out because they never caught the man. She never got justice. If he was behind bars she could put it behind her and move on.

Sometimes I fantasised about finding her attacker and giving him some of his own medicine, punching him until I broke the bones in his face, but that's all they were. Fantasies. I'm not really a fighter. Aside from those two bullies of Rob's, I haven't raised a hand to anyone else. My mind switched to think of my brother. I wouldn't have thought he was a fighter either, except the punches he'd pulled on the gunman in the restaurant told a different story.

Our Skype session with Susie's parents was its usual stilted affair with her mum trying too hard and her dad interjecting with odd little witticisms that kept falling flat. When Susie left me to talk to them alone, I jumped right in. I said, 'I know what Susie's job is.'

Her mother nodded. 'I see. I'll let you chat to Victor.'

Victor came into view. 'So she told you at last.'

'Yes.'

'I wondered if she ever would. It shows how much she trusts you.'

'She told me I can't lie very well.'

He smiled. 'I'm sure you'll find it in you to learn a new skill on her behalf.'

I smiled back, rather taken by the idea of getting a degree in duplicity.

'She's ambitious,' he warned me. 'I have every expectation she'll be head of her section before the year is out. From there she'll take another position, maybe working against digital threats or becoming a special emissary overseas, because one of the main requirements to become head of MI5 is a background of variety and experience. She's already been an agent, as well as recruited and run her own agents. She's done serious fieldwork in her time both overseas and at home. She's rising fast, son.'

'Head of MI5?' My voice didn't exactly squeak but it was definitely an octave higher than usual.

'Are you up for it?'

Bloody hell. Did I have a choice? Probably not, if I wanted a happy wife. 'I guess so.'

He smiled, a broad smile that lit up his face. 'Good, good.'

I left Susie for a little while, expecting her to finish the call but when I returned, they were still speaking. He was looking at her and she was looking back. She said, 'I'm sorry I'm not the daughter I used to be.'

'I know, my darling one.' He blew her a kiss. 'I know.'

I sneaked away, leaving them to their privacy.

Chapter fifteen

When we got home, we made supper and once we'd mopped our plates with some crusty bread and pushed our plates aside, Susie said, 'There's something else I have to tell you.'

There was more? I just looked at her.

She suddenly appeared unsure, but then she put her shoulders back. 'You're not going to like this either.'

I braced myself. Please God she wasn't going to confess an affair with James Bond. Not only would I never recover but I wasn't sure if I could take any more surprises.

'It's to do with Rob.'

I went blank. 'Rob?'

'Yes. I didn't meet him at any social events. I met him in the Office. He worked for us. MI5.'

'MI5? Rob?' I laughed. I couldn't help it. If I'd struggled picturing him commuting to London before, slogging his guts away in an office job, then this was right on the edge of credibility.

'You shouldn't laugh.' Susie frowned. 'He was, by all accounts, an excellent agent.'

I opened and closed my mouth.

'He didn't work for us for overly long. A year or so before he... vanished.'

'He wasn't a communications strategist?'

'No.'

'Jesus.' I tried to get my mind around it. Yes, Rob was a risk-taker, but even so, it was incredible. No wonder we hadn't a clue about what he'd got up to in London.

'What area did he work in?'

'I never knew, sorry. I just met him from time to time, that's all.'

She stood there, watching me. Her expression was deadly serious.

'Why didn't he tell me?'

She shrugged but I felt a cold finger of dismay run down my spine. Just like my wife, my brother probably thought I couldn't lie well enough to keep him safe. I closed my eyes. Pictured my parents' faces when we told them the news. They would be gobsmacked but not just that, they'd be so *proud*.

Despite myself, I gave a chuckle. 'Mum and Dad will never believe it.'

'You can't tell them, Nick.' Her tone was fierce. 'They'll want to know how you know and the more people who know what I do, the higher the risk of exposure. Even by keeping quiet at the wrong moment could alert someone and jeopardise me.'

'Ah, shit.' I rubbed the space between my brows. 'They'd have loved it.'

'I know. But it's impossible. Careless talk costs lives. It really does.'

I sighed. 'Just you and me then.'

She fiddled with her wine glass.

I said tentatively, 'Do you think it was Rob's work with MI5–'

'We call it the Office.'

'His work with the Office… could it have got him into trouble with the Saint?'

'Nick, I've already said I don't know what he was working on.' I could sense the irritation that she was having to repeat herself. 'But yes, it *could* have done.'

'Do you know who he worked with there?'

She looked away. It was a delaying tactic. She knew, all right, but didn't want to say. I switched subject.

'Do you think Rob was trying to take Abbott down?'

'What?' She looked startled.

'While he was working with MI5. That would explain it. He'd found something on the Saint that would put him away. That's why Abbott's after Rob. To silence him.'

'It's a theory,' she agreed.

I poured us some more wine. 'I want to talk to whoever ran Rob. His case officer, or whatever they're called. They'd know what was going on at the time.' I leaned forward. 'Perhaps we could find something that would finish Abbott for good, and Rob could *come home.*'

'It's a nice idea,' Susie said drily. 'But considering more experienced, trained people have tried to get Abbott and failed, I can't see how we'd do much better.'

'But what if Abbott gets to Rob before we do?' My mind was galloping ahead. 'He'll probably kill him. We need to get to Rob first… we could use him as bait and entrap Abbott and–'

Susie pushed back her chair and went to the sink.

'Leave it,' I told her. 'I'll do it tomorrow morning. Not now.'

She ignored me and started clearing up.

'Susie, come on.'

She turned round. I saw a spark of anger in her eyes. 'You want to take on George Abbott?'

'Not me personally.' I shifted on my chair. 'But if MI5 had something on Abbott, and Rob had been involved with it back then, wouldn't they have kept records? Couldn't we use them?'

Susie looked at me with a weird, angry light in her eyes.

'No.'

'No, what?' I flung up my hands.

'No, you are not going after Abbott. He's one of the most dangerous people in the UK, Nick. And I am not having my husband sniffing around the Saint who the moment he hears of it, will take him into the forest and kill him.'

Put like that, it didn't make my quest sound particularly wise.

'I still want to meet Rob's case officer though,' I said.

'No.'

This time I got to my feet. 'Why not?'

She looked away.

'Susie?'

'Look, he's way up the totem pole now. He's rumoured to become the next DG.'

Director General. Which, as she'd admitted the previous day, was her ambition. My wife. Superwoman. Who was looking particularly mulish.

'Come on, Suze,' I persisted. 'Just because he's a big cheese shouldn't stop us from asking, surely. What if he *knows* something about Rob and Abbott that could help us? There have to be files he can dig up. And aren't most of you guys known for your brilliantly retentive memories?'

She bent over and opened the cupboard beneath the sink and pulled out a pair of bright yellow rubber gloves. Ran the tap in the basin. Squirted Fairy Liquid inside. Started washing up. We'd talked about installing a dishwasher a while back but the kitchen area was so small we'd have no cupboards left and we'd be forced to store our canned goods, muesli and the like, in the sitting area. So we'd decided against it.

I watched her take a plate and dip it in the water. Soap it with a sponge. Her shoulders were set, her movements stiff and angry. When she was like this, I knew I shouldn't press any further, but I couldn't help myself.

'What's his name?' I asked. 'Rob's case officer?'

She spun round, gloves dripping water and suds. 'I can't tell you,' she said. 'You know that.'

'Ask him for me. Ask about Rob. Please.'

She turned back to the sink, didn't say anything.

'Suze?'

'Drop it, Nick.'

I took another glug of wine. 'No.' If she could give monosyllabic responses, so could I.

She paused. Finally, she turned around. Snapped off the gloves and placed them carefully on the draining board.

'Have you given any thought to me in all this?'

I looked at her blankly.

'I thought not.' Her voice was cold.

'What about you?' I said. 'It's no skin off your nose to ask a simple question about my brother. My brother who's been missing–'

'Shut up.'

Her voice was like a slap.

'Imagine this,' she bit out. 'I'm applying for my next job. Say it's with HM Customs & Excise. When they discover that I have a relative who has some kind of history with one of the most notorious smugglers in the country, how do you think they're going to react?'

'They can't tar you with Abbott's brush,' I protested. 'You're nothing to do with Rob.' I looked at her, my mind racing. 'Or were you involved with Abbott too?'

A look almost close to amusement crossed her face and for a strange moment I was reminded of the Saint.

'No,' she said. 'I had nothing to do with Abbott. I don't know about Rob, but…' She took a breath. 'Have you ever considered Rob might not be as snow white as you thought?'

'What does that mean?'

She folded her arms. 'What do you think?'

My brain was sluggish with wine but I finally got there. I gulped. 'You think Rob was on Abbott's pay roll? That he was a double agent or something?'

She didn't say anything. Just watched me.

'He wouldn't.' I shook my head. 'He's not an angel, but he wouldn't let someone like that get one over on him.'

'What if he was coerced? His family threatened?'

Another penny dropped.

'He'd disappear.'

She continued looking at me. Finally, she gave a sigh. 'I'll ask. Okay?'

I bit my lip. 'I don't want to mess things up for you…'

'Yes. But even so, I really don't want to abuse my position. Or become known for it. I'd like to keep Abbott and Rob out of my workplace, if it's possible.'

I fell silent. I couldn't think of anything more to say. It was up to her how she wanted to approach it, but I couldn't stop from having the last word because although a small part of me felt ashamed, the other part was still pissed off.

'I'd still like to meet his case officer though.'

We didn't talk much for the rest of the evening, and when we went to bed, she turned her back to me.

Chapter sixteen

The next morning, I was still feeling annoyed over Susie's reluctance to involve Rob's case officer, and when my mobile rang, showing *number unknown*, I answered it more brusquely than usual.

'Is that Nick?' a man asked hesitantly. He made it sound like *Neek*.

'Yes.'

'It is Etienne here. Robert's old sailing friend?'

'Hey, Etienne.' My voice immediately warmed as I pictured him, dark curly hair and blue eyes perpetually squinting as though looking out across a sun-sparkled sea.

'Is it true that Robert is alive?'

I'd forgotten he always used Rob's full name, never shortening it. 'Yes,' I said. 'It's true.' I took the phone to the sitting area window and looked out across the damp and wilted winter plants.

'Incredible. Has he contacted you at all?'

'No.'

'If he does…' He paused. I heard him say something to someone else in the background. 'Tell him I would like to see him.'

'Sure,' I said. 'Etienne… would you mind if I ask a couple of questions?'

'No, no…' There was a pause before I heard him speak to someone else once more, then he said, 'You have no idea where he might be?'

'No, sorry.'

'I see.'

'Etienne, can I ask when you last saw Rob?'

'Of course. I remember it clearly. It was in August, twelve years ago. Sunday the fourth.'

Three weeks before Rob disappeared.

'Where was this?' I asked.

'Ibiza.'

I blinked. I'd had no idea Rob had been anywhere near the Spanish party island around the time of his disappearance. 'What was he doing there?'

'He was taking a boat from Port de Sant Antoni to Hamble for a friend.'

'He delivered it okay?'

'Yes, no problem. I spoke to him just after he'd arrived.'

'When was that?' I asked.

'The twentieth of August.'

It was roughly a two thousand nautical mile journey, and if Rob hadn't stopped and sailed through the night, the timing made sense.

'What was he doing in Ibiza?' I asked.

'Sailing, getting some sun.'

I could almost picture Etienne's shrug as he spoke but something in his voice didn't sound right. My mind snaked away from the party scene. Had Rob been on assignment out there? Meeting someone on behalf of MI5 maybe? A suspect, a terrorist? Could he have been spying on someone? His professional yachting experiences would have made a great cover.

'What about you?' I added.

'The same... No–' I could tell he'd been interrupted and he'd partially covered the mouthpiece and was now talking to someone else but not in English or French. '*No, él no sabe, él no sabe nada,*' he was saying. He was speaking rapid Spanish. '*Te lo prometo yo no miento.*'

'Who're you talking to?' I asked, but he didn't hear me.

More rapid Spanish. My nerves tightened as it grew more heated.

'*¡Lo juro,*' Etienne said over and over. '*¡Lo juro.*'

'Etienne,' I called.

'Yes, Nick,' he came back. 'I am here.' His breath was short, almost panting. He was obviously under stress.

'Who are you talking to?' I asked for the second time.

'A friend of your brother's.' His voice was pitched higher than usual. 'He wants to know where Robert is.'

'This friend, he's Spanish?'

'Yes.'

More yammering in Spanish. This time Etienne sounded really panicky. Suddenly, silence.

'Etienne?' I said urgently. 'Etienne?'

Then he was back on the line. His words came in breathless bursts. 'This friend,' he said. 'You see, Robert owes him some money. He would like it returned.'

All the hairs on the back of my neck rose.

'How much money?' I asked.

'Tell Robert to help me,' he said. His voice was scared. 'Please.'

The line went dead.

My fingers were trembling as I rang the number for Etienne that Clara had given me the night before. I heard it connect, and then it rang and rang. No messaging service. I let it ring out and then I sent a text asking him to call me.

Then I rang Clara.

'What's this about Rob being in Ibiza before he disappeared?'

'What?'

I told her about Etienne's phone call.

'If he was in Ibiza,' Clara said, 'he never told me. I don't get it. If he'd been there he would have told me. He would have brought back presents for me and the kids, you know what he was like when he went away.'

I hadn't told her about the money Rob supposedly owed, just that Etienne sounded under stress from an unknown Spanish man.

'Had he been to Ibiza before?' I asked.

'A couple of times. We spent nearly a whole summer on the Med back in the day, do you remember?'

It had been when I was in my third year at uni. Both of them had helped crew a luxury catamaran from the UK to Greece and from there had found other crew work, island hopping and generally having a glorious time in the sun while I ground my teeth in fruitless envy. They'd returned soon after they discovered Clara was pregnant with Finn, and since then, she'd mainly stayed in the UK with the kids while Rob continued what I'd thought to be a feckless lifestyle. Until he'd landed the job in London, that was.

What did MI5 have to do with his owing money to this Spanish man? If MI5 were involved at all, of course. Perhaps Rob had suffered a mid-twenties crisis and hit Ibiza for some partying. I know he'd been struggling with family life at the time because he'd told me. We'd taken Dad's *Moody* out for a sail one Sunday, just the two of us, a crate of beer, and stacks of sandwiches cobbled together in his kitchen with Finn banging at our knees and Honey screaming next door.

'It's not that I don't love them,' he told me. 'But it just gets so *wearing*.'

'I think Clara would probably agree with that,' I said neutrally.

He pulled a face. 'I sound like a prize shit, don't I. I know she bears the brunt of it all, but I miss what we had before. Clara's permanently knackered, the house is a tip, the kids creating hell. Sometimes, I work late specifically so the kids are in bed asleep when I get home.' He ran a hand over his face. 'It will get better, won't it?'

I didn't have kids, but he looked so miserable that I did what many older brothers have probably done over the years and told him what he was going through was completely normal, that things would definitely get better, and had he considered getting a babysitter in so they could both have the occasional break?

'We can't afford it,' he said glumly. 'We can't afford anything much.'

'Mum and Dad will be happy to help,' I said.

'I don't want to ask them.' He set his jaw. 'Mum will look disappointed that I'm not the provider I should be, and you know

Dad. He'll take it as an excuse to rant about my getting a proper job, when am I going to grow up, all that crap.'

Fair enough.

'How about if I stump up for a babysitter every couple of weeks?' I offered. After all, I was single and earning a fairly decent wage so I could afford to be generous. 'Say every first and third Sunday so you and Clara can spend a day sailing together?'

A rush of emotion crossed his face and for a moment, I thought he was going to cry.

'Christ, Nick. You're tops.' He punched me on the shoulder. 'That's a great idea. I miss sailing with Clara so much and I know she misses it like hell too. I'll pay you back, I promise. Soon too. I didn't tell you because I don't want to jinx it, but I've got a job in the pipeline that may come off. It pays pretty well. But I won't know for a bit. Even though I've yet to meet the big boss, I still need extensive vetting, apparently.'

He wouldn't say what the job was, but now I guessed it was with MI5 because I only stumped up for four babysitting sessions, and in retrospect, this was the lowest I ever saw him. As Clara had intimated, from that time things had improved immeasurably. I frowned, trying to think why he might have been in Ibiza before he disappeared. I couldn't think how to make it work with the Saint and the security services, unless Rob had been undercover.

That would make sense.

A sense of urgency dropped over me. I had to speak with Rob's case officer. The sooner, the better.

I dialled Susie but got her voicemail. I left a brief message saying I'd spoken to Etienne, but no more. I didn't want to irritate her more than I had already.

Chapter seventeen

Checking my watch, I saw I was running late. As a family, we'd agreed to give one of the newspapers our exclusive story, and we were supposed to have congregated at Mum and Dad's ten minutes earlier. I pulled on my sailing jacket and jogged outside. My parents lived on the other side of the harbour, in a Grade II listed house called Sea Flax, originally a pair of coastguard cottages. With extensive harbour views, open fireplaces and oak-beamed ceilings it was probably worth a fortune but they would never sell, and we would never let them unless it was a dire emergency.

It was a house made for kids. Six bedrooms, loads of space and extensive gardens, and where Rob, Kate and I used to play endlessly in the garden – our tree house had been refurbished and rebuilt several times – or fix up our skiffs on the lawn. Rob's kids had done the same and we hoped the next generation would too.

Susie and I had talked about having children, but now I knew the extent of her ambition I wondered if it would happen. Perhaps if I offered to be a full-time house husband? That might work. I'd love to have kids. A brace of them, preferably. A boy and a girl.

As I neared the house, a journalist tried to ask me a question but I held up a hand, telling him I was giving an exclusive, sorry.

'Who with?'

When I told him, he cursed, but I was gratified to see him pull out his phone and move away.

We'd sold our story to one of the major national newspapers and were giving the money they were paying us to the RNLI since they'd worked so hard to try to find Rob the day he went missing. The paper had provided us with an experienced journalist and photographer both of whom were intelligent and empathetic, and exactly what we needed.

We'd agreed on a cohesive story between us, and it was Clara who told it. Lots of pictures of her and the kids, Finn looking awkward, probably due to his acne, and Honey in full make-up looking way too grown-up and sexy for a fourteen-year old. Talking about the past, Rob as a boy, a teenager, and how each of us remembered him took far longer than any of us had planned, mainly because every memory seemed to be fraught with emotion.

It was well past lunchtime when we wound up. I stepped outside and for the first time, didn't see a single journalist lurking. Word had obviously gone around.

A watery sun was trying to break through the clouds but the breeze was stiff and cold, so I zipped my jacket up to my chin. To save time, I walked across the harbour even though the path was slimy with weed. The tide had started coming in so I increased my pace, and I'd just made it to the other side when Susie rang.

'Etienne?' she asked. She was brusque because she was at work, so I was as brusque as I could be so I wouldn't waste her time. When I finished, she said, 'I'll arrange a meet between you and Rob's case officer. But I'll have to be there too, okay?'

I nearly fell over. I hadn't thought she'd do it.

'Brilliant,' I breathed. 'Thanks, Suze. I really appreciate it. I think once I meet him–'

'Sorry, Nick. I've got to go. Love you.'

'Love you too.'

After checking in with Ronja and catching up with various bits of work, I headed into Chichester and spent the remainder of the afternoon with the Sussex Police going through mug shots and supposedly trying to help them identify the two men who'd attacked Clara and me. I hated every minute, and loathed every lie. I knew I was doing it to protect Clara and the kids from any fallout from the Saint, but it didn't make me feel any better and I left as soon as I could, convinced I looked like one of their felons pasted on their wall: guilty and hangdog as hell.

It was dark as I left the station and most of the cars had left the car park, heading home after their working day. My phone gave a *ting* as I buckled up and I pulled it out to see it was Susie texting me. She was already at home and wondering where I was. I checked my watch to see she must have caught an earlier train. Spirits lifting, I texted her back. *On my way. See you in ten.*

I parked outside the cottage, glad to see the street was empty of journalists and photographers. I walked up our little front path and pulled out my keys but when I fitted the Yale into the lock it was to find it wasn't locked. I frowned. This was odd. Susie was a stickler for security and not just because of her job but because of her attack. I'd never known her not to keep the doors locked.

I pushed open the door, calling out, 'Hi Suze, it's only me.'

'Hi, only you.'

Barefoot and bare-legged, she padded down the stairs dressed in nothing but one of my V-neck sweaters that stopped mid-thigh. Damp hair indicated she'd just had a shower. God, she looked beautiful. I scooped her close. She smelled of ginger and some kind of spice.

'Hmmm,' I said. I slipped my hand to cup her naked buttock, smooth and warm and as round and sweet as anything I knew.

'Hmmm.' She reached up and wound her arms around my neck. 'Is now a good time?'

I put my head on one side and pretended to think. 'Well, I'm pretty busy right now, protecting the United Kingdom against malicious threats to national security from the proliferation of weapons of mass destruction and I'm–'

She pressed her open lips against mine, silencing me. Her tongue slipped inside my mouth, small and narrow, darting like a minnow. We must have kissed a thousand times, but whenever she did that I seemed to lose my senses and she knew it, because she'd then tease me, holding out until I felt as though I would happily murder someone, anyone, to be inside her. But I didn't want to be teased. I wanted her *now* and she seemed to realise it because she took my hand and drew me upstairs to bed.

When I came, I made an unholy sound as I half-groaned, half-shouted her name.

Afterwards, we lay curled together, her head on my chest, our limbs entangled.

'Sorry,' I said. 'It was a bit quick.'

She turned her head. Her eyes, as dark and deep as the night sky, bored into mine. 'Never apologise,' she said. Then she gave a snort of laughter. 'Sometimes it's useful. Remember the Marshfields?'

How could I forget? We'd been at their wedding and I'd been watching Susie from afar, admiring the way she moved, as slender and sinuous as a cat, and when our eyes met, she'd lower her lashes and send me a coquettish smile. She disappeared in the crowd for a minute or two, and then I heard her whisper behind me. I can't remember exactly what she said, it didn't matter, the lascivious invitation caused the effect.

We'd made frantic love in one of the guest bathrooms with people knocking on the door, wanting to use the loo, both of us caught in that sexual heat that made you do insane, crazy things you never would normally.

We weren't as in lust as we once were, it's not sustainable over the long-term, but she could still twitch her finger at me and I'd respond, a happy cohesion of love and lust twining between us.

After a while, we rose and showered, pulled on sweatpants and shirts and padded downstairs. I opened a bottle of beer while Susie moved to put on the TV, wanting to see the news.

'What's this?' She was staring down at the coffee table.

'What?'

She picked up what looked to be a plain white cardboard CD or DVD sleeve. Wordlessly she passed it to me. It had no image on the cover. Just a hand-penned message, in rough capitals, on the cardboard. IF YOU WANT TO SEE WHY YOUR BROTHER DISAPPEARED, WATCH THIS.

I withdrew a vivid blue and silver DVD.

'You've watched it?' she asked.

'No. I didn't know it was here.'

Her eyes widened. 'I didn't bring it in. And it certainly wasn't here when I got home. So who put it on the table?'

My heartbeat picked up. I licked my lips. 'The front door was unlocked when I came in.'

Susie stared at me. 'Fuck.'

We both went to the front door to find it locked. I'd automatically dropped the latch as I'd come in. We checked the rear door to find it was also locked. So were all the windows, apart from the one in the bedroom, which we'd opened a crack to air the room when we came downstairs. Susie closed it.

'It has to be one of your family,' she said. Her tone was tight.

We all had keys to one another's places, which didn't bother Susie as much as our somewhat lax attitude towards them. We'd let plumbers and electricians use them when necessary, as well as friends, and it didn't matter that we knew these people, had been to school with some of them, Susie still insisted on changing the locks, cutting new keys for everyone and labelling them against a list she held on her phone so she knew who had keys and where they were at any given time.

'They must have come in while I was in the shower.' Twin spots of red bloomed on her cheeks. 'Jesus Christ, Nick...'

Anger spiked in my gut, along with a sickening dose of fear. What if it wasn't someone in the family?

I was still holding the disc and looked down at it. 'I guess we'd better seen what's on it.'

Chapter eighteen

We booted up Susie's laptop and slipped the disc inside. Asked it to play. A grainy grey image appeared, shadowy and faint, but after a few seconds it steadied and became clearer.

CCTV video.

The camera was placed high above what appeared to be a reception area. Plain, no pictures on the walls, no comfy seats. An office block maybe. A male receptionist – Asian-looking, jacket and tie – sat behind a wrap-around desk. In front of him stood a computer and screen, two phones and what I took to be a reception folder. Automatic doors opened onto the street. Acres of tiled floor. People were walking across it. Mostly heading outside.

I checked the clock at the bottom of the screen. 1745.

Office workers, leaving work at the end of the day. All of them stopped at the desk and signed themselves out before they left the building. Very safety-conscious.

Then I took in the date.

Friday twenty-third August. Twelve years earlier.

The day before Rob vanished.

I heard Susie's breath hiss between her teeth. She'd obviously taken it in too.

Gradually the office-worker rush lessened. The receptionist packed up and left at 1803 handing over to what I assumed was a night watchman or caretaker. Nothing else happened for a while, then at 1810, the automatic door spun and a young woman stepped inside. Briefcase, plain white shirt with the sleeves pushed up, figure-hugging skirt, stilettos. Sexy but professional. I couldn't see her face clearly but even so, I might have been tempted to wolf-whistle, except of course it was now illegal and I was firmly married and standing next to my wife.

The woman signed herself in with the caretaker and walked away, to the lifts, I assumed.

Two minutes later my breathing hitched.

Rob walked inside.

He wore jeans and what looked like a linen jacket over a T-shirt. Deck shoes. His hair was shaggy and long enough so it almost brushed his shoulders. He looked casual and sporty, as though he'd just walked off the deck of a swanky motor yacht in the Mediterranean. He signed himself in. Walked in the same direction the young woman had taken.

Neither Susie nor I moved to press the pause button. We sat there, waiting for the CCTV to play out.

At 1813 another woman appeared. Middle-aged, grey-ish bob. Dark suit, flat heels, briefcase. She signed in, headed out of view.

A couple more people dribbled out. Then nothing happened for ten minutes. They had to be the longest ten minutes of my life, waiting for something to happen.

1828.

Suddenly, the middle-aged woman appeared at a run. Not a jog or a trot, she was sprinting for the door as fast as her sensible shoes would carry her. The caretaker rose to his feet in alarm. Then Rob appeared. He was running flat out too. It looked as though he was running after the woman.

My heart hollowed when I saw what he had in his hand.

A gun.

The automatic doors swung open. The woman tore outside, hotly pursued by Rob.

The caretaker was already on the phone. Calling the police, I guessed.

1837, the police arrived. Four of them, in a rush. They didn't sign themselves in. They spoke briefly to the caretaker, then raced out of view.

1842, two cops returned. One spoke to the caretaker. Another looked at the reception folder. The first cop jotted notes in a notebook. Took a photograph of the reception folder on his phone. The other kept talking to the caretaker.

Time passed.

The cops moved away from the reception desk. Disappeared back into the building.

More time passed.

We watched the caretaker fidget at his desk. I fidgeted too, but Susie remained perfectly still with her cloak of ultra-alertness wrapped around her.

1917.

The caretaker took a call. He went and stood by the door. Two large men in suits appeared. Behind them strode a tall figure in a suit I thought I recognised. My hand hovered near the pause button but there was no need.

It was the Saint.

1919.

They disappeared from view. They hadn't looked at the caretaker. Just swept through the doors and straight across the foyer.

1933.

The Saint walked back across the foyer and disappeared outside. He was alone.

1934.

The tape ended.

Chapter nineteen

I stood staring at the grey screen feeling as though I'd eaten a bag of razor blades. Susie didn't move for a while either. Finally, she turned and looked at me.

'What the hell?' she said.

I stood up and went into the kitchen area. Put my hands on the worktop and leaned over them, head bowed.

He must have been on assignment, I told myself. He was on a job for MI5, hence the gun. But why was he chasing that woman? What was all that about? Was she a criminal of some sort? A terrorist? She looked so unlikely. What had a dowdy businesswoman done to antagonise Rob?

I moved back into the sitting area and rewound the recording. I wanted to see it again. Susie watched it with me. We didn't say anything. When I saw the police enter this time round, something about the cop who'd photographed the reception folder caught my attention. Was it his body language? The way he held himself? Something about him was familiar but I couldn't work it out.

The Saint, on the other hand, I could identify with a blink of my eye. Same height, same breadth of shoulders and thick white hair. I wondered when it had changed colour. He was, according to the internet, sixty years old. He would have been forty-eight when this video had been taken, twenty-three years older than Rob, and aside from a few lines here and there, he'd aged pretty well.

For the second time, I watched my brother running after a middle-aged woman. He was running properly, no half-measures, the gun held easily in his right hand. He meant business. I wondered if he'd caught her. He wasn't far behind, and although she'd put on a fair turn of speed, obviously terrified, I doubted she'd outrun him.

When the screen turned fuzzy, I leaned forward and picked up the plastic case the DVD had been in. Re-read the note.

IF YOU WANT TO SEE WHY YOUR BROTHER DISAPPEARED, WATCH THIS.

I looked back at the TV screen. The CCTV footage offered more questions than answers as far as I was concerned, but there was still something niggling at me. I rewound the clip a little. Peered closely at the screen.

'What is it?' Susie asked.

'It's a logo.' I pointed at part of a grey blur on the front of the desk.

Susie bent closer for a better look. 'So it is.'

I enlarged it, and although it lost focus I was fairly sure it depicted a skyline. 'I'll take it to work,' I said. 'Get Ronja to have a look. If anyone can find out what it is, it'll be her.'

'I'll take a copy to work. Do the same.'

I leaned back, pressing my fingers against my forehead. Anxiety gnawed at me. Who had slipped into our house and left the disc here?

'Who's got keys?' I asked Susie.

She fetched her phone, checked her notes. She nibbled her lip. 'Um…' She put down her phone. Stared at the fuzzy grey screen on her laptop.

'Suze?' I prompted.

'The thing is…' She got to her feet and moved towards the kitchen area. 'I need a beer. Would you like one?'

I followed her. Watched her go to the fridge and pull out two bottles of beer, pop the tops. She passed one over and I took it, but put it on the worktop without drinking. When she glanced at me, I raised my eyebrows at her. She looked away. She said, 'The only people who have keys are you and me.'

'What?'

'I got everyone to return them.'

'Mum and Dad don't have a set?'

'No. Nobody does.'

I opened and closed my mouth. I felt broadsided. 'What if we have a problem, like the boiler blows up?'

'Then they ring one of us and we tell them where the spare is.'

The spare was in a watertight little tube buried to the left of our clematis. I'd used it several times.

'Nick,' she sighed. 'I know you've all spent your lives in and out of one another's houses, but I haven't had the same upbringing. And when I came downstairs once, dressed in nothing but a T-shirt and knickers to find your father fixing the tap outside the kitchen window, I just about had heart failure. I didn't know it was him at first glance, it was just a man, a *stranger*. Scared the shit out of me. This is our house, Nick. Your space, and mine. I don't want anyone to walk in at any time. I want to be in my home in the firm and safe knowledge that the only time I hear the key in the lock is when you come home.'

'I understand your point, but shouldn't you have said something?' My voice rose in indignation. 'Why didn't you tell me?'

Defiance crossed her face. 'Because I knew you'd respond like this.'

'No, I wouldn't,' I protested. 'I would have been fine if you'd asked me. It's just…' It was hiding what she'd done that had shaken me, but I didn't want to say that and cause a massive row. I took a breath. 'How did they take it?'

'They were fine.' She shrugged. 'They understood completely.'

Silence.

'I'm sorry.' She fiddled with her wedding ring. 'I should have said something but I never got the courage.'

'Am I that much of a tyrant?' I asked disbelievingly.

She gave a wan smile. 'No. Quite the opposite. It's just that you're… you love your family. I didn't want you to think I was shutting them out in any way.'

Which she had, literally, and I couldn't help seeing the humour in what she said. I put out an arm and she walked into my embrace. 'It's okay,' I told her. I kissed the top of her head. 'But next time, please promise to tell me if something bugs you.'

'Promise.'

Row diverted, I reached out and grabbed my beer, took a slug. 'Who do you think dropped the DVD in here?'

'If it wasn't you and me, it would have to be someone who knew where our spare was. When did you last use it?'

I tried to think. 'Before Christmas, I think. I accidentally left my keys in the office after our Christmas drinks. You?'

She shook her head. She'd never used them. No need. Unlike me – a bit shambolic from time to time – she had control of her life, and control of her keys. A bit of a stickler, my Suze, but thank God she didn't expect me to be like her because that would make life extremely tedious.

'I can't think someone would watch the house for weeks on end waiting for one of us to dig up a spare,' I said, but she wasn't listening. She was moving around the sitting area, checking the windows.

'What if one of my family kept a key?' I suggested tentatively.

'The exact number was returned.'

'What if someone had cut an extra copy?'

She paused. She said, 'I suppose they could have.'

'I'll check with them all tomorrow. And I'll get an alarm installed tomorrow too. As well as get the locks changed.'

'That would be great.' She gave me a smile but it didn't reach her eyes. She was anxious, I could see, and I couldn't blame her. I was anxious too. I wanted to know who had come into our home and left that disc on our coffee table. Whoever had done it could have put it through our letterbox, but instead they'd chosen to violate our space with a brazen gesture that said, *I can do anything I like, including walking inside your home while your wife is in the shower.*

Chapter Twenty

First thing the next morning, I rang an old pre-school friend who I still sailed with, Sebastian Potter.

'I need an alarm,' I told him. 'Like yesterday. We had a break-in last night.'

'Sorry to hear that.'

'And no saying "I told you so".'

'Would I do that?' He sounded innocent but I could hear the chuckle in his voice. He'd tried to sell me an alarm two years earlier and I'd asked what on earth for. Bosham was one of the safest places in the UK. Not anymore as far as I was concerned.

'I'm not at work yet,' he said. 'Do you want me to come over now? See what I can do?'

'Seb, you're a gentleman.'

'Your round next time, yeah?'

'Yeah.'

I left Seb installing a wireless kit with internal and external siren, part arming for night mode, and a panic button by the front door. I texted Susie to let her know and got a kiss back, then I went and knocked on my neighbour's door, asked her if she'd seen anyone entering our cottage.

'Sorry, love.' She closed the collar of her fleece against the chill breeze. 'Is there a problem?'

'It's not as much a problem as a puzzle. Yesterday, someone left something for us inside the cottage, and we're not sure who it was, that's all.'

'I only saw your father.'

'Really?'

'That's who I assumed it was.' She looked anxious. 'It was him, wasn't it?'

'Hang on a mo.' I quickly dialled Dad, asked the question. 'No,' I told my neighbour. 'It wasn't him. Can you remember what the man looked like?'

'Oh dear…' She screwed up her face while she thought. 'He was an older man. Which is why I thought it was your father.'

She couldn't recall anything further. Not what he was wearing, whether he drove a car or not. Believing he was Dad, her observational faculties had obviously switched off.

Thanking her, I walked to the car, hopped in and dropped the CCTV footage to Ronja to see if she could work out the logo, then I went around the family to see if anyone had a key of ours, or a copy of one. First stop, Clara and John, who said no. They could completely understand Susie's viewpoint.

'It's your home,' Clara said.

'But I have keys to your place.'

'That's different. We have kids.'

Neither Finn nor Honey had any keys of ours, nor my sister Kate or her husband Simon. Nor the paper shop, which used to hold a set beneath the counter for me. Which left my parents.

I found Dad in the shed, surrounded by cabinetmaker's chisels, mallets, plans and tenon joints. He'd finished making a kitchen table for a friend and was now absorbed with making a spice rack. 'Your mother wants a new one,' he told me. 'The old one's a bit of a mess now.'

When Rob "died", I remember Dad retreating to his shed. He always did that when stressed or needed time out from the grandkids or life in general. It was his escape, and back then, his lifesaver because Mum took Rob's death really hard. Not surprising I know, because no mother should lose a child – it's a wicked thing – but Mum seemed to make no effort to help herself and after six months, Dad was exhausted from trying to look after her. A rush of anger spiked in my gut. Didn't Rob know what hell he'd put us through?

I asked Dad about keys and he put down his pull-saw. 'Susie came ages ago wanting them back,' he told me. 'We had three sets, can you believe it? She took them all and I can't say I blame her. I felt really bad about giving her a fright that day. I'd sent a text telling her I'd be there to fix the tap but she hadn't read it. No excuse, mind you. I should have rung and spoken to her, made sure she knew I was coming over, especially after... you know.'

Her attack.

'It's okay, Dad.'

I nipped in to see Mum, who was taking in one of Honey's dresses. Mum had pins in her mouth and pink frothy material in her hands and she was pale and unhealthy looking, as though she hadn't seen the sun in years. She put down the dress and pins, greeting me with a hello and a hug. 'Any news, darling?'

'Not yet.'

'I can't imagine where he is.' She was shaking her head. 'What he's doing. Where he's been all this time. I can't sleep, let alone eat with worrying.'

We talked a bit about Rob, how angry we felt at his deception, how Clara and I were doing after our experience with the Saint – pretty good, considering, us Ashdowns are nothing if not robust – and then I turned the subject to keys.

'Susie took them all,' she said. Her words were flat and, unlike the rest of the family, she didn't add anything about understanding Susie's point of view.

'All?' I said.

'Three sets. Do you know how much they cost?' Mum looked indignant.

'But you can see her point. It's our place. Our space.'

She made a harrumphing sound. 'I don't see why she should act differently to the rest of the family. Set herself apart.'

I felt a stab of annoyance.

'She was attacked, remember?'

'As if we could forget it,' Mum snapped.

Jesus, just what I didn't want; Mum having a go at Susie. She'd never really got along with Susie and although Susie tried hard, Mum refused to be befriended, behaving like a typical mother-in-law who believed her son could do no wrong but the daughter-in-law was the devil incarnate.

'We've keys to everyone's houses, you know,' Mum went on. 'We were at Kate's last week, letting the carpenter in. Their windows are leaking like sieves. And we didn't have to bother Clara when Simon left his keys at work and Honey had accidentally taken their spare to her boyfriend's. He could simply nip in and grab a set. God alone knows how you'll cope when you have children.'

She allowed a silence to develop which I didn't dare broach. Anything I said would either be taken the wrong way or Susie would get shot down in flames for not yet having produced a grandchild for my parents to dote on.

'Neither of you are getting any younger,' Mum said, shaking her head. Which was true, and if I paused to think about it, concerned me as much as it did Mum now Susie had turned thirty-six and I was fast approaching forty.

'You do want children, don't you, darling?'

Her voice was gentle and a little gust of misery blew through me. If I was perfectly honest, I wasn't sure that Susie wanted kids anymore. When we first met she'd been really keen but now I knew how ambitious she was, I found it hard to see her embracing motherhood, even if I did turn into a full-time house husband.

Susie hadn't said so outright, but by prevaricating the way she had over the past couple of years – *Just let me get this promotion… what's the rush? Let's enjoy being just us a little longer* – I suddenly realised I might not become a father.

Something must have shown in my face because Mum put her sewing down and rose to her feet.

'Darling…'

I couldn't bear her sympathy.

'I've got to go,' I said stiffly. 'Sorry, Mum. I'll see you later.'

Chapter twenty-one

Still feeling emotionally wobbly, I walked down the corridor. I'd have to talk to Susie, I realised. Ask her outright about having children, because if we were going to start a family, we'd have to start soon. Like *now*. But something inside me already knew her answer and the little gust of misery abruptly turned into a full-blown monsoon.

I was so absorbed in my thoughts, I was already through the front door when I realised I'd forgotten to check the hall table for keys. I backtracked to the large bowl that always sat on top but didn't see any that looked like ours. I opened the top drawer. More keys jumbled among books of stamps, sunglasses and pens. Next drawer down, bingo. They even had a tag attached with my name on them.

My mind buzzed. Had Rob come here and borrowed the keys? He'd know where they were. Or had he told someone else where to find them? My stomach gave a little flip. Had it been my brother who'd left us the CCTV tape? And why had Mum blatantly lied to me saying Susie had every set of keys? Giving an internal sigh, I guessed her motivation: keep a set so when she saved the day, stopping the toilet from flooding or the roof from falling in, we'd be pathetically, apologetically grateful.

Gently I picked them up, put them in my pocket and headed to the office.

When I got there, Ronja greeted me with a hug and a kiss on the cheek. 'How are you doing, Nick?'

I was about to give my stock answer of *fine, thanks*, when my legs almost gave way. I don't know whether it was the concern on her face or whether it was because she wasn't family so I didn't have to present a strong front, but I suddenly felt incredibly tired.

'Hey,' she murmured and pulled out a chair for me. 'That bad, huh?'

I managed a rather weak smile as I sank into the chair. 'It's not been great.'

She made me a coffee and brought it over. 'Tell me.'

It was a relief to unload to someone I trusted. Unlike with the family, I didn't have to edit things as much and most of it (aside from Susie's job) came tumbling out. Rob and the people who wanted to find him, from DI Gilder to the Saint (but I never said his name) and onto Etienne and some unknown Spaniards who wanted their money.

'And then this CCTV video,' Ronja said. 'Left in your home. Scary. Have you changed the locks?'

'Yup. First thing this morning. We're also putting in an alarm.' I indicated her computer screen. 'What did you find?'

She turned the screen so we could both see. She'd played with the image, sharpening and expanding it, and I'd been right. It was a partial logo of what appeared to be the first part of a fuzzy M. Ronja clicked onto Google and the entire image appeared. A crisp skyline with an M beneath blurred into the word Mayfair. She tapped some more until a website appeared. The Mayfair Group. London Property Investment & Development Specialists.

'I'll leave you, yes?'

'Thanks heaps, Ronja.'

'Any time.'

I had a browse through their website. Learned it was founded by Anthony Abbott and Roger Marshall in the nineties, and that they'd helped private and institutional clients complete residential and commercial property deals collectively valued at many hundreds of millions of pounds.

My skin prickled.

The photograph of Anthony Abbott showed a man in his early thirties in a sharp suit, prematurely white hair, broad shoulders.

He was nothing if not a chip off the old block. He could have been a young George Abbott. Aka the Saint.

I grabbed the mouse and did some googling to confirm that Anthony Abbott was indeed the Saint's son. I then accessed Google Earth to check out Mayfair's head offices, which were, surprise surprise, in the heart of Mayfair.

When I had the right street, I switched the image to street view and had a look around. It didn't take long until I'd pegged the right building because most of them were around a hundred years old, Grade II listed buildings with architectural sculpture and putti on the façades, with big solid oak doors – but the Mayfair Group was housed in a modern construction – a ten-storey block of steel and chrome with automatic doors to the street. Overlooking St. James's Park, it was a stone's throw from The Ritz Carlton and Piccadilly Circus. Prime real estate. I mean *really* prime, like some of the most expensive on the planet.

What had Rob been doing there?

I leaned back in my chair and stared at the image of the building. Anthony Abbott, the Saint's son, had founded the company. With Daddy's money? My mind snaked onwards. Property development could be an easy way of laundering Daddy's dirty money as well. I trawled around the site but couldn't find any further reference to Anthony Abbott so I put his name into Google.

Instantly six images appeared of the man, all of him in a suit, all of him looking serious and businesslike.

The next reference was Wikipedia. I read that Anthony "Tony" Abbott was born on 5 December 1976 and was a property developer who'd won the Property Entrepreneur of the Year Award when he turned thirty-one. Most of the text was a plug for his business, but then I came to the last line.

Abbott was shot to death aged 32. He was buried in East Finchley Cemetery.

My eyes flew to the top of the page. I hadn't taken in the dates. He'd apparently died on Friday twenty-third August. Twelve years earlier.

My stomach rolled in ice.

Oh God, Oh God, Oh God. Please no, no, no no no.

Tony Abbott had been shot twice. Once in the chest, and then another bullet had been fired into the back of his head. Execution style. To make sure he was dead.

He'd been murdered in his office, on the third floor overlooking the park. He'd been murdered in the same offices on the same day my brother had been videoed arriving and then leaving at a run with a gun in hand. There were no witnesses and nobody knew who had done it.

Oh, dear God.

I felt shaky and sick.

I got to my feet, sat back down. Put my head in my hands. Tried to think. Had Rob killed the Saint's son? If so, it would make sense that the Saint had come looking for Rob. He'd want vengeance for Tony. Had it been a hit? Had MI5 told Rob to take Tony out for some reason? Or had Rob's cover been blown and he'd been forced to silence Tony? And then there was DI Gilder, also looking for Rob. Did he suspect Rob was the killer?

I thought of my brother, his love of the sea, his generous and compassionate spirit. Yes, he was independent and fun-loving, ebullient, but I would never have perceived him to be a killer. He didn't have a malicious bone in his body. He wasn't violent. He'd put spiders outside the house, rescued bugs and flies from the swimming pool, and once he'd come home with a kitten that someone had put in a sack at the side of the road to die. He called it Nelson even though it was female. The cat lived for another eighteen years. But then I recalled the CCTV film of Rob taking down the gunman in the restaurant, the efficiency and proficiency of his blows. Had he been trained to attack and kill? Or had it always been in him?

And what about me? Did I have that killer instinct too?

For the first time in my life, I felt my foundations shake.

I closed my eyes. Turned my mind to the police. If Rob had murdered Tony Abbott, why hadn't the police arrested him? That had to be why he'd vanished. Because he was wanted for murder.

Chapter twenty-two

I went back online. Found several newspaper reports. The one in *The Evening Standard* pretty much said it all:

BUSINESSMAN FOUND SHOT TO
DEATH IN MAYFAIR OFFICE
by Geoff Leipzig

Tony Abbott, a property developer, was found fatally shot in his office last night, and authorities say they are investigating the death as a homicide.

DI David Gilder of the Metropolitan Police reported they responded at 8pm to a report of a suspected gunman running out of the office building and onto Piccadilly. A caretaker told officers that the man was holding a gun, DI Gilder said. Police searched the building and found thirty-two-year-old Abbott dead behind his desk. He had been shot.

DI Gilder said there were no signs of a fight or altercation, and that nothing has been reported missing. Detectives have not recovered a weapon.

'We don't believe the people in the community should be concerned about this being a random act,' DI Gilder said. 'The fact the victim had no defensive wounds and hadn't even risen from behind his desk, means the victim probably knew the suspect.'

'Our detectives are busy speaking with family, friends and associates to try to determine any possible motivation for someone to take this man's life,' he said. 'Whoever it was is pretty cold-blooded. We owe it to the victim to find out who did this and make them answer for it. We will use all of our resources to do exactly that.'

DI David Gilder. I felt dizzy and shook my head to clear it. I'd brought the CCTV video with me, and I replayed it. This time I paused the video when the policeman took photos of the reception folder. No wonder I thought I'd recognised him. Same strong body, hard jawline, cropped pale hair. But it wasn't Barry Gilder I'd recognised, it was his father.

I searched for further stories about Tony Abbott's murder, but the few that were around – and there weren't that many – quickly dwindled to nothing. The last, dated two weeks after Tony's death, was also written by Geoff Leipzig. Why weren't there more? Usually the media hounded the police for weeks, wanting snippets and titbits to report as well as demanding why nobody had been arrested, but the investigation into Tony's death appeared to have been abandoned with an almost unseemly haste. Why?

Also, why did David Gilder give 8pm as the time the police received the report of a suspected gunman running through the building? The CCTV showed them arriving at 1837. If the reporter hadn't made a mistake, then what had happened in that hour and twenty-three minutes?

I picked up the phone. Dialled *The Evening Standard* and with little hope of success, asked for Geoff Leipzig.

'Who?'

'He was on your staff twelve years ago. He wrote a piece on Tony Abbott's murder.'

'Who did you want again?'

Hope dwindling, I repeated myself.

'Only person who's been around that long's Fredericka but she's in a meeting right now, can I get her to call you back?'

Without much confidence, I left my name and number and hung up. Then I rang DI Gilder. I said, 'I want to see you.'

'Has he contacted you?' Fervent, eager.

'No.'

'Then what–'

'Someone gave me a video,' I cut over him. 'I'd like you to see it.'

'I see.' He was cautious. 'Could you give me a hint as to what's on it?'

'I think you should see for yourself. I don't want you making any assumptions.' I also wanted to watch his expression, his body language, to see if he gave anything away. Whether he knew the full story or not.

'Can't you put it in the mail?'

'No.' I made a snap decision. 'I'm in London later today. You're in the City of Westminster, so what if I–'

'Don't come to the station,' he interjected sharply. 'I'll meet you at The Lord Moon pub on Whitehall. After work.'

'What time?'

'Seven o'clock.'

He hung up without saying goodbye.

I looked at my watch and did some calculations. Before I headed to the railway station, I texted Susie and told her about my evening meeting, suggesting we stay at her flat that night.

She texted by return, asking me to meet her outside the Office at five thirty. She had some news for me.

Spirits raised, I zipped back home to find Seb with his head buried in our little hallway cupboard, a toolbox at his feet.

'I'm away until tomorrow,' I told him. 'How are we going to arrange things?'

He showed me the alarm panel, already connected. 'What code do you want to use?'

'One, nine, four, seven,' I said. 1947. The year Thor Heyerdahl set out from South America on a 4,300 nautical mile journey across the Pacific Ocean in a hand-built raft, *Kon Tiki*. My hero ever since I'd received his book for Christmas when I was a boy.

Seb punched in the number. 'Just until you're back, mind. You change it afterwards.' He showed me how, then talked me quickly through the rest of the kit. 'If it goes off, it'll come through to your mobile, alerting you.'

'Useful,' I said drily. 'I wouldn't want to interrupt them.'

'Hopefully they'll see the box outside and not bother. It's all about a visual deterrent.'

'Thanks, mate.'

I packed some overnight things into my satchel, grabbed my laptop, thanked Seb again, and caught the next train to London.

I love London. The bustle and energy, the smell of exhaust, of cooking, coffee. People striding everywhere, strolling, meandering. Tourists, businessmen, lovers, students. Black, white and brown, a melting pot of every race and culture. I love Bosham too, don't get me wrong, but it's like comparing a rowing boat with a cruise liner, they're so different.

I headed to Piccadilly, wanting to see where the Mayfair Group was housed. One stop on the Victoria line and I was exiting Green Park tube station. Immediately the atmosphere became more rarefied. It wasn't just the breadth of the street and the broadness of sky giving the sensation of grandness and space, but the majesty of the buildings and the height of the ancient plane trees. Men were dressed in smart woollen coats over suits. Women wore cashmere, leopard print and leather. Taxis jostled alongside Ferraris and Bentleys, every other car worth more than I could earn in three or four years. I even saw a shimmery purple Lamborghini. I was in one of the most affluent areas in the world and I was glad I'd changed out of my usual uniform of jeans and fleece and pulled on a decent pair of trousers and jacket, and my best leather shoes. Oh, and I'd shaved too.

When I passed through the automatic doors into the Mayfair Group's building, I felt a wave of déjà vu. Everything was familiar to me, but not known. The wrap-around desk appeared to be the same as the one on the CCTV tape, with its logo proud on the front. Same acres of floor space, but this time I could see straight ahead and to the bank of lifts and emergency staircase.

'Can I help you?'

I shifted my satchel on my shoulder and approached the desk where a smart whippet-thin woman sat, alert and expectant. Her name tag read *Gillian Wade*.

'Hi, Gillian,' I said. 'My name's Nick.' I glanced down at the reception folder. It looked as though it could be the same one from twelve years earlier, a ring binder with loose leafed photocopied pages punched through. *Name. Company. Visiting. Time In. Time Out.*

'Hello, Nick,' Gillian said.

I'd rehearsed what to say several times, but everything went out of the window. I decided to be up front.

I said, 'It may seem a bit out of left field, but I wanted to speak to the caretaker who was on duty when Tony Abbott died. Do you know who that was?'

She stared at me. She didn't blink. 'Why do you want him?'

'It's a personal matter.'

'I'm sorry, but we don't give out details of employees to the general public.'

'Does he still work here?'

'I'm sorry.'

'Look...' I turned my head as a man arrived, signed himself out. I watched him leave before glancing at the folder. *Edward Lilley. Jacobsen Co. Visiting Brian Armstrong. In at 1425. Out at 1510.*

Rob had signed in all those years earlier and so had the middle-aged woman he'd chased outside. Who was she? What had she witnessed? She hadn't been mentioned once, not in the newspaper reports, not anywhere. Why?

'I'm trying to answer a couple of questions for someone close to me,' I told Gillian. 'It won't take long and I'll pay him for his time.'

She considered me at length. Seemed to come to a decision. 'You're talking to the wrong person. I don't know who was on duty then. You'll need to talk to HR. They'll have the files.'

'HR it is. Who do you think would be the best person?'

She mulled a bit, then said, 'I think Helen might be the most receptive. I wouldn't see Sara, she's a bit of a dragon.'

'Helen then,' I agreed. 'Is she available now?'

Gillian made a couple of calls. 'She's free in ten minutes. Would you mind waiting over there?' She pointed at two leather chairs tucked to one side, with a table in between covered in property magazines.

'Sure.' I gave her a smile. 'Thanks.'

She returned the smile with a nod. All very polite and accommodating. So far, so good.

I flipped through Mayfair's International Luxury Collection catalogue, where every other page depicted tropical villas with infinity pools and endless views of palm trees fringing achingly gorgeous ocean fronts. It made me want to grab Susie and head straight for Heathrow, jump onto a plane to the Caribbean and forget all about everything that was going on. I'd never been to the Caribbean but of course Rob had. He'd said the sailing was fantastic, the rum cocktails even better.

'You can go up,' Gillian called. 'Third floor.'

I had exited the lift and was following the arrows to HR along a plush royal-blue carpeted corridor, when a group of men came around the corner and walked towards me. Four of them. Three of them were listening to the one in the front who was speaking. The boss. For a moment I couldn't believe my eyes. What the hell...?

Then my adrenaline kicked in and my heart banged like a great big drum. Bang-bang-bang. It was thumping so hard I wondered why I didn't faint. I was about to walk away – God knew where, all I knew was that I had to leave *fast* and without being seen – when he looked straight at me and said, 'Well, well. If it isn't the artist.'

Chapter twenty-three

'Hi,' I said, my voice a croak.

The men with the Saint spread out slightly in a defensive half-circle but he waved a hand at them. 'It's okay. He's a comic book artist.'

The men relaxed. I didn't.

He came and stood in front of me. He wore a camel coat, flung casually over his shoulders. Sharp suit, immaculate shoes. A silk tie with little white dogs dotted all over it. He saw me looking. 'My niece gave it to me.'

'Nice,' I managed.

'She thought it was cute.'

Inside, an endless stream of swear words shrieked through my mind. *Fuck fuck fuck.*

He said, 'What are you doing here?'

I licked my lips. 'Trying to find my brother.'

'I see. And how do you plan to do that?' He looked genuinely interested, not surprising since he wanted to get his hands on Rob to kill him for killing his son. If that's what had happened of course and if not, I wanted to find out the true story so I could prove Rob innocent and he could come home.

'I was going to talk to the caretaker who was here the day...' I cleared my throat. 'Er, your, er...' I didn't dare say the word *son*, let alone the word *died*. I didn't know how he'd react.

For a moment he looked stunned. Then he caught my upper arm and twisted me aside, away from the men. His grip was so strong I could feel the bruises forming but I didn't protest. I didn't dare.

'So now you know why I want your fuck of a brother,' he hissed.

I gulped.

'He ripped out the heart of me.' The hiss was low and vicious, laden with venom. 'He stole the best thing in my life, do you understand?'

I gave a jerky nod.

'I thought he was fucking *dead*, you get it? And then there he is on my fucking TV screen having fucking lunch in the same fucking city as though nothing's fucking happened, the fuck.'

He pushed me hard, away from him. I knocked into the wall. He stood there motionless, gazing at me, his expression cold.

He said, 'Call me when you get any information on him. *Anything*. Understood?'

He clicked his fingers at one of his goons who reached into a pocket and withdrew a business card. Handed it to me. I didn't look at it. Just stood there until they'd vanished inside the lift and the door had closed. I was trembling and felt chilled to my core. I hadn't considered the Saint might be here, but of course he'd be involved in the company. He was Tony's father.

Shit, shit, shit.

Did it matter that he knew I knew the story? I didn't think so. He'd *want* me to find Rob of course. No wonder he hadn't thrown me out of the building, which at first I thought he might.

I just about jumped out of my skin when a voice said, 'Nick?'

A sweet-faced young brunette was walking towards me.

'It is Nick, isn't it?'

I unstuck my tongue from the roof of my mouth. Managed a hoarse, 'Yes.'

'You know Mr Abbott?' She was looking at where the Saint had disappeared into the lift.

'Oh, yes.' My tone was slightly dry as I recovered a fraction of equilibrium, rather like a minnow that had just escaped the jaws of a barracuda.

'Great,' she said. Obviously the exchange between Abbott and me hadn't triggered anything to alarm her because she smiled at me. 'I'm Helen.' She put out a hand. 'How can I help?'

I cringed as we shook because my hand was horribly sweaty but she was polite enough not to wipe it on her skirt immediately, but waited until we were in her office and she thought I wasn't looking. Bless her.

'I want to speak to the caretaker who was on duty when Mr Abbott's son was, er… died.'

Her eyes widened. 'Oh.'

'I assume you keep a record of your employees?'

'Oh,' she said again. She looked flummoxed.

'Is there a problem?'

'It's just that we never mention it. That day. I mean, *ever*.'

'Ah,' I said. 'I see.'

'But if Mr Abbott has given you the go-ahead, then I will do everything I can to help.'

'Thank you.'

She wheeled her chair closer to her desk. 'When was it? The day, er… I'm afraid it was well before my time.'

I gave her the date. Watched her tap away.

'I'm afraid I don't have a record of who was on duty that day. We don't keep rosters for more than a year at a time.'

'Could you tell me who the caretakers were then?'

More tapping while I gazed outside at the park, the dull green grass crossed by paths, the avenues and scattered leafless trees. The sky was leaden and aside from the odd flash of a red scarf or blue gloves, no colour. I felt a longing for spring. Or the Caribbean. I'd had enough of winter.

A soft whirring sound indicated a printer was at work. Helen passed me a sheet of paper.

She said, 'None of them work here anymore.'

I ran my eyes down the list of three people and their dates of employment. Two men, one woman. One man's address was in Wandsworth, the other in Ealing. The woman's address showed Peckham. Each had a phone number attached. I had to hope none of them had moved.

'Anything else?' Helen asked, bright-eyed and keen.

'I'd like the same printout for everyone on the payroll at that time.'

She blinked. 'Everyone?'

'Everyone.'

'It might take a while.'

'I'm happy to wait.'

I spent the time half on my laptop, half looking out of the window, thinking. What had Rob been doing in these offices? Who had he been seeing? I'd have done anything to see the relevant page of the reception folder when Rob had signed in.

Finally, Helen reached across to me and I had another list. A swift count showed it had twenty-three names on it.

'Thanks.'

She arched her eyebrows prettily, waiting for another request.

I tapped the list she'd given me. 'Who on here is still around?'

She looked at her screen. 'Roger Marshall.'

'The co-founder.'

'Yes. Along with Eryn Deroukakis and Tim Kelly.' Helen looked further. 'And Steve Smith and…' She glanced at me. 'I know what. I'll print off who's employed here today and you can compare the lists.'

'I'm very grateful,' I told her sincerely, which won me another pretty smile.

The next list contained forty-one employees from the directors to general counsellors and administrative assistants. The company had almost doubled in twelve years, and out of the twenty-three people in Mayfair's employ twelve years earlier, six were still here.

'Who's available for me to speak to this afternoon?'

'I'll see.'

I let her ring two people, who had no interest in wasting time with a stranger who wasn't interested in buying a multimillion-pound property in the Turks and Caicos, and then I leaned forward. 'Tell them I'm a friend of Mr Abbott's, and it's at his behest I'm here.'

Chapter twenty-four

Five minutes later I was with the main man himself, Roger Marshall, fifties, dark spiky hair, open shirt beneath a casual jacket.

'George sent you?' he said.

'Yes.' I was getting good at this lying lark. Everyone seemed to believe me even though to my ears my tone sounded slightly off.

He steepled his hands in front of his face. 'Helen intimated it was about Tony's death. I'm surprised. Usually George won't have it mentioned.'

'He wants to find the person who did it.'

Both eyebrows lifted. 'It's not before time. Are you a private detective?'

I couldn't help it. It was so far from how I imagined myself, I blinked.

'Cold case,' I said wildly. 'We both want to know definitively who was in the building that evening.'

'I told the police at the time.' Roger frowned.

'I know it's old ground, but in my experience things that people thought irrelevant at the time, become relevant later.' I waited for him to smell the bullshit, but he gave a nod.

'It was just the two of us,' he said. 'It was Friday. Everyone else had gone.'

'Two?' I prompted.

'Myself and Tony.'

Not Rob, nor the pretty young woman in the white blouse, or the middle-aged businesswoman. Odd.

'Could you tell me what happened that evening?'

Roger leaned back in his chair and put his hands behind his head briefly before dropping them to rest on his desk. 'Not much really. The first I knew anything was wrong was when a police officer stuck his head around my door. He was checking on a report that a man with a gun had run through reception.'

'What time was this?'

A guarded look came over Roger's face. 'After nine or so. I think I told the police nine fifteen.'

I frowned. 'Are you sure about that?'

His expression remained guarded. 'Absolutely.'

'It's late to be working. On a Friday.'

'I take it you haven't set up your own business.' His tone turned contemptuous. 'Turned it into a multi-billion company with seven offices in London, fifteen provincials in the UK, and eleven more in different countries around the world? Like Dubai, Hong Kong and New York?'

Point taken, but I wasn't going to kowtow.

'Who did you see that evening?' I asked.

He moved his hands to pick up a pen and twirl it between his fingers. 'Just Tony. He came around just after five. We shared a beer. Everyone had pretty much gone by the time he left to go back to his own office.'

'When was that?'

'Well before six. We both had shed loads of work to get through.'

'Did he have a family?'

Another frown. 'You know this, surely.'

'I'm asking because–'

'Yeah yeah, you said the thing about relevance coming later. Yes, he had a family. Beautiful wife, two kids. He was devoted to them.'

Something in his voice wasn't right so I said, 'But?'

'But what?' His tone was irritated and defensive.

He looked at me and our eyes locked. I hoped he saw nothing but steely determination. 'May I remind you,' I said coolly, 'who sent me.'

Marshall looked down at his lap. Let loose a long breath. 'Okay.' He lifted his head. 'But you've got to promise you won't tell Lily, Tony's wife. And for Christ's sake be careful what you say, and how you say it to George. He'd have ripped Tony's bollocks off at the time, and God knows I don't want his memory of Tony besmirched.'

I waited.

'This is between us.' He sent me a fierce look. 'If you say I told you, I will deny it one hundred per cent.'

'It's between us,' I echoed.

He closed his eyes briefly. Opened them. He looked down at his desk as he spoke. 'Tony liked the girls… fancied himself as a bit of a ladies' man. They didn't seem to mind him either.'

I'd been ready for him to say that Tony was a closet gay with a gambling or BDSM addiction, nothing as straight as being a bit of a womaniser. My mind flashed to the gorgeous creature who'd arrived at 1810. Had she gone to see Tony? I brought out my laptop. Fast forwarded through the video until I came to her. I turned the laptop round. 'Do you recognise this woman?'

Roger leaned forward. Took in the video's details. 'How the fuck did you get this?' He sounded shocked.

I let the silence hang.

'Jesus.' He was blinking rapidly. 'George is serious, isn't he? He really does want to know.'

'Do you recognise her?'

He had another look. 'No.'

Then he took in the date and the time. He said, 'Sweet Jesus. She was in the building then.' He sounded genuinely stunned.

I didn't answer. I let the video run until the middle-aged woman arrived. I pressed the pause button once again. 'And her?'

He studied her at length, frowning. 'No. Sorry.'

I switched off the video and snapped shut the laptop lid.

'Both women were here?' he asked. 'That night?'

I'd worked out I got results perfectly fine if I didn't answer any of his questions and kept asking my own, so I said, 'Do you think the younger woman was Tony's type?'

He stared at me. 'You think she was here to see him?'

'What do you think?'

'In all honesty?'

'Yes,' I said. 'In all honesty.'

'I think she's too classy.'

'In what way?' I was genuinely curious.

He had to think about that one. 'I'm not sure. She looks as though she's from the upper side. I guess it's her clothes.' He shrugged. 'He liked them more tarty, a bit more obvious.'

I was about to move on and ask about DI David Gilder and the detective's police work on the case, but the sleek chrome phone on his desk buzzed. A woman's tinny voice said, 'Mr Palmer's on his way up with Mr Abbott.'

I tried not to make an unseemly bolt for the door and rose in what I hoped was a casual fashion. 'I've already seen George today,' I said. 'I'll leave you to it.'

I didn't offer to shake hands. Nor did Marshall. I walked out of his office. Tried not to run for the lifts. Tried to keep a steady pace across the foyer.

It wasn't until I was outside and on the opposite pavement and passing Fortnum & Mason's when the muscles in my body finally relaxed.

Chapter twenty-five

I stood waiting for Susie beside the entrance of MI5, housed in Thames House, an impressive Grade II listed stone building decorated with statues on the north bank of the River Thames. The Secret Intelligence Service's distinctive "ziggurat" fortress-style building, often mistaken for the Security Service's HQ, was on the other side of the river. The tide was as high as it was going to get. The water swirled in dark shapes and shadows beneath a looming cement sky.

I looked at the closed-circuit TV cameras dotted around and felt amazed that I'd married such an incredible woman. A real live spook.

I was still mentally shaking my head in wonder when my spook swept out of the doors and came towards me. She was wearing a tiny-checkered pencil skirt suit and high heels. Her hair was pinned up in a no-nonsense knot and she looked smart and efficient and very, very sexy.

'How do you run in those?' I pointed at her shoes.

'I don't.'

'But what if there's an emergency?'

'I kick them off. Or I put on a pair of trainers.' She kissed my lips. 'You're looking smart. I like it.'

'Perhaps I should dress up more often?'

'Don't,' she said, smiling. 'I like you the way you are. You're the yang to my yin and I wouldn't have it any other way.'

I hadn't known anything about Taoism until I met Susie. She'd given me a beautiful black and white sculpture, a ball depicting the Taijitu symbol, on our first wedding anniversary, which sat on my desk at work. It was a stunning piece of art that invited you to touch it, feel its smoothness and weight. You couldn't feel where the white stone connected with the dark, the point I supposed, since yin and yang describes how opposite or contrary forces are actually complementary, interacting to form a dynamic system in which the whole is greater than the assembled parts. Or something along those lines.

She looped her arm in mine and looked up at me.

'Where to?' I asked.

'You're meeting Gilder in a pub, so I thought we could go to Tachbrook.'

'Don't tell me, you fancy a chocolate éclair.'

'Me?' She pasted an innocent expression on her face. 'Chocolate?'

Tachbrook was a bakery and patisserie on Tachbrook Street. I'd met her there before, when I believed she worked in the Home Office on Marsham Street, just around the corner from MI5. It was only a few streets away so I wouldn't have to go far to get to the Lord Moon pub later.

We settled at the window. It had started to rain, a steady patter that dribbled down the window. We ordered coffee and pastries. Both came with a smile from a young man with pink stripes in his hair and a bolt through his eyebrow.

'So,' Susie said, biting into her éclair. 'What's new?'

When I got to the part about meeting the Saint in the corridor, she choked on her pastry. 'Jesus Christ, Nick.'

'Yeah, I know.' I had the smarts to look shamefaced.

'You shouldn't have gone there.' She leaned forward, expression intent. 'At least not without telling me. What if he'd abducted you? Or *worse*?'

I took a leaf out of my new investigative book and instead of answering, asked a question instead. 'Do you think the Mayfair Group is a legitimate business?'

'On the surface, sure, but if Abbott's around it's bound to have some murky bits. Property development's a great way of laundering money.'

I brought out the lists of caretakers and employees Helen had printed off for me. Showed them to Susie.

'Holy cow, Nick.' She looked at me, astonished. 'You'll be taking over my job soon.'

I grinned, delighted to have impressed her. 'Not bad for an amateur, eh.'

She scanned the list while polishing off the last of her pastry, licking the tips of her fingers until they were clean. 'Nobody there rings any bells,' she said. 'But let's pass it by Mark Felton tomorrow.'

'Who?'

'He's Rob's ex-case officer. He's my boss… So you'll have to behave. I've arranged for you to meet him tomorrow, first thing.'

My jaw dropped. 'You have?'

'Yup. We're meeting him for breakfast in Pimlico. Then he and I can walk to work.'

For the first time, I felt as though I was making ground. I was getting more and more questions answered, and once I'd seen Mark Felton, maybe I'd know how to find Rob. I wanted to see my brother *so much*. I wanted to go sailing with him. Have a pint with him. Go walking along the shore, identifying the waders probing in the mud for shellfish and crabs, chatting about nothing in particular alongside the sound of curlews. I wanted to see my little brother and give him a hug. After punching him first, of course.

I was still daydreaming when Susie touched my arm, pointing at her phone and excusing herself from the table. I nodded and as she moved to the far end of the café to talk, I read the lists again. Then I rang the caretaker in Wandsworth, but he'd moved, no forwarding details. Next, I called the caretaker in Ealing, who'd stopped working for the Mayfair Group a month after Tony Abbott's murder. The number rang and rang, and I was about to hang up when a man said, 'Hello?'

'Hello,' I said. 'Is that Mr Choudhuri? Mr Arun Choudhuri?'

'Yes, it is. Who's calling?'

'Hi, my name's Nick Ashdown. I wanted to talk about the time you worked for the Mayfair Group.'

Short pause.

'What about it?' His voice was cautious.

'You were on duty on Friday evening the twenty-third August, am I right?'

'Are you a journalist?' Still wary.

'No. Just someone wanting some answers as to what happened that night.'

'Who are you again?'

'I'm gathering information that I hope will find who killed Tony Abbott. I've been in touch with the police. They know I'm on the case.'

'What, like you're a private detective?' He sounded amazed. 'After all this time?'

'Which is why I would like to talk to you.'

'I can't.' He sounded surprisingly regretful. 'Sorry. I signed a confidentiality agreement. I can't break it.'

Excitement quickened in my gut. He knew something. He knew what had happened.

'I see,' I said. 'But you were on duty that night, right?'

'Yeah. But I can't talk about it. No point in continuing this conversation. Sorry.'

Meticulously polite, he apologised once more, then hung up.

I brought up a map of London on my phone and punched in his address. Checked my watch. 6.30pm. I hoped Arun Choudhuri would be home this time the next day, because I was going to make a house call. By then I would have seen Rob's boss as well as DI Barry Gilder.

Sophie returned, and I was going to give her an update but she said, 'Sorry. I've got to go. There's a bit of a flap on.' Her eyes were bright and glittering, and although she pressed a swift kiss against my lips and said she could be late, don't wait up, she wasn't actually seeing me. She was already at work, wherever that was, and the adrenaline was obviously pumping.

I watched her go, her slim form exuding energy and focus, and I tried not to think where she might be headed, or whether it might be dangerous. There seemed little point since I could do nothing about it. She loved her job with a passion I admired, although admittedly, sometimes I resented the time it took her away from me. And imagining her pregnant or with a toddler in hand was almost impossible.

I sighed, and in the interests of self-preservation and my general sanity, I turned my mind firmly away from my wife and to Rob and what I'd learned, and when I finally hit the pavement outside, I had a bit more of a spring in my step. I was getting closer to my little brother with every hour.

Chapter twenty-six

Earlier, I'd read that the Lord Moon of the Mall pub used to be a bank, and it still exuded a sense of dignity. Behind the classic pale pink sandstone façade was lots of dark woodwork, arched windows and vaulted ceilings. It was impressive and imposing, the clientele mostly businessmen and women in suits – Whitehall civil servants and MOD employees – and the odd tourist.

I couldn't see Gilder so I went to the bar and ordered a pint of Butcombe bitter. I was about to pay when he said at my shoulder, 'Same for me, if you don't mind.'

Pints in hand, we sat at a table next to a bookcase. Gilder took a long draught of beer, emptying the first quarter of his glass.

'Tough day?' I enquired.

'Always is.' He put down his glass, licked his lips. Exhaled. 'So where's this video?'

I brought out my laptop and he shifted his chair so he could see the screen clearly. I angled my body in order to watch his face. Pressed play.

It took him a nanosecond to realise what the video was about. 'Where the hell did you get this?'

'Have you seen it before?'

He didn't respond. Nor did he move his gaze from the screen.

When the sexy young woman in the white blouse appeared, I saw his gaze flick to the time. He did the same when the middle-aged woman arrived.

'Nothing happens for ten minutes,' I told him. I spun the laptop round so he couldn't see the screen and pressed fast forward, letting it run past the middle-aged woman running away from

Rob. I wasn't going to let Gilder see what looked to be hugely incriminating evidence against my brother until I'd got the whole story.

I turned the screen back to him and although I was sure he was doing his best not to react, I'd bet the last coin in my pocket he hadn't seen the video before. When the police arrived, he recognised his father immediately. His mouth slackened. He looked shocked.

Together we watched Barry's dad make notes in his notebook, and photograph the reception book. When the Saint appeared forty minutes later, Gilder's face became pinched, but it didn't show any surprise.

Eventually the video ended.

I closed the laptop lid.

Gilder sat there for a moment, then took a gulp of his beer. I did the same.

'Did your father send you to ask me where my brother is?' I asked.

'Where did you get this video?'

'I asked first.' I made sure my tone was mild.

The muscles in his cheeks bunched.

'No,' he gritted out. 'It wasn't him.'

'Was it the Saint?'

He wouldn't meet my eye, which I took to mean *yes*. Did that mean Barry was on the Saint's payroll? I'd have to tread carefully, if he was.

'There's a time discrepancy I'd like to talk to your father about,' I went on. 'As you saw, he arrived at the Mayfair Group at six thirty-seven, but he told a reporter that the police responded to a call about a gunman in the building around eight o'clock. I wonder what happened during that hour and twenty-three minutes?'

His nostrils flared. 'You may not believe this, but it's the first time I've heard about any time discrepancy.'

I raised my eyebrows.

'It's the truth.' He picked up his beer and took three more gulps, then he put down his glass and stood up. I rose too.

I said, 'The caretaker had to sign a confidentiality agreement about what happened that night. Does your father know why?'

He stared at me. 'I don't know. But you can rest assured I'm going to ask him.'

He walked outside. His shoulders were stiff, his body language forceful. I decided to let him go.

Chapter twenty-seven

Susie was back in the Office. Her nerves were tingling, her body alert. Her mind buzzed with the papers Nick had shown her. Was he crazy walking into the Saint's lair like that? Pride mingled with terror for him. How could she keep Nick protected in all this? She couldn't be with him every minute of every day. Plus, she had a job to do. She was part of the team tracking down several men suspected of planning a large-scale attack in central London, suggesting multiple targets, and her team had just alerted her of a new development.

As she strode down the corridor, she saw one of her team had emailed her, telling her that the Vauxhall car she'd seen near Clara's the night the Saint had threatened Clara and Nick, belonged to a DI Barry Gilder. It couldn't be a coincidence, could it? She looked at his photo. Something about him seemed familiar. Had they worked together perhaps? She undertook enough operations alongside the police for it to be possible.

There was a report attached which she hastily read. Lots of guff on training and official assessments, but the bottom line was that Barry Gilder seemed to be a pretty solid cop, and clean. The same couldn't be said for his father, however, who was rumoured to have been on the Saint's payroll. No evidence. Just speculation. But deep down she knew David Gilder was dirty, having seen him on that CCTV video and exposed his lies about when he'd arrived at the Mayfair Group the night of Tony Abbott's murder.

How far does the apple fall from the tree? she wondered. She couldn't work out whether Barry Gilder would help or hinder her and Nick's search for Rob, and she wondered if she ought to meet him. Or should she let Nick continue his haphazard but surprisingly effective investigation undisturbed? But what if he got hurt? What if he *died*? It didn't bear thinking about. Dear sweet Jesus. Nick was her rock, her island, her perfect companion, her lover, her defence, her guard and her protection against the world. Without him, she'd be back where she started; alone, unhappy, angry and confused. Never again. She would do just about anything to keep him safe because by doing so, she'd be kept safe too.

And then she was talking with fellow officers Ryan and Theo and her mind did its little shiver, and her husband and DI Gilder were no longer at the forefront of her mind, they were tucked neatly into a box right at the back while another box opened before her and she became absorbed in planning her next mission, executing it perfectly, a hazardous operation that might end her life – but it was at these times when she never felt more invigorated, more animated or more *alive*.

Chapter twenty-eight

The bus dropped me off on the Kings Road, just before Lots Road. It was raining, and I pulled up my jacket collar in a vain attempt to stop the water trickling down my neck. I increased my pace, looking forward to pouring myself a drink in Susie's flat and turning on the oven, heating up the takeaway I'd bought on the way home: prawn masala and garlic naan for me, beef rendang and rice for Susie and some samosas, a couple of onion bhajis with accompanying sauces.

Lots Road was full of auction houses, interior design stores and high-end wine shops for the wealthy. Broad shop windows showed antiques, hand-tufted rugs, glass tables, crystal lamps, French fabrics and wallpapers. Everything the average millionaire needed to furnish their home.

Apparently Susie had employed an interior designer to furnish her flat from top to bottom, including bed sheets, pictures on the walls, kitchen crockery and utensils – even the little knick-knacks like the Sri Lankan fan made out of papyrus on the mantelpiece and the cheerfully rude sculpture of Sheelanagig in her bathroom. I'd obviously shown my surprise – or was it disappointment that she hadn't collected these intriguing items herself? – she'd turned defensive.

'I didn't have the time,' she told me. 'It would have taken hours, *days*, to make it look even half as good as it does. You know I'm not into that stuff anyway, prettifying things. I'd rather spend the time down the range, shooting targets.' Out of nowhere, she suddenly switched from being self-protective to anxious. 'Would you like me to?'

'Like you to, what?'

'Be that woman who prettifies a home. You know, buying flowers and making little padded hearts to hang in the kitchen, stitched with *Home Sweet Home* or something equally...' She struggled for words and settled for, 'homey,' but I knew deep down she really meant *nauseating*.

I couldn't help it. I gave a snort of laughter.

'It's not funny.' She looked indignant. 'I want to know.'

'Considering you can't sew,' I told her, 'I can't begin to imagine what shape the heart would be.'

She looked glum.

I reached over and took her hand. Her insecurity always brought out the tenderness in me. 'Seriously, my love,' I told her. 'I wouldn't want you any other way. You should know that by now.'

'I know,' she sighed. 'But sometimes I wonder if I'm a bit OTT for you. You will tell me if something bugs you. If I get too bossy or short-tempered.'

'Sure,' I said, 'as long as you do the same for me.'

However, when I did mention a particularly foul mood of hers where she snarled and snapped at anyone and everyone during a family weekend, she vanished to London for three days and refused to take my calls, so I was careful how I approached that particular aspect of our relationship. We all have our dark sides and at least Susie's wasn't tucked away festering but open for everyone to see.

Not for the first time, I wondered what she was like at work, and I was picturing her sneering at some poor sap at the bottom of the food chain when two men appeared from behind the florist's booth outside Chelsea Harbour, and walked towards me.

'Nick?' one said.

'It is Nick, isn't it,' said the other.

I slowed down. 'What?' I didn't recognise either of them. Young, mid-twenties, jeans and hoodies. Fit-looking. They were smiling, hands wide, their appearance unthreatening, but instinct told me to back away.

'Hey, don't worry,' the first one said.

'We don't mean any harm.'

Yeah right.

I glanced quickly around to see who else was on the street. A taxi stood in the bay opposite the flower shop, a woman was walking towards the harbour ahead, a man on a scooter driving past. Not exactly busy but not deserted either.

I kept backing away.

'We just want your satchel.'

One of them extended his hand. At first I thought he was wearing a knuckleduster but then I realised it was a knife. A knuckle knife, with a steel blade.

For a moment I was immobilised. I couldn't even open my mouth to yell.

The other man held out his hand.

'Hand it over like a good boy and we won't hurt you.'

Dial 999, my mind screamed, and at the thought of the police, adrenaline flooded into my veins.

I dropped the takeaway and ran.

I heard one of them say, 'Shit,' and felt a second's gratification I'd surprised them.

I raced back the way I'd come. Head down, I charged along the street, heading for the pub. It was past eight in the evening. Loads of people inside to call the police. Loads of help.

I could hear the men's footsteps pounding behind me as I pelted along, my eyes fixed on bright lights of the pub across the mini roundabout and praying they wouldn't catch me before I got there.

When I reached the junction I was totally unprepared for another man to run full tilt from my right, straight at me.

I went down like a sack of sand.

One of the men behind me landed on my legs, pinning me down. The other punched me hard on the jaw. It was a stunning blow and for a moment I went limp. I felt my satchel tugged away, hands rummaging through my pockets and I raised my hands to ward them off but I got punched again. Lights flashed behind my eyes.

I heard an engine revving hard. The slick skid of tyres through the rain as someone jammed on the brakes. Doors opened and were slammed shut.

I struggled to my knees to see a grey sedan rocket back up Lots Road.

'Jesus, mate.' A man came galloping out of the pub. 'Are you all right?' Several people joined him, shocked and indignant.

The man hefted me upright and I stood there, swaying slightly, trying to get my head around what had happened.

'You need a witness, call me.' A woman gave me her business card. Two more people did the same.

'Heavens,' said another woman. 'I can't believe they mugged you so close to the pub. Almost in broad daylight.' The taxi that had been standing outside the florist's arrived, the driver asking if I needed a hospital. I shook my head.

'Barman's called the cops,' someone said.

I remained silent, rubbing my jaw, my aching cheekbone, and staring up Lots Road.

Chapter twenty-nine

The police thought it a routine mugging until they discovered I'd been attacked and tied up by unknown assailants in my sister-in-law's house two days earlier.

'You're not having a very lucky week, are you?' Detective Constable Wendy Doherty asked me.

'No,' I agreed.

I hadn't wanted to go to the police, but when I'd made moves for Chelsea Harbour after my attack – and a much-needed double whisky – the do-gooders wouldn't let me.

'But you've got to make a statement,' said a woman, looking shocked. 'You can't let them get away with it.'

Murmurs of agreement and nodding heads all round.

'Look, pal,' the taxi driver said. 'I'll give you a lift. On the house. Police station's only around the corner.'

I already knew a police interview was going to be tricky without having spoken to Susie. I'd tried her several times, thanking the heavens that although the thugs had snatched my satchel, they hadn't taken my mobile phone which had been tucked in the breast pocket of my jacket. I left another message for her, but I knew if I didn't report the assault, people might wonder why.

So here I was, sitting in a small windowless room with two chairs and a metal desk bolted to the floor, fluorescent lighting and the smell of peppermint air freshener.

'Do you think there's any connection between the assaults?' The DC's eyes were sharp.

So far, I told myself, I hadn't lied.

And even though I knew I couldn't tell the police what was going on without putting Rob in the frame for murder, I still felt as though I was hovering on the edge of what felt like a bottomless chasm.

I shook my head. 'I don't think so.'

'Just unlucky.' Doherty's eyes continued to bore into me like drills.

'Unlucky,' I murmured. My face was sore and I suddenly felt exhausted, as though I could sleep for a week. The reaction to all that adrenaline leaving my body, I supposed.

'There were four of them,' she said.

'Yes.'

'Two who approached you.' She checked her notes. 'One who tackled you when you ran away, and another driving the car they got away in.'

'Yes.'

The silence hung in the air as Doherty continued gazing at me. Her disbelief was palpable. *This is not a normal mugging, is it.* I tried to return her look with some kind of equanimity, but it was difficult. I was a fraud and she knew it too but she couldn't seem to do anything about it, because eventually she got me to sign my statement, and let me walk outside.

The rain had stopped but a chill mist had descended, wrapping the streetlights in gauze and making them resemble glow-worms. Needing to clear my head, I walked back to Susie's.

It didn't take long – fifteen minutes or so – but the walk down Lots Road felt much longer because I was so jumpy. But nobody came for me a second time, nobody showed me a knife. Amazingly my takeaway was still there, albeit hanging from one of the white posts next to the taxi rank. I plucked it free and had a look to see that everything seemed to have survived intact thanks to being stored in airtight plastic containers.

Susie rang just after I'd put on the oven.

'What's wrong?' she asked. She sounded breathless, as though she'd been running.

'It can wait until you get home.'

'Sure?'

'Yes.' I reached for the glass cabinet door, pulled out a whisky tumbler. 'I got curry.'

'Perfect. I'll see you in forty.'

Susie arrived home wired, almost rabidly energetic. 'Sorry I couldn't call you,' she said as she zipped into the bedroom, stripping off as she went. 'I was in the field. I desperately need a shower. I reek.'

Which meant she'd probably been running up and down streets with a gun in her hand chasing bad guys, much as I'd been running along a street being chased by them.

'Join me?' she called.

Although I'd had my whisky – a double, drunk on her balcony while cancelling all the credit cards that had been in my wallet, along with blocking my phone – I hadn't yet had a shower to wash away the fear-steeped sweat crusted over my skin.

'Coming,' I called back.

Susie's bathroom was a lush sanctuary with a feature wall in lavish white gold mosaic, cleverly partitioning the bathing area from the double-entry walk-in shower zone. The overhead showers were enormous, big enough to wash a rugby team so I wasn't worried about lack of space.

I'd barely stepped beneath Niagara Falls, as I liked to call it, when Susie slipped her soapy body against mine. Her hands were everywhere, her breathing coming fast. Out of nowhere, I felt a total and uncharacteristic loss of control. My mind abruptly emptied of everything but the need to be inside her. My heart roared, and there was a mute pounding in my skull. I couldn't hear, couldn't speak. I was only aware of how much I needed her. I was no longer terrified of my life, no longer fearful for Rob. I vanished into Susie like a dying man in the desert diving into an oasis of clear, cool water.

And then it was over.

Slowly, I came to.

I brushed strands of wet hair from Susie's face. Kissed her gently on the lips, on the forehead.

'I didn't hurt you?' I asked.

Somehow we'd ended up wedged against the marble-edged bath. Not the most comfortable environment.

She giggled against my chest. 'Trust me, if I get any bruises I won't be complaining. I needed that.'

Me too, I thought, and I had a flash of perspicacity that Susie had probably just used sex as I had, as a way of shutting off the turmoil in her head. A way of releasing tension after a dangerous mission.

'What were your calls about?' she asked. 'You sounded really stressed.'

I kissed her again. 'I'll tell you over the curry.'

Chapter thirty

Susie was quietly sympathetic over my attack and went and fetched some arnica, and gently tended my bruises. She didn't say much when I told her what had happened, but later, in bed, she curled into my arms and said, 'I know you want to find your brother but please, Nick, be careful. I don't want to lose you.'

I stroked her spine, listening to her breathing deepen as she fell asleep. Where part of me was surprised she hadn't demanded I stop looking for Rob, the other was glad she hadn't. She'd let it be my choice. I couldn't imagine many wives letting their husbands continue what others might call a reckless undertaking. Typical Susie, and why I loved her so much.

I slept badly, worrying about my stolen laptop along with its incriminating video of Rob. What would happen if it fell into the wrong hands? The police hadn't given me any reason to think they might retrieve it and it took me most of the night to realise I could do nothing except cross my fingers and hope that the CCTV footage never came to light.

When Susie looked at me the next morning I knew I looked bad. Cupping my face she tenderly kissed my bruised jaw, the bruise beneath my right eye, high on my cheekbone. She applied more arnica. I didn't bother shaving. Too tender, and there seemed little point.

Just past seven o'clock, Susie and I took a number eleven bus to Victoria Station. From there, we walked to Pimlico. It was raining again; dank and grey with people hunched under endless mushrooms of umbrellas.

The Regency Café stood on the corner of Regency and Page Street, and was one of those places that if we'd had one in Bosham,

I'd be there every day. With its tiled walls, linoleum floor, gingham curtains and boxing photographs on the walls, the English diner looked as though it hadn't changed since the 1950s. It was also packed: brickies, lawyers, city construction workers, a couple of Japanese tourists. Suits and coveralls jostled noisily together and the food smelled fantastic.

I followed Susie as she weaved her way to a window table where a man in a suit sat with a large glass of orange juice and a copy of *The Times*. Fifties, gold-rimmed spectacles, soft grey hair, paunchy jowls. Skin as pale as the underbelly of a fish.

He half-rose from his seat when she approached but sank back when she waved him down. She gestured for me to shuffle along the bench and, ever cautious, leaned past me to make sure the curtains, covering the bottom third of the window and giving diners privacy from the street, were pulled tight. Susie sat next to me. She made the introductions.

Mark Felton offered his hand and we shook. His grip was damp, surprisingly weak. A pair of level grey eyes surveyed me. Not a flicker of reaction over my bruised face.

'So,' he said. 'You're Rob's brother.'

'Yes.'

'Susie's filled me in.' He glanced at Susie over his spectacles. 'While she gets us breakfast – set breakfast deal for all of us, perhaps? – you can start asking your questions, but please remember that I may not be able to answer them fully, if at all. A lot of your brother's work was very sensitive.'

Susie rested her hand on my thigh for a moment before she rose and joined the queue at the counter.

I cleared my throat, trying to get my thoughts in order.

'Thanks for seeing me,' I started.

A brief nod, but there was a twitch of impatience that told me I shouldn't waste any more time and that I should dive in with the most important questions first.

'How long did he work for you?' I asked.

'Just over a year.'

I leaned forward, lowering my voice despite the echoing din. 'Was he involved in trying to bring George Abbott to justice?'

'Not directly. But he had some dealings with his organisation.'

'In what way?'

'He was undercover.'

I felt a hop of excitement. I knew it!

'In Ibiza?' I asked.

He expression turned neutral.

'He was there before he disappeared,' I added. 'His sailing friend told me he took a boat from Port de Sant Antoni back to the UK.'

'What friend?'

I could see no reason not to tell him. 'Etienne Dupont.'

Still, the neutral look. Did this mean I'd touched on a *very sensitive* part of Rob's job?

'I spoke to Etienne yesterday,' I told him. 'He said Rob owed some people money. They sounded Spanish. They wanted to know where Rob was.'

And they didn't particularly sound nice, either, I wanted to add, but didn't. I recalled Etienne's voice, filled with fear. *Tell Robert to help me. Please.*

'How much money?' Mark Felton asked.

'He didn't say.'

At that moment, Susie returned. 'What money?' she asked.

'The money Etienne mentioned,' I told her.

Felton looked at Susie while she looked back. 'Was it a sting?' she asked him.

When he didn't respond, she added, 'Was it an investiture?'

Although he didn't move a single facial muscle, approbation gleamed in the back of his eyes.

'Ah,' she said. She leaned forward. Spread her hands on the tabletop. 'Now everything is beginning to make sense.'

Chapter thirty-one

Susie spoke softly. I leaned close to listen but Felton stayed where he was. He obviously had better hearing than me.

'Rob had massive sailing experience,' said Susie. 'I'm thinking this could have been his inauguration into the organisation. Doing a drug run. Or maybe carrying money.'

Felton said neutrally, 'It would be a good way of inserting him into the thick of it. Gain everyone's trust.'

'Is that why he was at the Mayfair Group the day before he disappeared?' I asked.

Felton didn't make any movement or gesture that could have been taken for an answer, so I ploughed on. 'Was he delivering cash to Tony Abbott? Drugs?'

'And something went wrong?' Susie suggested.

'Very wrong,' Felton agreed.

I took a deep breath. Felt as though I was standing on a beach about to plunge into a huge wave, cresting over me, ready to crush the life out of me.

'Did he kill Tony?'

No response. Nothing. Not a glimmer, not a spark.

'What happened?' I meant the question to sound neutral but it came out harsher than I wanted. 'Please, tell me. I've seen the CCTV tape. Who was the middle-aged woman? Why was Rob chasing her? Who was–?'

Susie put a hand on my arm. Our breakfast had arrived. Egg, bacon, sausage, beans, tomato, toast and tea. Momentarily frustrated at being interrupted, I held my tongue, watching Susie and Felton tuck in with gusto. Spook food, obviously. I, however, had no appetite against the questions burning inside me, and struggled to take a bite of anything.

'Please,' I said again. 'Tell me what happened.'

Felton shot Susie a look. Shook his head.

'Sorry,' she murmured. She squeezed my thigh. 'Try another angle.'

I took a breath. 'Was David Gilder involved?'

Nothing.

'At the time he was a DI,' I added. 'He became Assistant Commissioner Specialist Operations. He's now retired.'

Felton returned his attention to his breakfast. Like Susie, he was a fast eater. They probably had to be in their line of business – not much time to dawdle over meals when there was more important stuff to be doing – but their insouciance was doing my head in.

'Come on,' I said, unable to stop the anger rising. 'You must be able to give me something more.'

'Nick…' Susie's voice was warning.

I leaned forward, getting in Felton's face, interrupting him mopping up the last of his egg.

'Did you help him disappear?'

He looked at Susie. Picked up his mug of tea and drank it straight down as though it was a glass of water.

'Time to go,' he said. 'Join me?' He was looking at Susie. I no longer existed to him.

He began to rise.

'Wait.' I wanted to rise too, but I couldn't push back because the table and bench were affixed to the floor and Susie was blocking me in. 'Where did Rob go? What's he been doing? Is he still working for you?' My heart was beating hard and I pushed against Susie, willing her to move. 'Where does he live? I want to see him, dammit, just fucking tell me, or I'll–'

'Nick,' Susie snapped. 'Shut it.'

She was holding my arm, gripping it with a strength I hadn't felt before and reminding me of the Saint, the bruises his fingers had left.

'And don't move,' she added in the same commanding tone. 'Or I swear I will plug my fingers into your carotid artery and disable you in such a way you may never speak to me again.'

Her words were like ice daggers in my consciousness. Mouth dry, I stopped fighting.

Without so much as another look in my direction, Felton left the café. I craned my head over the curtain to see him vanish fast down Page Street.

'Fuck,' I said.

'Thanks a bunch.' Susie still held my arm in her death grip to stop me bolting after him. 'You've really pissed him off.'

'What was I supposed to do?' I jerked my arm free. 'Sit here and watch him hoover up his fucking breakfast? Jesus Christ. What a waste of time.'

'No it wasn't. And once you've calmed down, you'll see you've got far more than you thought. Okay?'

No, I thought. *Not okay. Mark bloody Felton knows everything but he's not willing to tell me.* For a wild moment I pictured waiting outside the MI5 building and kidnapping him, forcing him to tell me the whole story. As if that was going to happen. I'd put a single finger on him and a dozen agents would drill me with a dozen bullet holes.

'I'm going to catch him up,' Susie told me. 'Do not follow me. Do not embarrass me any further.'

I stared at her. *I'd embarrassed her?*

'Fuck you,' I said.

'We'll continue this conversation at home,' she said icily and, after picking up her handbag, she slipped away.

I was sliding after her, fully intending to follow, catch her and Mark Felton up and confront him, when a waitress stood right in my path, blocking me. Fat, dressed in pink and white tiers like she was a sandwich cake. 'You haven't paid.'

'I'll be back in a flash,' I told her. 'My wife's left her phone behind and–'

'Whoa, there. Do I *look* like an idiot?' She folded her pudgy arms over a wobbly layer of pink frills.

'God no. Of course not.' I tried to step around her but she moved fast, blocking me. 'It's just that her phone's incredibly–'

'The quicker you pay me, the quicker you can get after her.' Thin smile. A glint in the eye that told me she wasn't going to budge an inch.

I scrabbled in my pocket for my wallet. *Shit, fuck.* It had been stolen the previous night. Then I remembered the loan Susie had given me that morning and delved into my inner jacket pocket, pulled out two twenty pound notes, shoved them at the waitress.

'Keep the change,' I snapped.

'*Excellent,*' said the waitress, her stubby fingers grabbing the money.

Chapter thirty-two

Even though I knew there was little chance of catching them up, I still tore outside. Jogged down the street – the Office was only half a mile away – but I didn't see them. They could have taken any myriad of routes, and considering how furious Susie had been with me, she'd probably chosen one I didn't know specifically to avoid me catching up with them and *embarrassing* her further.

Infuriation dogging every step, I changed direction. Made my way to Victoria station and a mobile phone shop. Fortunately, Susie had loaned me her card to our shared credit card account as well as giving me some life-saving cash, and with my contacts backed up on iCloud, I was soon back in business. This time I was tucked right at the back of a nice quiet Caffè Nero.

First, I called the lovely Helen at the Mayfair Group. Since I didn't have her direct line, I had to go via the receptionist, who put me through. When Helen picked up, she sounded bright and cheerful.

'Helen Flynn,' she sang.

'Hi, Helen. It's Nick Ashdown here. You were kind enough to help me yesterday with some lists.'

There was such a long silence I thought for a moment we'd been cut off.

'Helen?' I said. 'Are you still there?'

'Er… I – I… I mean, yes I am.'

'I'm really sorry, but I've mislaid the lists. I didn't have time to make a copy and I was wondering if I could beg you to print them off for me again.'

'I… I… n-no. I d-don't think so. No. Sorry.'

Gone was the helpful nice young woman and in her place was a stammering nervous wreck.

'What's wrong?' I asked.

'I shouldn't have given y-you those papers yesterday. I'm s-sorry.'

'What happened?'

'Two men,' she said. Her voice was trembling. 'They c-came and saw me last night. At home. They t-told me not to help you again. Not under any circumstances.'

'Oh, Helen.' I pushed my forehead into my hand. 'I'm so sorry. If I thought this was going to happen I would never have asked you.'

'P-please,' she said. 'Don't contact me again.'

She hung up.

It took me a little while to gather my nerve to ring *The Evening Standard* in case they had also had a threatening visit, but I needn't have worried. I was put straight through to Fredericka, who hadn't a clue who I was.

'You want to talk about the Tony Abbott case?' Surprise threaded her tone. 'That was years ago.'

'Twelve,' I agreed.

'What's your name again?'

'Nick Ashdown.'

'And your interest in the case?'

'I've got a few questions.'

'In that case, try Wikipedia, Mr Ashdown. I'm not a help desk.'

'No, please wait. I'm really curious as to why there was so little coverage of Tony's murder. I saw Geoff Leipzig did a big splash to start with, but he never followed up.'

'I'll ask the same question again. What's your interest in the Abbott case?'

I watched a businessman settle at a table nearby with his coffee. I said, 'I have new information.'

'Like what?'

'I'm trying to find Tony Abbott's killer. And I've uncovered some stuff. I can't say what, right now. But let's say it's significant.'

'*Significant.* I like that. Geoff would have liked that. Except he's now working in the Far East for another publication.'

'Oh.' I rubbed my forehead. 'I don't suppose you have a contact number for him?'

'No.'

Brief silence.

Then she said, 'Does this have anything to do with your brother?'

For a moment I froze. *What?*

'While we were chatting, I looked you up on the internet, Nick. Brother to Kensington Superhero, whereabouts currently unknown. You're his brother, right?'

I let out a sigh. 'Yes,' I confessed. I felt like a complete idiot for giving her my real name. I had to sharpen up.

'Let's talk.' She suddenly sounded cheerful.

'My family and I have signed an exclusive,' I warned her. 'Sorry.'

'But that's over your brother,' she said. 'Not about you and Tony Abbott's murder.'

'True,' I admitted cautiously.

'So we can do business.'

'Perhaps.'

'Come on, Nick. I need more than that.'

'If you help me, I'll try to help you.'

'Try?' There was exasperation in her tone but it wasn't nasty, more like wearily resigned.

'Yes, try.' My tone was wry.

'Okay then. With regard to your initial question, about why there was so little press coverage, the answer is that we were warned off.'

'What?'

'We heard about the murder late Friday night and Geoff managed to scramble something together for the weekend papers – it was a huge story, crime boss's son shot dead in his office – but the papers had barely hit the shops before the police were in our faces, trying to shut us up.'

'Can they do that?'

'No, but they went to our boss who told Geoff to drop it. Geoff dug a bit more on his own, but he was warned off by a couple of thugs waiting for him on his doorstep. Really nasty types too.'

'Abbott's men?'

'We assumed so.'

'Did they threaten your boss?'

'Jury's out on that one, but let's just say it was obviously a bigger story than just Tony's murder. Any idea what?'

'Not yet,' I said, grateful she couldn't see me and spot the lie.

'Come on,' she cajoled me. 'I've shown you mine. Now you show me yours.'

The businessman sitting near me had finished his coffee and was absorbed with his phone. I kept my voice down as I spoke. 'I'm trying to find out why there's a time discrepancy between the police arriving at the murder scene, and the time the police actually said they turned up. There's an hour and twenty-three minutes unaccounted for.'

'How do you know this?' Her voice was sharp.

'CCTV.'

'You've got footage of that night?' Her voice went up an octave.

'Yes.'

'Sweet mother Mary of God,' she breathed. 'Any chance I could see it?'

I didn't want to say a flat *no* and antagonise her so I batted another question right back. 'Did you or Geoff have any idea who might have killed Tony?'

'The field was wide open from an inter-gang hit to some poor sap looking to avenge someone The Saint had killed. Greed, lust, envy, hatred – take your pick. That family is immersed in all that shit up to their ears. Why is your brother involved?'

'He isn't,' I said quickly. 'He's got nothing to do with any of this. This is personal, to me.'

'Why? You're a graphic designer, not some corrupt town planner or drug dealer.'

'Let's just say I'm trying to help someone.'

'Who?'

'Did Geoff have a file on the case?' I asked. I needed another lead. Another angle to follow.

'I'd like to say yes, so we could do an exchange – CCTV tape for Geoff's file – but I'd be lying. I do, however–' her voice turned sly 'have his email address.'

'If you get me a good lead,' I told her sincerely, 'and I get a good story from it, you can have an exclusive.'

'Promise?'

'Promise.'

Chapter thirty-three

It was just after six thirty by the time I got to Ealing, and Arun Choudhuri's street. Houses were being lit from inside, cars parked in the resident zones as people returned home from work. Smells of cooking drifted, making me salivate. I hadn't had much to eat since the previous night's curry. A mouthful of fried egg at breakfast, then a supermarket-bought ham sandwich for lunch, half of which I binned. The bread had been dry and tasteless, the ham slimy. I'd been happy to go hungry.

I strode down Craven Avenue, a quiet residential street just off the main road. Trees, shrubs, little clipped hedges fronting handsome red-brick buildings with crisp white paintwork. Arun Choudhuri lived in a period conversion flat that was, when I looked it up on Zoopla, worth around half a million pounds. Or was he renting? Not that it mattered because the area wasn't by any stretch of the imagination cheap, making me wonder how much a caretaker got paid, or whether he'd found another job that paid a whole lot better. Maybe he'd just won the Lottery. Or maybe he'd got paid a shedload of money for signing that confidentiality agreement with the Mayfair Group.

I walked up the path to the front door. Motion sensor lights flooded the area as I approached. From the lights shining upstairs and downstairs within the building, it looked as though everyone was home. I rang the bottom bell, marked *Garden Flat: Choudhuri.* I heard its trill deep inside the building. I waited. After another minute had passed, I rang the bell again. Still no response. I backed away a little, hoping for a glimpse inside, maybe to see some movement, but the blinds were drawn.

One last time.

I rang the bell again, firmly, letting it trill for a rude six seconds. Nothing.

Perhaps he'd nipped out to the shops. To the pub, to see a friend around the corner. But why leave the lights on? Security?

I stepped close to one of the windows and cocked my head, listening. I could hear voices murmuring faintly. The TV was on. I tapped on the window, nice and light, nothing threatening. Tap-tap-tap.

Nothing.

I took out my phone and rang him on his landline; the number I'd got from Helen and recorded on my *recently called* list. The phone inside the flat rang, and rang. He was either ignoring it or he was out, at least that's what I hoped because a warning of something dangerous hovered at the periphery of my consciousness. Nothing solid, nothing I could put a finger on, but my unease grew.

Stop being such an old woman and get your imagination under control, I told myself. A car passed then slowed, came to a halt. I heard it reverse into a parking space. A door slammed shut. An alarm beeped. Then quiet.

Unsure what to do next, whether to wait a bit more or go home, I cautiously stepped to the side of the house and peered around the corner. The area was well lit and showed a little gravel path leading round the back. I didn't want to trespass, and I was about to turn away when behind me a man said loudly, 'Can I help you?'

I jumped a mile.

A young man stood on the front path. Smart suit, briefcase, black shoes. He was eyeing me suspiciously.

'I'm here to see Arun Choudhuri,' I said. 'He's not answering his doorbell.'

The man looked at me, expression flat. My bruised face wouldn't have inspired confidence and I wondered how to persuade him I wasn't a wrongdoer.

'He's not answering his phone either,' I added. 'His lights are on. I was worried, that's all.'

'And you are?'

'A friend. We spoke yesterday around this time. I expected him to be in.' The young man's expression didn't warm, so I said, 'My name's Adam Boden.' Having had the journalist look me up on the Internet, I'd decided to be more cautious. As I said the name, I stepped forward, offering my hand. Reluctantly, he took it. Gave me a nod.

'Isn't he usually home now?' I said.

He glanced up at the top floor windows. 'I'm not sure. Ellie will know though.'

'Could he be down the pub?' I suggested. 'The shops?'

He thought that one over. A tiny frown appeared. He said, 'Give me a moment.'

I watched him open the front door and step inside, close it behind him. I moved to the front door, close enough to hear him knocking on a door inside and calling: 'Arun? It's me. Justin. Arun? Are you there?'

Then, silence.

A minute later, I heard the phone ring inside the flat. I guessed that the young man, Justin, was calling Arun.

A handful of minutes passed before Justin returned minus briefcase but with two keys on a black rubber key tag. Spares, I assumed; they'd have one another's keys so they could let people into each other's places just as my family did for tradesmen, plumbers and such like.

'Ellie says Arun's always home now,' he said. 'She's called his mobile, but he's not answering that either. She thinks we should check. His front door inside is double locked so I can't get in. I'm going to try the back.'

My unease increased, and it must have shown because he tightened his lips.

'You wait here,' he told me.

I waited until he'd vanished down the side of the house before I followed. I was about to turn the corner when I heard him say, 'Oh Christ.' His voice was filled with horror.

I dived after him. He was standing motionless, staring through a window. But it wasn't a window anymore. It had been shattered, the glass knocked out. Inside, a man's body lay across a kitchen floor. A savage wound across his throat gaped open, a gash that spewed great clots and gouts of blood the colour of tar down his chest and across the floor. His eyes met mine but there was no expression. They were milky white.

I'd never seen a dead body before. Let alone one that had been brutally murdered. He had the most beautiful hands, I noticed, elegant with long tapered tips, like a surgeon's. Then the smell hit me. Rank and pungent, sickeningly sweet, I was reminded of rotting steak drenched in liquefied sewage. My gorge rose. I felt the blood drain from my head. My ears sung.

'Oh Christ,' Justin said again. His skin had turned the colour of putty and I guessed mine had turned much the same colour. I quickly turned aside. Walked away from the stench. Gulped in clean air. I felt my stomach steady but my fingers were trembling. Fear tingled through my veins. The singing in my ears turned to a roar.

I saw Justin reaching for his phone, patting pockets, muttering 'Dear God' over and over. I listened to him summoning the police, an ambulance, trying not to listen to the voice in my head screaming, *Get out, get out, get out.*

'H-help's coming,' Justin stammered.

'Okay,' I said. My voice sounded as though it came from a long way away.

Justin suddenly moved away. Strode purposely to the far end of the garden. Bowing his knees, he bent double. I heard him throwing up.

I walked to the front of the house. Got out my phone and rang Susie. My fingers were trembling so hard they slipped the first time and I had to redial. I told her what happened. I wanted to ask what I should do, but didn't want to put her in that position, let alone look weak, so I remained silent. When she didn't say anything, I said, 'Susie?' For a moment, I truly thought she was going to hang up to punish me for my behaviour in the café earlier.

'Wait, Nick. I'm trying to think.'

I held the phone. Let her think.

She said, 'You say you gave this young man another name?'

'Yes. Adam Boden.'

'It could be a good thing, but it could be bad because the cops will want to know why.'

I closed my eyes. In the distance, I heard a siren. My nerves tightened into balls of barbed wire. 'They're coming,' I said. 'I can hear them.'

Silence.

Then Susie said, 'I wish I could help you, my love.' She sounded tired. 'But I don't think I can. All I can say is that if you stay, you'll get grilled by the police, possibly become a suspect, but if you leave you'll have the police make you a person of interest.'

I didn't like either option.

'What on earth's going on?' she said, but she didn't seem to want me to reply. 'What have you got yourself into?'

'I'm trying to find Rob.'

'I know. But this is crazy.'

At the end of the street, I saw flashing blue lights reflected against windows. Part of me desperately wanted to leave, run away and forget I'd ever been there, but the law-abiding citizen in me was petrified it might make things worse and riveted my feet to the ground.

'They're here,' I said.

'Give me the address,' Susie said. Energy suddenly filled her voice. 'I'll be there as soon as I can.'

I hung up and watched a patrol car pull up against the pavement. A uniformed constable stepped out and walked briskly towards me, his radio crackling. He reached me and said, 'You found a body?'

'Yes.' I pointed to the side of the house. 'Round the back. There's glass everywhere. It looks like someone broke in.'

The constable nodded. 'Thanks for calling it in.' He was in his late twenties, wiry, with short-cropped russet hair. 'If you could wait here, I'll talk to you in a moment.'

Chapter thirty-four

The moment stretched to ten minutes, then half an hour. I watched two paramedics arrive but they didn't stay long. Another patrol car turned up. By this time, news had spread and people were peering out of windows, a handful hovering on the pavement trying to get a look.

The constable finally came over. 'The DI's arrived. He'll want to talk to you.'

He jerked a thumb over his shoulder at a Mazda MX-5 where a man with dark curly hair was climbing out of the driver's side. The passenger door opened, and my pulse hopped when I took in the man's chunky build and big navy overcoat.

DI Barry Gilder.

His gaze was already fixed on me and I wasn't sure, but even from that distance, I thought his expression was one of dismay.

Both men came over. Gilder's eyes swept over my bruised face as he said, 'What are you doing here?'

I wanted to ask him the same – his station wasn't in this jurisdiction – but I decided to be prudent. 'I came to see Arun Choudhuri.'

Gilder turned to the curly-haired man. 'I'll take this one.'

Curly-hair surveyed me coolly before walking away.

'Why?' DI Gilder said.

'He was the caretaker on duty the night Tony Abbott died.'

I watched a van pull up and two people stepped out. They were carrying protective suits and shoe covers, a couple of large, heavy-looking cases. They gave Gilder a nod before disappearing to the back of the house.

'Who knew you were coming to talk to him?' Gilder asked.

'You,' I said.

His nostrils flared. 'No, I didn't.'

'You could have worked it out.'

He thought that one over. 'Who else?'

I didn't know how much to tell him and opted for giving him more rather than less in the hope it might help build some trust between us. I told him about visiting the Mayfair Group. That I was attacked by four men who stole my briefcase and the lists. That Helen Flynn had been threatened by two thugs into not talking to me again. I finished telling him about Etienne, and the money Rob supposedly owed some Spanish men.

Gilder looked at me hard. 'Tell me, exactly what was your brother involved in?'

'That's what I'm trying to find out.' My tone was weary. The shock of seeing Arun Choudhuri's body was taking effect and I was beginning to crash.

'He still hasn't contacted you?'

'No.'

A light tap-tap of a woman's heels entered my consciousness. Susie, dressed in a tailored woollen coat and an A-line skirt with a sexy little flare. As she approached, Gilder's head switched round. He watched as she came and stood next to me and gripped my hand. 'Are you all right?' she asked.

I nodded.

She looked at Gilder. 'Hi.' She put out her hand. 'I'm Susie Ashdown. Nick's wife.'

They shook. 'DI Gilder,' he told her.

She studied him with interest. 'You visited Nick in his office, wanting to find Rob.'

'Any idea where he is?' the policeman asked her.

'No.' She kept looking at him.

'He hasn't contacted you at all?'

'No.'

'May I ask how well you knew him?' Gilder asked.

'I didn't.'

Susie's voice was smooth and if I hadn't known it was a lie, I wouldn't have heard anything to alert me otherwise.

She added quietly, 'I met Nick a year after Rob… vanished.'

Which was the story we told everyone. It had been Susie's suggestion, but even I'd seen the sense in not broadcasting the fact we'd met at Rob's memorial. It wasn't the most romantic of histories.

I was opening my mouth to ask if maybe I could go now when the man with the dark curly hair reappeared. He glanced at Gilder then at me. 'I'd like to ask some questions. Down at the station if you wouldn't mind.'

Once again, I found myself in an impersonal interview room but this time with two cops. DI Gilder and Inspector Hayden. After the preliminaries – taking down my date of birth, address and so on – the questions started, all revolving around where I was the previous night.

For the first time I was glad I'd gone to the Chelsea Police Station because, apparently, the processes of decay gave a reasonable indication that Arun Choudhuri had been murdered the previous night, and although I couldn't understand why they might think I killed the poor man, I was mightily relieved I had a pretty cast iron alibi at least for part of the evening.

'After DC Doherty had taken your statement, you went home?' the Inspector asked.

'To Susie's, yes.' I gave them her address.

'Did anyone see you? Aside from your wife?'

'Er…' I tried to replay that evening in my head. I could remember picking up my takeaway that some kind person had hooked onto the railings, then I walked past the harbour and let myself into her block. I pictured getting into the lift and pressing 3.

'Oh,' I said. 'I saw Mrs Gabb.' She'd had her usual moan about Susie's newspaper, complaining that having *The Sun* lying outside Susie's flat in the communal hallway brought the tone of the place down.

'What time was this?'

I hadn't looked at my watch because I'd seen no need. 'Around ten or so, at a guess.'

Gilder made a note. 'And you spent all night there.'

'Yes.'

'Why did you give Justin Goodhew another name?'

Exhaustion pulling at my eyelids, I made an effort to protect myself. 'I didn't.'

'Arun Choudhuri's neighbour says you told him your name was Adam Boden.'

'I can't think why.' I shook my head. 'But maybe he got confused. He got a huge shock seeing the body. He threw up in the garden. He was in one hell of a state.'

The Inspector considered this for a moment. Then he gave a sigh and looked over at Barry Gilder and raised his eyebrows. Gilder gave a nod. And with that, I was allowed to go.

Chapter thirty-five

'I'm sorry about Mark Felton,' I said. 'I didn't mean to embarrass you.'

Susie didn't respond. Just took another bite out of her toast.

We were in her flat, having breakfast. Tea, toast and marmalade. The most English of breakfasts. Raindrops spattered against the windowsills but otherwise the harbour was quiet. No rumbles of diesel engines of clatter of halyards. No rich playboys and girls going out on their yachts. Too grey, too wet. I could see our reflections, distorted by wriggles of rain. Where Susie looked fresh and rested, I looked haggard and bruised and ten years older.

After we'd got back to the flat it had been just before midnight and we'd gone straight to bed. But where Susie had fallen asleep almost immediately, I'd struggled, haunted by visions of poor dead Arun Choudhuri and his wide-open milky-white eyes. He'd sounded nice on the phone. Polite. And genuinely sorry he couldn't help me.

I wondered if he'd had a family. If he had children, parents, brothers and sisters. Who would mourn him? Who would hate me for bringing a killer to his door? Because I didn't doubt that's what I'd done. Somehow, someone had guessed I was going to see him and had wanted to silence him before we spoke.

Would he have told me anything? He'd told me he'd signed a bit of paper. A confidentiality agreement. *I can't break it.*

I'd lain next to Susie sleeping for an hour or so then got up and spent the rest of the night on the sofa, gazing out of the balcony window and listening to the rain rattle against the glass, my soul as bleak as any midwinter's day and wondering if this was how Rob felt after he'd vanished.

Now, I glanced at Susie, who was still ignoring me, still obviously pissed off with my behaviour in the café.

'I was just so... *frustrated*,' I told her. 'It was like talking to a brick wall.'

She sighed. Put her toast down. 'I know, Nick. But considering he met you as a huge favour to me, you got more than most people would have.'

I tried not to feel guilty. Had I jeopardised things for her? Disturbed the groundworks of her ambition? But no matter how I replayed it, I couldn't have done anything differently. I'd needed to speak with Rob's old boss, and Susie had – eventually – arranged it.

'Thanks,' I said sincerely. I wasn't going to apologise again and Susie seemed to realise it, because she sighed again. I was relieved that the storm of anger she'd shown the previous morning seemed to have blown over. Another thing I love about my wife: she doesn't hold grudges.

'I haven't seen him yet to apologise,' she told me. 'But I'm pretty sure he'll be okay because if he was pissed off, he would have dragged me into his office for an arse-kicking by now.'

I reached over and put my hand on hers, gave it a thank-you squeeze. I was forgiven. She patted my hand. Popped the lid back on the marmalade. Turned to look at me. 'What's next?' To my surprise, a twinkle started. 'I'm not sure if I should let you out on your own, you know, as your Batman cape is at the dry cleaners. Oh, and your Superman pants are in the laundry and–'

'My Iron Man powered armour suit has rusted solid in the basement.' I tried a smile but my lips felt stiff.

She rose and came and stood behind me. Wrapped her arms around my shoulders and pressed a kiss against my neck. 'Do what you have to. But be careful. And I mean *careful*, okay?'

'Okay.' I sighed. My motivation to find Rob had been shaken by the events of the past forty-eight hours and all I wanted to do was go home. Maybe go for a sail if the weather cheered up, and try to forget about everything for a bit.

Susie moved away and put the breakfast things away while I stared glumly out of the window.

'Fancy an exhibition or something?' she asked. 'There's bound to be something at the Royal Academy, or the Tate. We could have lunch at The Wolseley.'

Susie's favourite weekend place to eat. Sometimes I couldn't understand why she liked the Viennese-style brasserie so much. I thought it overpriced and overcrowded, but she said she found the grand art deco glamour characterful and charming and she loved spotting the smattering of celebs over her eggs benedict. Personally, I'd rather go to the Regency and have a monster fry-up rubbing shoulders with a brickie rather than some posh nob in a Saville row suit.

'I think I'll go home,' I said gloomily.

There was a pause, then Susie said, 'If I stay here, would you mind?'

It wasn't often we had a weekend apart and normally I'd grumble, but I thought some time on my own in my current mood was probably a good thing. I could brood as deeply and darkly as I liked and also drink as much as I liked without having Susie lift her eyebrows at me. I suddenly felt like getting drunk. Absolutely totally falling down drunk so I wouldn't have to think, and wouldn't have to see Arun Choudhuri's savagely cut throat and his beautiful elegant hands with their long-tapered tips waxy and grey in death.

'Sure,' I said. I got up. I wanted to be in The Anchor Bleu pub with my head buried in a pint and talking of nothing but sailing, dinghy suppers and sailing club lottery draws. I wanted to put back the clock and never to have seen Rob on the TV screen. I wanted things to be the way they were. Even if it were just for a day.

I barely felt my wife's touch or her soft kiss goodbye, nor did I take in the tube ride to Victoria. My journey home was a blur. I parked outside the cottage but didn't go inside. I walked straight to the pub, uncaring it was chucking it down. It was only when

I stepped into the warmth of the pub that I realised how wet and cold I was.

Charley the barman greeted me. I ordered a pint of winter ale. Drank it standing at the bar. Then I ordered a double whisky. Drank that. Then I drank another pint and another double whisky. I settled on a barstool. Drank some more. Darkness fell. The rain increased. I could hear it lashing against the windows. People came in with dripping waterproofs. Lots of laughter, shaking clothes dry.

'Nick. Nick, it's me. I've been trying to find you.'

I turned my blurred gaze to a tall curly-haired figure standing at my side and said thickly, 'Go away.'

'Jesus, Nick. Give me a break. I'm not in a happy mood right now. I want to know what the hell's going on. Where's Rob, do you know?'

I stared hazily at the rows of bottles shining cheerfully behind the bar, the nautical bric-a-brac Charley had collected over the years. 'I dunno an' I don' give a fuck either.'

'I think he's had enough, don't you?' said Charley. 'Take him home for me?'

'Merde.' Etienne swore. '*Est-ce vraiment nécessaire?*' Do I have to?

'Someone's got to do it,' Charley said reasonably. 'And since you're friends…'

As Etienne put his hands on me, I pushed him away and nearly fell off my stool. 'Ooopsh,' I said. I reached for the rest of my pint but Etienne scooped it out of reach.

'Charley's right.' He sounded tired. 'Time to go home.'

'Don' wanto. Wanto toasht my bruvva. Who is the biggesht arshole thish shide of Bozz… ham. Here'sh to Rob. My shite of a bruvva.' My voice was loud, causing people to turn and stare.

'Come on, Nick. Let's go.' Etienne took my arm. 'You're embarrassing everyone.'

'A-run ish dead,' I said. 'He'sh dead ash a fuck-in' doornail. Nishe guy. A-run. Wanted to 'elp me but couldna do it. Had an agree-men. A shined piesh of paper.'

I felt Etienne's hand on my shoulder and I slid off my stool to stand, swaying, in front of the pub crowd who were staring at me. Not just staring, *gawking*. I suddenly felt a stab of aggression. 'Wassyou lookin' at?'

Their eyes skidded away.

'Bet ya don' have a bruvva like mine,' I managed. 'Who'sh dead then comsh backto life.'

Etienne took my elbow and guided me to the door, people parting like fish to let us through. Outside, it was still raining. I raised my head to the rain and opened my mouth, trying to drink it.

'Nick, let's get you home. Try to sober you up.'

'Don' wanna.'

'Let's get you to bed. You can sleep it off.'

I pushed his hands away and overbalanced, only catching myself from falling by grabbing a lamp post and hanging on.

'Sorry,' I said. 'I'm pished.'

'As if I hadn't noticed.' His voice was dry.

'I'cn get myshelf 'ome,' I told him. 'I'm fine.' When he stepped towards me again I waved him off. 'Bye bye,' I said. I pushed myself off the lamp post and walked carefully along the street, concentrating with every step as the ground oscillated and rocked beneath me, making me think I was at sea rather than on a tarmac pavement.

I made it to my front door without mishap. The last thing I remember was the alarm beeping wildly at me in a completely different tone to what I was used to and my drunkenly praying I was punching in the right code.

Chapter thirty-six

Susie normally loved the rare occasion when she had the weekend to herself, but this time things were different. She felt as though she was skating across an enormous frozen lake, and if she lost a moment's concentration, the ice would crack and buckle, plunging her straight into the inky black water below.

She would get through this. She had to. And what about Nick? He'd looked awful yesterday. Shattered. Not surprising considering he'd seen his first dead body. He wouldn't forget that in a hurry. She could remember her first corpse quite clearly, but the second, third and fourth held less of an impact, didn't feel so shocking.

She hadn't liked the fact Nick had gone home on his own, but she was also wise enough to know that he'd needed to. He'd called her briefly from the pub last night, wasted, barely able to string a word together, and after she'd hung up she'd called Charley, who promised her he'd make sure Nick got home safely. She wouldn't ring or text Nick for a while. Let him have some space.

Meanwhile, she had things to do. She wanted to know why DI Barry Gilder had stepped out of his jurisdiction the previous night. She'd done some research on both Barry and his father first thing, and now it was time to take their measure.

Barry Gilder lived in Cockfosters, in a neat semi-detached brick house with a single garage and clipped shrubs in the small garden that ran down to the street. The front door was painted blue. Very appropriate for a police officer, blue. She rang the bell.

A child's voice called inside, and then she heard scampering feet, followed by a woman's yell. 'In a minute!'

Susie waited, taking in the bay windows, the freshly swept driveway. The paintwork on the house wasn't fresh, but it was in good condition, as was the brickwork.

The door opened to reveal a woman with spectacles shoved onto her forehead and ink on her cheek. Auburn hair and green eyes. Freckles. She was prettier than in the photographs Susie had viewed that morning. The boy at her side had soft brown hair and grey eyes like his father. He looked at her curiously.

'Who are you?' he asked.

'I'm Susie Ashdown. I've come to see your dad.' She looked at Hayley Gilder. 'It's police business, I'm afraid.'

'Noah, go and get your father,' Hayley said.

The boy darted away and down a long corridor of polished floorboards that Susie could see led to a flood of light at the rear of the house.

Neither woman said anything while they waited. Susie liked Hayley for that. For not mindlessly filling in the silence with chat that neither wanted. And for not closing the door in her face, which Hayley had every right to do, considering she was married to a cop and didn't know Susie from Adam.

When Barry Gilder saw her, his mouth narrowed. 'I'll take it from here,' he told his wife. Without looking at Susie, Hayley vanished inside. Barry stood on the doorstep, arms folded.

'Mrs Ashdown.'

'DI Gilder.'

'How did you get my address?'

She reached into her bag and brought out a wallet. Flipped it open and showed him her ID card. If it had said she was a vampire with a licence to rip his throat out and feed on his heart, he couldn't have looked more surprised.

'It's not something I normally shout about,' she told him. 'But I wanted you to know.'

'I see.' His voice was stiff. 'You'd better come in.'

He brought her into the front room, the one that overlooked the street. He closed the door behind them. No offer of tea or coffee. He came and stood opposite her. 'What's this about?'

'I was thinking if we combine forces we might be able to find Nick's brother before something catastrophic happens.'

Gilder raised his eyebrows.

She put her handbag on the coffee table. Folded her arms, mirroring him. 'Nick probably didn't tell you, but the man who attacked him and his sister-in-law last Tuesday was George Abbott.'

'No, he didn't tell me.'

He didn't look surprised, which made her alarm bells ring.

'Good. I told him not to.' She held his gaze. He was intimidated by her. She could tell by the way he tried to broaden his shoulders, stick his chin out.

She continued. 'Nick told me he showed you the CCTV tape.'

He nodded.

'But not all of it.' She withdrew her phone from her bag. She'd copied the footage onto her laptop in Bosham before downloading it to her phone. She found the video and handed her phone to him. 'Press play.'

She stood so she could see the screen as well as his face as he watched. He maintained a steady expression, not giving anything away until Robert Ashdown came belting across the reception floor in hot pursuit of the middle-aged woman. 'Shit,' he said. He glanced at Susie. 'I didn't realise.'

She reached over and took her phone, put it back in her bag.

'I can only imagine what the Saint will do to get his hands on my brother-in-law,' she said. 'Which is why I want to find him before the Saint does. If we can discover who sent this to Nick, then we'll find Rob.'

'You don't think Rob sent it?' Gilder said.

She put her head on one side. 'Why would he do that?'

'He might not have killed Tony Abbott. He might be wanting to stir things up, to prove his innocence.'

'If I were him,' she said, 'I wouldn't want anyone to see that tape whether I was guilty, or not. It has to be the most incriminating evidence I've ever laid eyes on.'

He shrugged. 'Just thinking aloud. Hypothesising.'

'If we're doing that,' she said smoothly, 'I'd like to know what the responding police officers got up to in that one hour and twenty-three minutes that is unaccounted for.'

Her gaze held his.

'Any ideas?' she asked.

No emotion crossed his face.

'How is your father these days?' she asked, still holding his gaze.

In the fall of silence, she heard footsteps outside the room. Little Noah calling to his mum. Her calling back.

'Enjoying his retirement?' she added.

She saw the fear. Gilder's face wasn't blank anymore. She had to force herself not to smile. She was twisting the knife. She knew Barry's father worked for the Saint. Knew it was him on the CCTV tape. Knew his father was corrupt.

'What do you want?' Barry's voice was hoarse.

Chapter thirty-seven

'To work together.' Susie widened her eyes to make them appear innocent. 'Pool resources. Share information.'

'Okay,' he said, but he didn't look happy about it. She guessed the last thing he needed was an MI5 officer poking about, exposing every dirty secret.

'For instance, I'd like your father's take on what happened the night Tony Abbott was killed.'

'So would I.'

She was startled at the sudden anger in his voice.

'He's…' Barry Gilder ground his teeth for a moment. 'Gone fishing.'

'I hope he's on the Test,' she said, 'and that he hasn't gone anywhere like Norway.' *And where there'll be no phone signal.*

His cheeks flushed. It wasn't embarrassment, she realised, but fury.

'He's gone to Norway?' Her voice held disbelief.

'Finland. It's a place called Kotka.'

Susie grabbed her phone and looked it up on the web to see it was slap bang between Helsinki and St Petersburg. Barry's father could be on the moon as far as she was concerned. Was that the intention? To be utterly out of touch, out of reach, while the Saint tried to find Robert Ashdown? Was David Gilder being sensible, removing himself from danger, or had he simply run away? Turned into a coward?

'He's got his mobile with him.' Barry's words were clipped. 'But I haven't been able to reach him.'

'How do you feel about that?' Susi asked. 'His leaving you in the shit?'

The rage in his face gave her no doubt he would have happily hit his father if he were standing with them right now. Which cheered her immensely because it appeared that where David Gilder was a crooked shyster in bed with the Saint, his son was cut from a different cloth.

'I'm sorry,' she said. 'You must be really frustrated with him.' Her voice was gentle, letting him know she understood his anger and shame over his father. She'd learned over the years that occasionally this kind of empathy worked wonders when you wanted to bond with someone.

Barry ducked his head, in a gesture of embarrassment perhaps, she wasn't sure, but at that moment, with the light on one side of his face, she remembered where she'd seen him. It hadn't been at work, as she'd originally thought, and her pulse quickened as she processed the new information.

'Since we're sharing,' she said, putting her head on one side. 'Is there anything else you'd like to tell me?'

He pulled a sorry-that's-all-I've-got face.

'I thought you might least have shared the fact you were staking out Clara's house last Tuesday.' She shook her head in a parody of disappointment. 'You were staking it out, weren't you?'

He licked his lips. 'Sorry.'

'It wasn't your idea, was it?'

'No.'

'And nobody else knows about it, am I right?'

He swallowed, looking sick.

She considered the photograph of Hayley and Noah on the wall, both smiling, both looking happy. Barry's eyes followed hers briefly, before returning to hold her gaze.

She tucked a strand of hair behind her ear. 'I don't want to get up your nose, and I certainly don't want you to get up mine, but it's worth my saying that I'm not after you here. I just want to find my brother-in-law before he gets himself killed, and if you can help me do that, then I would be very grateful. Okay?'

It was a peace offering.

'Okay,' he said.

'Anything on Arun Choudhuri's murder?' she asked.

He thought for a moment. 'George Abbott thinks Robert Ashdown killed him.'

'Does he indeed?' She mulled this over. 'I may not like the idea, but I suppose he could be right. Arun Choudhuri was a witness to that evening, after all.'

'He threatened my family,' Barry finally admitted. He didn't have to say exactly who. She knew.

She didn't look at him as she said, 'I guessed as much.'

When she left, although she was reasonably certain he'd keep her secrets safe for the moment – no doubt hoarding them to be used in the future when it would benefit him to maximum effect – she still didn't trust him an inch.

Chapter thirty-eight

My consciousness crept awake. My back was stiff, my neck aching. I was sweating but I was cold. My head was a red throbbing balloon of pain and my mouth as dry as sand. I realised I was fully dressed and that I was lying on a floor. At first, I had no clue where I was and felt a moment's panic. I forced my eyes open to see the hallway ceiling.

Thank God. I was at home. I rolled to one side and what felt like twin knives stabbed through both eyes and lodged themselves in the back of my brain. I took in the pillow beneath my head and the duvet from our bed upstairs that had been tucked around me. A bucket had been placed strategically beside me and as I looked at it, the urge to vomit rose.

I galloped upstairs, making it to the bathroom just in time, where I stayed for another half an hour.

Finally, dosed with paracetamol, showered and shaven and dressed in clean clothes and smelling of toothpaste, I stepped gingerly downstairs. Picked up the duvet and pillow and reinstated them in the bedroom. Put the bucket back beneath the sink.

'Thanks,' I said to the figure on the sofa, who was watching breakfast TV, the volume turned down low.

'It's okay,' said Etienne.

I poured myself a glass of water, then another. 'Coffee?'

'I've already had some.'

I considered putting on the machine but decided I wouldn't be able to stand the noise. I fanned out the mail which Etienne had put on the kitchen worktop but had no interest in opening it. I went and sat on the floor next to the sofa. Stared at the TV where a weather woman was showing a group of tight isobars over the west of England.

'Zebra's arsehole,' I said.

'Yes.'

'Sorry,' I said again. I closed my eyes. I hadn't had a proper hangover in years. Now I knew why. I felt truly dreadful. It really wasn't worth it.

'What's going on, Nick?' Etienne turned off the TV and came and squatted opposite me, expression intent.

I looked into his eyes, as blue as the sea, and felt so ill, so tired, I could sleep for a thousand years.

'I killed a man.' I closed my eyes.

'What are you talking about?'

'I killed a man called Arun Choudhuri. He used to be a caretaker for the Mayfair Group.' I spoke in a monotone, and as I spoke, pictures paraded themselves across my eyelids. Pretty smiling Helen Flynn being threatened, my satchel being snatched, Barry Gilder and his DI buddy interviewing me, Arun Choudhuri's throat a gaping wound. The words poured out of me in great gushes and stops, unthinking, unrehearsed and uncoordinated, like a bottle of water upended.

Eventually I ground to a halt.

'Dear God, Nick. You're talking about George Abbott? The underworld boss?'

I opened my eyes to Etienne's appalled expression. I hadn't been able to keep the Saint out of it, since he was pivotal to what was going on. 'Don't tell anyone,' I said, a bit late in the day. 'It might threaten your life.'

'You're saying Robert was dealing with Abbott?' He leaned forward.

'Yes.'

'You know, it makes sense.' Etienne nodded. 'The people who came to me are nasty types, just like him. They break bones and heads. They're part of a narcotics gang working out of Ibiza. They want their money. Did I not mention that when I called you?'

'How much money?' I pushed myself upright and staggered into the kitchen area for another glass of water.

'One million.'

'One million, what? Albanian leks?'

'Pounds.'

I nearly dropped my glass. 'Holy crap.'

'Now you see why I have to find him. These men, they gave Robert thirty-four kilos of MDMA to deliver, and he screwed them over.'

I felt my legs soften and had to clutch the kitchen worktop to stay upright. My insides turned greasy. I licked my lips.

'Why did these men come to you?' I croaked.

He looked away.

'Etienne. I have to know.' Despite my thumping great headache and nausea, my tone was fierce. 'I don't care if it tarnishes your impeccable reputation. You've got to tell me.'

He took a breath. 'Robert said he wanted to make extra money. I knew a man who knew another man. It was he who introduced Robert to this Spanish gang.'

'His name?'

'I never knew it. I didn't want to know, okay? Your brother took this gang's drugs from Ibiza to England. He was supposed to return with the money, but he didn't. The drugs and the money disappeared with him.'

'Which gang? Does it have a name?'

'La Familia de Sangre.'

'The Family of Blood?'

'They're one of the biggest gangs in Spain. They have a strict allegiance. It takes two years to be fully initiated but once you're in, there's no turning back.'

I could hear Susie's voice and see Mark Felton's bland pale face as though I was back in the Regency Café.

Rob had massive sailing experience. I'm thinking this could have been his inauguration into the organisation. Doing a drug run. Or maybe carrying money.

Mark Felton's voice. *It would be a good way of inserting him into the thick of it. Gain everyone's trust.*

'Etienne,' I said. 'What I tell you now, is to be kept one hundred per cent confidential between us. Nobody must know. Nobody must find out. No matter what. It's extremely serious and extremely dangerous.'

Etienne's eyes widened. 'Go on, Nick.'

I poured another glass of water. Looked straight at him. 'Rob was working for MI5.'

The Frenchman stared at me. 'I beg your pardon?'

'Rob was an MI5 agent. You know, the British security service responsible for protecting the country.'

Etienne continued to stare at me. Then he said, 'Is this a joke?'

'No.' I started to shake my head but stopped when it felt as though my brain might implode. 'He was working for them for maybe a year before he disappeared.'

'No way,' Etienne responded. He scrambled to his feet. 'This isn't possible. Not Robert!' He flung up his hands. 'You know how he was. He could no more be a spy than… than…' He trailed off and then he threw back his head and laughed. 'Robert, a spy! Good God! This is the most incredible, ridiculous thing I've ever heard!'

I didn't say anything. Simply stood there and looked at him.

Gradually, his humour evaporated. 'You're serious?'

'Yes.'

'You actually know this to be true?'

'I've met his ex-case officer.'

Etienne sat down suddenly, as though he was a puppet who'd had his strings cut. His mouth opened and closed. He was gaping like a fish and his skin colour had paled. 'Fucking hell. Fucking *fucking* hell.'

I didn't say anything. I knew how he felt, because I'd gone through exactly the same shock and disbelief. Leaving him to assimilate this new information, I opened the fridge, wanting to eat something, preferably sweet and fatty, but couldn't find the energy to make anything, so I turned to our tiny grocery cupboard and dug out one of the Mars bars that we kept as snacks to take on the boat.

By the time I finished it, Etienne's face had regained its colour and he was pacing our miniscule sitting area.

'You say he was working for MI5 for perhaps a year?'

'Yes.'

'What do they have to say about where he went? What happened?'

'They won't tell me. It's classified.'

'Fuck that.' He stopped pacing and came and stood in front of me. His eyes held an electrical storm of fury. 'Don't they realise the danger they've put me in? The men who came to me, they'll cut off my balls and make me eat them if they think I have introduced a spy into their organisation. Fucking hell, Nick! Who has the money? Do they have it? If so, they have to give it to me so I can give it to *La Familia* and get them *off my fucking back.*'

Somehow, I didn't think that was going to happen but I didn't say so. I didn't want him to get any angrier so I said, 'I'll ask them, okay? But I can't promise anything. They're as tight as ticks and the entire operation appears to be classified. I was incredibly lucky to meet Rob's old boss, but I don't think he'll want to see me again.'

'What's his name?'

I shook my head. 'Sorry. I can't tell you.'

'What's his *fucking name!*'

If I gave Etienne Mark Felton's name Susie would never speak to me again, so I held my ground. 'I can't say.'

'How did you find out about him?'

'Rob told me,' I lied. 'Ages ago. He wanted one of the family to know who he worked for.'

And how I wished it had been true. It would have made things so much easier if I had known, and I could have told him how proud I was of him. But right now, I'd lost all understanding or compassion since Arun Choudhuri's murder and if Rob turned up that minute, I'd be hard pushed not to punch him square in the face.

'Fuck.' Etienne spun round, his hands clutching his head. 'Fuck, fuck, *fuck!* I'm never going to find Robert, am I? Never!'

Chapter thirty-nine

While Etienne paced and ranted some more, I opened a couple of envelopes. One from a medical insurance company wanting to sign us up so they could fleece us into our old age, the other a programme of what was on at the Chichester Festival Theatre which I put to one side for Susie. I preferred the movies, but she was a complete theatre buff, fascinated by the actor's performances and how they could play a character so unlike themselves so convincingly.

When Etienne calmed, I said, 'What boat did he sail in? With the drugs?'

'It was the gang's boat. They want that back also. It was a nice little boat, twenty-five foot, six berths. Worth fifty grand or so. Your brother fucked off with that too. You see what a mess this is?'

'What was its name?'

'*Jovita.*'

'You've tried to find it?'

'I've asked around, but it's twelve years ago, Nick. He could have sold it, sailed it to the Caribbean for all I know. The chances of finding it now are zero.'

I mulled things over, vaguely noticing that the Mars bar was doing a reasonably good job of settling my stomach. I ate another, and mulled some more. 'Etienne... now I've spoken to you, I'm wondering if Rob isn't in some kind of witness protection.'

That brought him up cold. 'You could be right,' he said. 'The fuck. When I get my hands on him I'll throttle him. I really will.'

'You'll have to get in line.'

He gave a long sigh. Ran his hands over his head. 'I'm sorry, Nick. This must be terrible for you.'

I gave a half-hearted nod and opened the last envelope. This one was A4, quite bulky, addressed in blue felt pen to me, Nick Ashdown. Puzzled, I pulled out a handful of photographs. A paperclip attached them together with a handwritten note in the same blue felt pen.

NOW YOU KNOW THE TRUTH BEHIND WHAT HAPPENED TO TONY.

There were six pictures. They were all in full colour. It took my sluggish hungover brain a few seconds to assimilate what my eyes were seeing. 'Oh my God.' I put them down on the worktop. I had to swallow several times to prevent the nausea from rising.

'What is it?' Etienne said, and before I could snatch them back he'd picked them up. 'What the...' He flipped through them. Looked at me. 'What the fuck is this?'

I couldn't answer. My hands were cold. I was having trouble breathing.

'Are they for real?' Etienne asked.

'Yes,' I managed. 'I'm pretty sure they are.'

He stared at them. 'Fuck.' He put them carefully on the worktop. Stared some more.

Trying to be objective, not think about what I was actually seeing, I looked at them again. Each picture was of a murder scene, taken from varying angles. The victims were in an office. A man and a woman. Both had been shot in the chest. Both had had their faces bludgeoned. Tony Abbott's face was recognisable but the woman's was a pulped and bloody mess. It was the young woman I'd seen on the CCTV tape dressed in a plain white shirt with the sleeves pushed up, figure-hugging skirt, stilettos. Sexy but professional. She still wore her skirt, tights and shoes but otherwise, she was naked. She had a black leather studded collar around her neck, nipple clamps on her breasts. A gimp PVC mask with zips forming the eyeholes and a zip where the mouth should be, lay next to her left hand.

Tony wore a leather full body harness. He was spread-eagled on the floor, each wrist handcuffed to the legs of his desk. He'd been ball-gagged. A long whip lay to one side, along with a pair of wet-look gloves and a roll of black bondage tape. There was a Polaroid camera too, and a couple of pictures lay on the floor along with the woman's shirt.

The blood stood out shockingly against their pale skins. A bright vivid red. The photographs had been taken fairly soon after they'd been killed, I guessed. But then I saw a great smear of blood against the wall. Where had that come from?

'What's this, Nick?' Etienne asked. His voice was hoarse.

In answer, I went and fetched the CCTV tape from the cupboard, and put it into the machine.

'This was also given to us,' I told him. I didn't have to compare the handwriting between the two notes. I already knew they were identical. Whoever had slipped into our house to leave the CCTV footage that day had also sent the photographs of the murder scene.

We watched the recording in silence but when it showed Rob running from the building, tearing after the middle-aged woman, gun in hand, Etienne erupted. 'He killed them?'

'I don't know.'

'Merde.' He was scrubbing his face with his hands. 'I cannot believe this. Robert takes down a terrorist in a restaurant, is a hero, and then I see this… my old friend. Did I know him?' He turned to me. 'Did you?'

I couldn't answer. I had no idea.

'This is all so fucked up!' He flung his hands in the air. 'What do I tell *La Familia*? I cannot tell them he was a spy. I cannot say he seems to have killed two people. Merde. I should never have come.'

I watched him get to his feet. He looked down at me. 'I think I shall go now.'

I clambered upright. Opened my mouth to say something, I wasn't sure what, but I didn't want him to leave. Perhaps I was hoping he might help me, become an ally in my search for Rob, but Etienne didn't want to hang around.

'This is the Saint's son that Robert has killed,' he said. 'I want nothing to do with this. I shall return to Spain. I will tell *La Familia* I found nothing.' He gave a Gallic shrug. 'Which is true when you think of it.'

I spent the rest of the day nursing my hangover and on Sunday, when I awoke to a clear bright day with a brisk westerly, I went for a sail. Sailing has always helped clear my head and for a while, I seriously thought that I was going to drop the whole idea of finding Rob, but I was in too deep, the questions burning too furiously, and when I returned to Bosham Harbour, mooring *Talisman* back onto her buoy, I knew what I had to do.

Chapter forty

I caught the same train Susie usually took to London on Monday morning – the six twenty – and was in Richmond in time to grab a cappuccino before the offices of Missing People unlocked their doors.

Finally, people drifted inside. Black, white, Asian, men and women of all colours and ages. A truly mixed bag of employees. Or were they volunteers? I had no idea. I finished my coffee. Crossed the road and walked inside. Lots of posters on the walls, some plants, the smell of coffee and donuts. A young woman greeted me. She reminded me of Helen Flynn at the Mayfair Group with her friendly open smile.

I brought out the two photographs I'd enlarged and cropped. They showed the sexy but professional young woman who'd been murdered with Tony. 'I'd like to see if she was reported missing,' I said. 'On, or around, Friday the twenty-third of August.'

Her face immediately turned sympathetic. 'Of course.'

'The only trouble is,' I went on, 'I'm talking August twelve years ago.'

'I see.' She nodded as though this happened every day. 'What's her name?'

'This is where it gets strange, because I don't know.'

She blinked several times.

'But you might have her image on record?' I gestured at the posters, the photographs of men and women of all ages. MISSING. SEEN HIM? SEEN HER? CAN YOU HELP?

'I'm sorry,' she responded, tapping my photos with her fingers. 'But I have to be a little honest here. These photographs, well,

161

they're terribly blurred. I'm not sure if we would be able to find a match. Do you have anything that shows her face better?'

I'd done my best enhancing the pictures from the CCTV tape, but she was right. My expression must have turned gloomy because she said, 'Can I ask you something? If you don't know her name... can I ask your relationship to her?'

'I might have some information about her,' I prevaricated. 'Which might help her family. If she was reported missing.'

'I see.' She was frowning as she rose from behind her desk. She gestured at my photographs. 'Would you mind if I borrowed these for a moment?'

'Sure.'

She vanished for three minutes, no more, and returned with a short compact-bodied woman. Freckles, a bright interested face. Another warm smile.

'Hi,' she said. 'I'm Ginny.'

'Hi,' I said. I didn't give my name.

She gave a nod, as though acknowledging the fact and accepting it. She passed back my photographs. 'Kirsty says you're after information about this young woman.'

'Yes. I'm sorry I don't have her name. My friend refused to give it to me. I want to know if she went missing when he thinks she did.'

She surveyed me. It wasn't an unfriendly look. More curious. 'We've had far stranger requests, believe me. Was she reported missing to the police?'

'I'm sorry, I don't know.'

'You haven't contacted them?'

'It's complicated.'

She sighed. 'In order for me to help you, I really need you to report her missing to the police. Then I can check our involvement is appropriate.'

'What if I don't go to the police?'

She raised her eyebrows.

'Couldn't you have a look at your records?' My tone turned pleading. 'See if someone resembling her was reported missing around that time? That's all. I don't need any other information. Nothing at all.'

'I'm sorry.' She shook her head, genuinely apologetic. 'We have a very good relationship with the police and I wouldn't want it jeopardised. I know a sympathetic sergeant at our local station though. It's only in Kew Road. I could ring her for you? Set up an appointment?'

'You're very kind.' I gave a smile but it was forced. 'I'll think about it.'

I picked up the photographs and walked outside. I was glad they didn't have my name. I wondered if they'd report my visit, but what would they say? A man wanted to know if a woman with no name had gone missing twelve years ago?

As I walked to North Sheen Station, I rang Susie. We hadn't spoken since I'd left her flat and although we'd texted, I wanted to talk to her about Etienne's visit. Her phone went to voicemail. I left a message. An airliner roared above, heading for Heathrow. I looked up to see the sun was making a feeble effort to break through the cloud but I couldn't see the aeroplane. I bought another coffee and drank it while I waited for the train.

I was at Victoria Station when Susie rang me back.

'How's the hangover?' she asked.

I blinked. 'Er… better, thanks.'

'You can't remember, can you?' She sounded amused.

'What?'

'You rang me when you were at the pub.'

'I did?' I had no memory of it.

'You were hammered.'

'Mmm.' I felt abashed.

'After you'd hung up, I called Charley. He said Etienne looked after you.'

'Yes, he did.'

'I'm glad.'

There was a pause. I heard her talking to someone her end but it was muffled. I thought I heard her say, *Two minutes*, and then she was back on the line.

'Sorry,' she said. 'I don't have much time. Shall we talk at home tonight? Unless there's anything urgent I need to know now?'

'Not really.'

'Quickly,' she said, 'just so you know, I saw DI Barry Gilder earlier. I showed him my badge. He's agreed to team up. He won't make it official, so we're safe for the moment. He's pretty okay, I think. He'll help, where he can.'

'Wow,' I said.

'One thing though. I didn't tell him who Rob used to work for.'

'Oh.'

'Let's keep it that way for a bit. See what he comes up with for us first. Gotta go, handsome.'

'Love you.'

She was gone.

I spent a couple of hours that afternoon at work, trying to pick up the threads of the HAPS account, but it was difficult to concentrate, so I didn't hang around and headed home just as it was beginning to get dark.

I was climbing out of my car – an ageing BMW that was going to become a classic one day soon – when a huge shape appeared at the corner of my vision.

'Christ!' I leaped back, heart pounding.

The man held up his hands as though to show he wasn't armed, wasn't going to hurt me. He said, 'I bin waiting.'

The man was the size and shape of a hay bale and wore a white shirt beneath a jacket that bunched beneath his arms. Short-cropped brown hair. Reflective sunglasses. He looked like the elder brother of Tommo, the man who'd accompanied the Saint at Clara's. I was tempted to ask if they were related, but decided I didn't have the guts.

'Waiting?' I echoed. My heart was still galloping like a demented horse.

'Got here at seven. Bin waiting all day.'

'Oh,' I said. 'I caught the six-twenty train this morning.'

'Shit. I was told you didn' move till eight.'

I felt a tap of dismay beneath my breastbone. 'What do you mean?'

'You get up at eight, normally. Right?'

'I'm being *watched*?'

He didn't reply. Gave a shrug of his hay-bale shoulders as if to say, *Yeah, sure, but don't gripe to me about it.*

'Jesus.'

He held out a hand.

I said, 'What?'

'Your phone.'

'No,' I said.

He reached up a hand and opened his jacket. He showed me a gun sitting snugly in its holster. 'It's loaded.'

'You'll shoot me for my phone?'

'Stop being such a dick and just fucking hand it over, would you? The boss wants to see you and he doesn't want you to have your fucking phone on you.'

'No.' I stood my ground. I wanted to see what he'd do.

He looked at me but since I couldn't see his eyes it was hard to tell his expression.

'Open the car,' he told me.

'No,' I said. Then, 'Why?'

'Jesus, you are a pain in the backside. Throw your phone inside. Lock the car. Then we're all happy.'

I thought it a decent compromise so I did as he said. I chucked the envelope with Jane Doe's pictures inside as well, but I didn't leave the phone in view in case it tempted a passer-by to smash one of my windows and steal it. I tucked it under the driver's seat.

The thug indicated a silver Mercedes parked down the road. 'Get in.'

'Look, I'm dying for a piss. Could you–'

'Get in or I'll thump you so hard you'll see fucking stars for a week.'

No negotiation then.

The Merc whisked me northwards. Along the M3 and around the M25. We exited at junction eighteen and after Chorleywood and Little Chalfont, swept through the pretty market town of Old Amersham, its main road lined with ancient timbered coaching inns and several old pubs, all lit up and looking cosy and friendly in the wintry dark.

Then we were winding our way through the Chilterns, along narrow country lanes, the car splashing through muddy puddles. We climbed up a long hill and then the Saint's goon swung left to pause in front of a pair of tall wrought-iron gates. He wound down his window, pressed a button, and as the gates swung open, dozens of artfully hidden lights came on, illuminating the way ahead.

The drive was lined with beech trees, trunks shining black in the rain. A few yellow leaves clung on but mostly the branches were bare. CCTV cameras took in our progress. I turned in my seat, looked through the rear window, but nothing was there. Just tall trees, dripping rain. I faced forwards, my palms damp, my stomach filled with dread.

Chapter forty-one

As we swept through a garden – lots of topiary and box hedges – I saw Tommo's brother, or whoever he was, glance at me in his rear-view mirror. He'd taken off his dark glasses and I was surprised to see he had a pair of large round brown eyes, like a deer.

The Saint's house was a stunning Queen Anne-style country mansion in fine red brick with tall, elegant windows and four whopping great chimney stacks sprouting through its roof. Twin cedars flanked the building, accentuating the symmetry of the design. I was dropped outside the front door, where a man in smart trousers and jacket ushered me inside. A huge stone fireplace gave off a welcoming glow and the air smelled sweet, as though someone had been baking biscuits.

I caught a glimpse of a red-velvet dining room on the right, a green and gold drawing room on the left, where a woman sat with an iPad on her knee. Round spectacles. Late fifties, faded curly red hair. Overweight. As I passed, our eyes met in the briefest of glances. She looked sad.

I was led past a grand staircase and along a narrow passage into a library. One wall was adorned with photographs of the Saint with his family. Tony as a toddler, as a man. Two daughters. I recognised the sad-looking woman as his wife. Books lined the two other walls. Another fire glowed in another huge fireplace. Deep leather chairs, lots of dark wood, crystal decanters and glasses. Very old school. Very classic. Which was why I was surprised when I saw the dog. I would have expected a wolfhound or a Labrador, but instead a small hairy creature with a pushed-in snout, bulging eyes and stained beard came over to sniff my trousers.

'She's a Brussels Griffon,' the Saint said.

Knowing how proud people could be of their dogs, I said, 'She's cute,' even though it had to be the ugliest dog I'd ever seen.

'You should be a diplomat, artist,' he said. His mouth twisted. 'Now, before we get down to business, I want to show you something.'

He took me to a cabinet at the far end of the room, away from the fireplace. Inside, to my astonishment, lay a selection of highly collectible comic books, including early editions of Batman, Captain America and the Fantastic Four.

He tilted his head, awaiting my reaction.

I licked my lips. 'Wow. They're in incredibly good condition. They must be worth a fortune.'

He opened the glass lid and withdrew the Batman comic, passed it to me. Sweat trickling down my back. I handled it reverently, carefully.

'It's Catwoman's first appearance,' he told me.

It would be worth thousands. He wanted me to look through his collection, obviously proud, and very much an enthusiast. Normally I would have enjoyed talking about how each artist developed the characters, the storylines, over the years, but my mouth was dry, my heart fluttering. I was in the lion's den and nobody knew I was here. The Saint could have me murdered and buried beneath one of his box hedges and nobody would know.

'So, artist.' He returned the comics to their cabinet and closed the lid. 'It seems nobody's telling me anything. I've already had to chastise someone for not volunteering information, and now I've got you.'

·'Me?'

He tilted his head again. 'You were at the scene of Arun Choudhuri's murder, and you didn't think to tell me?'

I opened and closed my mouth.

'Come, come, artist. What's your excuse?'

'I didn't think.'

The Saint drew his lips back over his teeth in a humourless smile and I felt my lungs contract. 'You didn't think.'

I didn't know what to say or do to diffuse the sudden penetrating menace in the air, so I remained silent.

'Please tell me you won't be so stupid again.'

I shook my head.

'Promise?'

I nodded.

'So, artist, who killed my faithful ex-employee?'

'I don't know.'

He did the head tilt again. My sweat poured harder.

'What about Robert? Your brother? Where's he?'

'I don't know. I swear it.'

'You're not much use, are you?' he said, baring his teeth once more.

I wanted to ask him about the woman in the photograph I'd seen that morning, lying alongside Tony with her face smashed in, but after Roger Marshall's warning about besmirching Tony's memory, I didn't know how the hell I could.

'You saw Missing People today,' he said.

'Yes.' I saw no point in not admitting it since I appeared to be under surveillance.

'Why?'

With a surge of annoyance, brought about by sheer fear, I said, 'Why do you think?'

'Ooooh.' He flung up his hands. 'I'm scared. Big scary Nick Ashdown grows balls. Now that's a headline.'

He held my eyes, dropping all pretence of humour. 'Why. Did. You. See. Them.'

'I, er... I don't know if you know... that, er... there was a woman with, er...' I frantically licked my lips. 'Tony, er, that night...?'

It was as though a switch had been flicked. The Saint's moderately frightening expression vanished and in its place stood one far worse. Pure rage.

'How the fuck do you know that?'

He took a step forward and I couldn't help it, I cringed.

'Someone, sent me something. Anonymously.'

'Show me,' he snapped.

'I don't have it with me.'

'What was it?'

'Photographs.'

'Of what?'

I looked away.

'Of what?!' he screamed. His face turned purple. His fists bunched.

'Tony,' I blurted. 'And… her.'

The Saint was breathing heavily. His nostrils were dilated. 'You saw them. Together?'

I nodded.

'You saw the murder scene?'

Dread sat like a stone in my stomach. I nodded again.

He took several breaths, obviously trying to get himself under control.

'Who sent them?'

'I don't know.' I gulped. Dragged my courage up from my boots. 'Who's the woman?'

For a moment he stared at me. He was, I realised with shock, surprised.

'You don't know?'

'No.'

He gave a choked snort which I took he meant to show he found this funny, but there was no amusement in his eyes which remained as flat and cold as slate. 'She was your brother's girlfriend.'

My jaw softened. Rob was cheating on Clara?

'You don't have a fucking clue, do you?' he said pityingly.

I decided there was no point in answering that one and remained silent.

He put a finger on his lips, as though he was in deep thought. 'If you didn't know she was his girlfriend, I suppose you know jack shit all else.'

'Who was she?' I asked again. 'What was her name?'

'Fuck knows.' He flung his hands in the air. 'Some bint who had the morals of a cat and if she wasn't already dead, I'd kill her myself. Because it was your fuck of a brother who followed this bint of a girlfriend to my son's office and when he saw them, what they were doing, he killed them both in a fucking jealous rage.'

His voice grew louder again, his colour rising.

'What happened to her body?' I asked.

'Don't ask that question again.' He gave me a look that sent an ice pick to my core.

I tried to hold his gaze, but my eyes slid away and when they did, he walked over to me. Stabbed my chest with an iron-like forefinger. 'You dare mention the situation in which my son died to anyone else and you'll regret it. I do not want Mrs Abbott's memory of the son she adored dragged through the mud by a little worm like you. The same goes for my daughters. It would kill them. And I'll come after you, and I'll slice you open and let you die trying to stuff your entrails back into your body. Understood?'

I nodded. Unstuck my tongue from the roof of my mouth. 'C-can I ask…'

He surveyed me at length. Finally gave me a curt nod.

'W-where did m-my brother get the g-gun?'

My legs were feeling shaky, so I put a hand on the back of one of the leather armchairs to steady myself.

'Fuck knows.' The Saint turned away as he shrugged. 'From the street, from the Blood fucking Family in Spain, eBay, Amazon, take your pick. He was a drug runner. He could have picked it up anywhere.'

'He ran drugs for you?'

'Are you hard of hearing or something?'

Through my fear, my brain was overloading with conflicting information. Rob, running drugs, working undercover for MI5. Rob the jealous boyfriend, cheating on his wife. Rob who'd vanished to keep himself safe. Rob, who I had to see to get some fucking ANSWERS.

'Oh,' the Saint suddenly remarked, sounding startled. 'Look at that.' He strode to the window, clicked his fingers. 'Come and see, artist.'

On unsteady legs, I walked over. He was looking outside and pointing. I saw a soft shape move on the lawn, just outside the arc of light shining from our window. It was a badger.

'You've brought me luck.' To my astonishment, he beamed at me. 'I haven't seen a badger in ages.'

I couldn't think of anything to say. I seemed to have lost the power of speech. I didn't say another word, not when he ushered me outside, nor when Tommo's look-a-like dropped me off at home.

I had to drink two whiskies before I could speak to Susie, and when I did, it took an immense effort not to cry.

Chapter forty-two

A strong wind came in just after dawn. Susie had already left for work, planning to spend the rest of the week in London, and I lay for a while listening to the rain rattle the windows, the wind whistling around the eaves. I felt snug and secure beneath the duvet, and I had to force myself to get up. Normally I'd head straight for a slash and a shower, but after the previous day's revelations, I peeked outside to see if I could spot anyone watching me.

No silver Mercedes, which was a relief, and as far as I could tell, the parked cars appeared to be empty. I studied the street, looking for anyone twitching their curtains or blinds, but all I could see were endless puddles and lashing rain. Trees swayed in the wind, yellow and brown leaves gusting through the air. That the Saint was watching me, I had no doubt. He wanted my brother. What easier way to find him than keep tabs on me?

While I showered, I tried to make a plan but my head was muzzy, my brain having trouble computing everything I'd learned. My body felt tired, from all the adrenaline flowing the previous day probably, and I was toying with the idea of going back to bed and pulling the duvet over my head, when the landline rang.

'Nick,' said Ronja. 'You're at home.'

'Yes.' I was about to say I was going to come into the office – I felt as though I needed a dose of normality – but she interrupted.

'I need to run something past you. About the HAPS account. Put on your coffee machine. I'll be with you in twenty minutes, okay?'

'But I was going to–'

She hung up before I could finish my sentence. I tried to ring her back but her phone went straight to voicemail. What was going on? Was it really to do with work? Unnerved, uncertain, I paced the cottage until the doorbell rang.

I scooted to the kitchen window but since whoever it was stood on the porch step, I couldn't see who it was. I went to the front door.

'Who is it?' I called.

'Ronja.'

I opened the door a crack, keeping it on the chain. Not that it would hold if a large shoulder smashed against it, but at least it would give me a couple of second's warning. I paused, trying to see past her rain-spattered raincoat. She was holding a folder over her head in a vain attempt to keep her great mane of wind-whipped hair dry.

'Come on, Nick. I'm getting soaked out here.'

I quickly unlatched the chain and opened the door. She stamped her feet on the mat, then kicked off her boots. Dumped the folder on the hall table. Fluffed out her hair.

'What are you doing here?' I asked. She never came to my home. We normally met at a pub or café if we saw each other out of working hours.

'I'm your boss, remember?' She gave me an arch look.

'Yes, but…'

'I told you to put the coffee machine on, yes?'

Yes, Herr Commandant. I refrained from saluting and led the way into the kitchen area. Put the machine on. Brought out a couple of cups. Made the coffee. Gave her a cup of Rosabaya, which I knew she liked. Made myself an Indriya, super strong. I thought having too much caffeine in my bloodstream was the least of my concerns.

'So,' I said.

'So,' she repeated. 'I want you to listen to me, okay?'

'Okay,' I said cautiously.

'I don't want you looking out of the window or making any phone calls, or doing anything out of the ordinary. I'm here as your boss. I brought a folder to do with work.' She pulled out her mobile, made a call. She said, 'He's here,' into her phone and then passed it to me.

'Nick,' a man said.

One word. That was all it took. I felt as though I was in an express lift with its cables cut.

'You…' I could hardly speak I was so flooded with emotion.

'Sorry,' he said.

'Fuck,' I added. My tone was strangled.

I saw Ronja's hands come up. 'Be calm,' she hissed. She flicked a look at the windows, then back. I struggled to breathe.

'Sorry,' my brother repeated.

Silence.

I was trembling but whether it was from relief, anger or fear, I hadn't a clue.

'I didn't want it to be like this,' he added.

All my emotions abruptly narrowed into a single laser beam directed at the source of all my trouble.

'You little fuck, did you even think what–'

Ronja reached across and snatched the phone from my hand. She said, 'We need you to be calm. We're having a business meeting. We're talking, not shouting.'

I said, 'Ronja, for Chrissakes…'

Then I pulled myself together. Getting angry with her wasn't going to do any good. And she was right, if anyone was watching, I needed to act normally. I must not let them think anything untoward was going on.

I held my hand out for the phone. She passed it back.

I said to Rob, 'Sorry about that. I've been under a bit of stress lately.' My tone was stiff, but at least it was calm, and although I wanted to add a sarcastic comment like, *I wonder why?* I refrained.

'Understood,' he said. 'Let's meet.'

Chapter forty-three

I wanted to ask Rob: *Do I bring the family? Mum? Dad? Oh, and what about Clara's husband?* But I managed to desist. I could punch him on the nose when I saw him.

'Where?' I said, my tone only lightly curious, but my nerves were tightening, coming alert.

'Remember that day with the Christophers? The trouble we got into? Let's have a re-enactment.'

I glanced outside. It had to be force seven at least. A moderate gale.

'What, now?'

'No time like the present.'

I wanted to ask if he'd checked the tides, and also the forecast to see if things might deteriorate into more severe weather, but I didn't want to give anything away.

'See you there,' I said.

He hung up.

I stared outside. The Christopher boys. I hadn't thought of them in years. Like us, they were grown up, one a solicitor in Portsmouth, the other working for a sports clothing company out of Nottingham. We'd had a race with them from West Itchenor to Hayling Island. I'd been fifteen, Rob thirteen. The Christopher boys had been that little bit older than us, which made us all that more determined to beat them. It had been Rob, clever, cunning Rob, who'd noted the way storms the week before had changed some of the sea bed. He didn't tell me though, or what his plan was. We were just about neck and neck with the Christopher's yacht, clipping along nicely in a stiff breeze, when Rob suddenly screamed at me, *Tack starboard, now!*

He was at the yacht's prow and I assumed he'd seen something dangerous dead ahead – some debris that might damage the boat perhaps – so I'd pushed the tiller hard and we swung round, cutting away fast, seemingly off course and making an error, and I was yelling at him, *What is it? What's wrong?* when he grinned and pointed behind us. The boys were laughing, their yacht flying like an arrow for the island when suddenly their bow lurched and dipped and the boat slammed to a stop. It was as though it had hit a brick wall.

Both boys were flung violently forward. One broke his wrist, the other his collarbone. Their yacht had to be towed off the sand bank, and both boys sent to hospital. We'd got hell, but we'd won.

I passed Ronja her phone. 'Thanks.' Then I gave her a twisted smile. 'I think.'

She didn't smile back. 'It's okay.'

'How did…' I gestured at the phone, wanting to know how he'd contacted her, wanting the whole story.

'He called me.' She pushed one shoulder up in a hey-it-was-nothing gesture. 'I'm easy to find. My phone number is on our website. He asked me to come here. He asked me to be careful. He wanted to speak to you. And he has, right?'

'Right.'

She looked at me. A deep long look. 'How much trouble is he in?'

'Lots.'

'I thought so.'

She came to me and put her arms around me and turned her cheek so we could hug. She squeezed me close, strong and firm and steady. A proper hug from a friend. A hug of compassion, of empathy. It felt good. I lowered my head a fraction so it rested against hers. We were nearly the same height, but not quite. 'Thank you,' I whispered.

She leaned back. Held my gaze. 'You need me, ring.'

I watched her drive away, her Firenze-red baby Rangie splashing through the puddles. I could remember the day she'd taken delivery of the Range Rover Evoque. She'd driven it into the office car park as excited as a kid in a sweet shop, showing me all the gizmos, the parking sensors and cameras, the head-up display on the windscreen, lane-keeping assist, blah-blah. Pricey as hell, but even I could appreciate its design, and the fact she'd worked her socks off for it.

Before she vanished around the corner, I took the opportunity to casually study the street, but could see nothing to alarm me. It was odd because although intellectually I knew I was being watched, I found it almost impossible to believe. I couldn't see anyone suspicious – I couldn't see anyone at all – but Rob had taken precautions. He'd send Ronja with a phone call cover: *I need to run something past you. About the HAPS account.* And she'd brought a work-style folder with her. A prop to add to her deception. Which, I realised, she'd left behind.

I quickly closed the door. Picked up the file and had a flick through. Lots of pictures of bathrooms, boilers, flues and cylinders, documents drafting *Our Products, Plastic Plumbing* and *Tools and Workwear.* Dear God, when this was over, please could I have a sexier account? Something to do with Caribbean holidays at least, or luxury leather handbags, designer watches, anything that didn't involve bifold doors, stopcocks, bib taps and draw-off fittings. I flipped through more achingly dull pages, nearly bypassing a photocopy of columns, but there was something about it that made me pause.

Name. Company. Visiting. Time In. Time Out.

There were twelve lines. The page appeared to have just been started and there were only three lines which had been filled in. At the top was the date. Friday twenty-third August. Twelve years earlier.

My ears rang.

It was the Mayfair Group's reception folder.

Carefully, I looked at each column. The times spanned were between five fifteen and five forty-five. Three people had signed in, but hadn't signed out.

Susie Fleming.

Danya Benesch.

Robert Ashdown.

I could feel the blood drain from my head but I didn't move, didn't do anything. I was like a statue. Cold as marble, as stone, as ice.

I stared at Susie's name for a long time.

Chapter forty-four

I glanced astern and to starboard. Across a hundred feet of dirty grey water, the sapphire-blue bow of a boat called *Jovial* sliced into a dark wave and kicked water over her foredeck.

Jovial. Jovita. As Etienne had said, it was a nice little boat, twenty-five foot, six berths, and Rob seemed to have looked after her well because although she was no longer in her prime, her paintwork was immaculate and her hull was shining clean, no growth or slime to be seen.

The wind was blowing hard from the west, where bloated clouds came off the sea. Luckily the wind had come down from force eight, gusting nine, a big relief. I spun the wheel and *Talisman*'s nose turned through the wind. The aluminium boom clanked across, the jib sliding smoothly around the front of the mast. She leaned in again, to starboard, heading for *Jovial*. I saw Rob's mouth open, a wide grin splitting his face. The gap of water between our boats narrowed. Inch by inch, we were coming together.

Talisman's nose dug up a lump of water and sent it down the deck into my face. It tasted flat and cold and salty. I looked around but couldn't see anyone else out on the harbour, not surprising since it was such a shitty day.

As *Jovial* approached, Rob released his jib and main sail, depowering, slowing down. I did the same. Slowly, steadily, we slopped and tossed our way towards one another, our sails flapping and roaring. I was sweating with anxiety and tension, wondering how this was going to work. I could understand the location. We could see anyone approaching for miles, but how were we to have a proper conversation if we had to shout across the wind-capped waves?

Finally, we turned into the wind. We were barely six feet apart. Then Rob called out.

A woman appeared at *Jovial*'s hatch, glanced my way. Curly yellow hair, a Norwegian fishing sweater, oilskins. Her face was expressionless. She skimmed around the boat like a professional, putting out fenders. Then she took the helm from Rob and eased *Jovial* toward me until we were nearly touching.

A puff of wind made *Jovial*'s slack sail jump and billow. The boat shuddered. Rob walked across the dipping heaving deck as though he was on land. The fenders squeaked against my hull.

'Give me your hand!' I shouted.

He ignored me and in three quick capable movements, he'd swung himself on board. Immediately, the woman tightened a sail and swung *Jovial* away.

For several seconds, we looked at one another.

'Hey, big brother. It's good to see you.' He smiled at me, the smile I remembered of old, full of mischief and daring and joy.

'You bloody bastard,' I said.

He punched me on the arm, hard enough so it hurt, just as he used to, and then we were hugging one another and I was shouting *you bastard!* over and over and we were laughing, tears streaming down our cheeks, choking, yelling nonsense.

The deck surged under our feet, causing us to lose our balance and forcing us apart. I grabbed the helm, Rob the hatch.

'Let's go,' I said. We needed to get some headway so we could stabilise the boat.

Rob went to the winches, tightening both sails and settling the boat into a steady cruise. The sound of the water against the hull, the cold wet air in my lungs, the sight of my brother on my boat. I could hardly believe it. It felt fantastic.

He came and stood beside me, bracing a hip against the gunwale.

'So, who's your friend?' I asked.

'Sorcha.'

'A close friend, I assume.'

'Yup. We live together. Have done for years. We couldn't get married, obviously.'

'She knows about Clara?'

'Yup.'

'Jesus.'

'Sorcha knows everything.' He faced forwards, his cheeks glowing apple red, his hair damp from the spray. 'It was the only way.'

'Where did you meet her?'

'In rehab.'

I could feel my eyes bulge. 'Rehab?'

He smiled, but it held a tinge of sadness. 'I had a bit of a problem with drugs. I did some bad things, but I turned my life around and I'm all right now.'

'Bad things?' I repeated. Although my tone was relatively level, my blood pressure had begun to rise. 'Does that include putting your family through hell and back? Crucifying Clara? Crucifying Mum and Dad...' I had to lasso my emotions which were threatening to stampede for the horizon. 'Jesus, Rob. What the hell did you think you were doing?'

His eyes narrowed. 'What do you know?'

'I hardly know where to start.' My tone was biting.

'Try the beginning.'

I noticed a bit of disturbance in the forward part of the mainsail, checked the telltales, and adjusted my course in order to increase the headsails' efficiency.

'I know you were running drugs for the Saint. That you owe that Spanish gang a million quid...' The shock of it came at me anew and I said again, 'a *million quid*. Jesus Christ, Rob, do you realise what trouble you've landed Etienne in? They're squeezing his balls in a vice and he's going insane trying to find you.'

'Ah, shit.' He shook his head. 'I'm sorry.'

'And you've still got their boat.'

His eyes gleamed. 'Nice little cruiser, don't you think? We lived on her for over three years, until we managed to get it together to get a mortgage. Settled down like normal folk.'

I was overcome with questions – where did he live, did he have any more kids, what did he do for work – but before I could say a word, he said, 'Come on, Nick. Tell me what you know, and I'll fill in the blanks.'

'You ran away to protect Clara and the kids, us, from the Saint. All very laudable but do you realise the hell you put us through?'

'Yes,' he said simply. 'I do. And I'm sorry, truly sorry, but there was no other way.'

We sailed on in silence for a bit.

I said, 'Did you kill Tony Abbott?'

Chapter forty-five

'No.' Rob's tone was firm. 'I did not kill Tony Abbott.'

'What about the woman who was killed with him?'

'Absolutely not.'

'Was she your girlfriend?'

His head snapped around. 'My *what?*'

'That's what the Saint told me.'

His colour paled. 'You've met him?'

'Twice.'

'Oh, Jesus.' He ran a hand over his face. 'I'm so sorry. That's the last thing I wanted.'

'He wants your head on a plate.'

'I know.' Rob gestured around the wind-chopped harbour. 'Why do you think we're here?'

Jovial had eased in front of us and now she tacked, keeping away from the buoys ahead warning of low water.

'What happened?' I asked.

'Let's tack,' he told me. 'We don't want to end up like the Christopher boys.'

Talisman's deck came level as I turned her nose through the wind. The boom went across, and the jib, accompanied by a spatter of spray as she leaned to port.

'What else do you know?' He was looking at me with an intense expression, penetrating, and I knew it was time to come clean, whether Susie liked it or not.

'I know that you worked for MI5.'

For a moment, his jaw slackened. His eyes rounded into golf balls. 'My, my. Wherever did you hear that?'

'From an old colleague of yours. Susie Fleming.' I took a breath. 'She's my wife.'

A minnow of caution swam briefly in his eyes.

'Is she, indeed?' he said. He stared at me for a long time. His expression had turned smooth, unreadable. It was a look I didn't recognise. I'd thought Rob an open book, but he could be planning mass murder or buying a bunch of flowers for his Norwegian sweater-wearing paramour for all the emotion he showed.

He turned to face forward for a while, then he turned back to me. 'What else do you know?'

I swallowed. Looked ahead and past the sails, at *Jovita*. Plucked up my courage, and looked back at him.

'That she was there that night too.'

He didn't move, didn't say anything. This wasn't the brother I remembered, who'd been a bit crazy, happy-go-lucky, everyone's friend. This man was calm and self-possessed. Rational. In control. And at that moment, I could see him being an MI5 agent. I could see him being anything he wanted, and out of nowhere I felt something shift between us and it was as though I was the younger brother all of a sudden, and he the more experienced elder.

'You were working together?' I asked.

'Is that what she told you?'

No, I thought. *I just found her name on the company's reception folder for that night.* At that point, a thought crashed through: if she was there in an official capacity, would she have left her name, evidence she'd been there? Or had she been there in an unofficial capacity? Wouldn't she have used an alias? Or had someone else put her name there? If so, why?

'Nick?' he pressed.

I wanted to say, *I have evidence she was there*, but I wasn't entirely sure if that was true without a handwriting expert. Plus, I didn't want to be disloyal. I wanted to talk to her first.

'What were you doing there that night?' I asked instead.

He considered my question briefly as though weighing things up, then he said, 'I was there to bug the place.'

'Ah.'

'I was a trusted "employee" of the organisation. I'd been given some pretty high-end kit to use by the boys in blue. We knew it was risky as I wouldn't normally be there, but someone had to do it and since I was the only person who might get away with it…'

'Risky,' I said. 'Because if you'd been caught…'

'I wouldn't be here,' he agreed, suddenly looking cheerful. 'But as it is, everything went to rat shit and I scarpered, and now here we are.'

'What was Susie doing there?'

'I think you'd better ask that one yourself, don't you?' He raised his eyebrows at me.

'You chased after a woman. You had a gun.'

'Ah,' he said, nodding. 'You got the CCTV tape then.'

'Who was she? The woman you chased after.'

'I have no idea.'

'Why were you chasing her?'

His facial muscles didn't change, but his eyes grew watchful. 'Ask me another.'

'No. I want to know. Were you going to shoot her? Did you catch her? What happened to her?'

He held up a hand. 'Enough.' His voice cracked like a whip.

'You may not want to talk about it–' my tone grew angry 'but I do. Did she see what happened?'

At that, he gave a groan. The tension went out of his shoulders. He closed his eyes. He nodded.

'So,' I said. 'She's a witness.'

He opened his eyes and gazed across the water, expression closed. He didn't confirm or deny it.

'Did you catch her?'

'No, I didn't. She ran like a bloody jack rabbit on speed. I lost her outside.' He opened his eyes. 'Can we stop with the twenty questions? I'm sure Suze will fill you in. What I really want to know is what's next?'

I wasn't sure "Suze" would fill me in at all. She may have dragged Mark Felton out for me, but that had only been under duress. She'd concealed her involvement in all this, hiding behind half-truths and lies, and the betrayal had yet to hit me. Did she have a good excuse for not being honest? Would she cover it up under the guise that it was "classified"? I thought of us sitting on our sofa and watching the CCTV recording together. Had she seen it before? From her response, I thought not, but I could be wrong. She could be a good actress when she wanted. Which was why being a spook suited her so well. Mirrors and veils, secrets and shrouds. That was her world. But it wasn't mine.

I watched *Jovial* execute another neat turn, so she was facing back the way we'd come.

'What do you think should happen?' I responded.

This time, dark emotion filled his face. 'The Saint,' Rob said. 'I want to bring him down, and I want to come home.'

I couldn't help it. I had to ask. 'What about Clara and the kids?'

His gaze became distant. 'We need some kind of resolution.'

'She's remarried. John, he's a nice guy…'

Rob looked at me again. 'I'm not going to mess things up for anyone. I just want to be able to sail into the harbour with Sorcha and have a beer at The Anchor Bleu without someone turning up wanting to kill me. Did you know there's still a bounty on my head? Half a million quid and the queue isn't getting any smaller, I can tell you.'

He leaned forward, adjusted a cleat, and went on. 'When I say "coming home", I mean that I want to drop in on Mum and Dad for a cup of tea without looking over my shoulder. I want to see Honey and Finn…' His voice broke and for a moment I thought he might cry, but he quickly got himself under control. 'I want to see my kids without bringing homicidal maniacs to their door. Coming home means I want George fucking Abbott locked up, behind bars for the rest of his life, and to be *free of fear*.'

'Okay.' I nodded. 'I get it.'

I reached over and gripped his arm briefly. He nodded back. Then he looked at his boat – or rather the Spanish gang's boat – and said, 'We need to make a plan.'

'Coming about,' I said, and wound the wheel, spinning the boat so we came in front of *Jovial*. 'What kind of plan?'

He grinned, and the brother I remembered returned, his eyes lit with excitement and adventure. 'Something clever, that doesn't get anyone killed.'

Chapter forty-six

When I returned to moor *Talisman* on her buoy, I saw two men outside the sailing club, standing in the rain, watching me. Usually I would cover the boat with a tarp, but since I didn't know when I might need it again, and maybe in a hurry, I decided against it. I padlocked the hatch and went for'ard and grabbed the dinghy. As soon as I started rowing for the shore – obviously alone – the men disappeared.

In the shallows, I splashed the dinghy up the muddy bank and secured it against a wooden piling. No men watching me, as far as I could tell. I wondered if they had followed me here and watched me sail out into the harbour, or whether they were simply tourists, maybe a couple of walkers taking in the view. They'd been too far away for me to make out their clothing, let alone their features. All I knew was that I hadn't seen them earlier.

I walked home, keeping an eye out, but I didn't see them again. Just a woman walking a small brown dog, and an elderly bloke in a tatty old Barbour. If anyone had followed me in the hope I'd lead them to Rob, they'd have needed a drone to track my progress across the water. You couldn't follow us by car because of all the inlets and tributaries – you'd have to drive twenty times the distance that we would do by boat. Which was why Rob's chosen meeting place had been so perfect, because while I'd headed *Talisman* north for Bosham, Sorcha and Rob had gone in the opposite direction, perhaps toward Hayling Island, or even the Isle of Wight. I had no idea. Before he left me, he'd given me a mobile phone, a cheap second-hand Nokia worth about ten quid.

'So we can talk, undetected,' he told me. 'It's pay as you go. I've put my number in there. However, if you think anyone's seen it, send me a text with the word Avalanche in it. Then chuck it. Thereon, I'll post or leave messages in post office box number 2113.' He went on to give me a Chichester PO box office service address.

I said, 'It's around the corner from work.'

'Dead handy,' he agreed, indicating he'd chosen its location specifically for my convenience. He gave me a key to the mailbox.

It was still raining when I arrived home, and despite my wet weather gear I felt cold and damp, so I ran a bath, the age-old cure for chilled-to-the-bone sailors around the world. While I soaked, I leaned back and closed my eyes but all I could see was Susie's innocent expression, hear her voice in my head.

No, I wasn't working with Rob. You know that already, Nick. I told you, remember? And no, I had nothing to do with Abbott.

I remembered us watching the CCTV recording. My absorption with the grey blur on the front of the desk. Her asking me what I'd spotted. *It's a logo*, I'd said. *So it is*, she'd said, as if she didn't know. As if she'd never been there. The liar.

Rob's death had felt a bit like this. Denial, yes, and shock, but what distressed me the most was that I recognised the same data ticking through my synapses, telling me nothing would ever be the same again. It wouldn't matter what she said in her defence, if her excuse was MI5 sanctioned, certified by the Prime Minister and authorised by the Queen herself, my wife had lied to me. And it hadn't been a little white lie like when she told me she liked the shirt I was wearing to give me confidence before I met her parents (even I knew it was crap), but a monster lie over the day my brother had vanished.

I'd bet my last penny she had been there that night. And she hadn't told me.

Would I be able to forgive her? Or would I never be able to trust her again? Would I spend time in the future wondering if she was being honest with me? Or would I stop listening to her, tune her out, unable to know if she was lying or not? It would, I thought, rot me from the inside out. It would destroy us.

Emotions rioted through me. Anger, fear, apprehension. But right at the top sat a deep-rooted sorrow. I'd trusted her, and she had ripped up that trust and set fire to it before flushing it down the toilet.

When the water cooled, I added some more hot. I kept doing this until my skin was pink and I started to sweat. Then I towelled myself dry, put on jeans and a sweatshirt. I made tea. Went and fetched some logs from the log store at the side of the house. Lit a fire. I quickly cooled and felt shivery, slightly ill, and I knew it was shock. Shock of seeing my brother, shock of Susie's duplicity.

The fire was blazing merrily when my mobile went. I had a quick look at the display. *Unknown.* Since Susie used blocked numbers from time to time, I wasn't sure whether to answer or not. What would I say to her?

Cautiously, I answered. 'Hello?' If it was Susie I'd make an excuse, like someone was at the door, and hang up. I wanted to be ready when I saw her. I wanted my head straight, my questions in line. Basically, I wanted all my ducks in a row.

'Hello, Nick.' A woman's cheery voice. 'How are you going with our little investigation?'

I'd forgotten about Fredericka, the journalist. 'Er, it's... er, complicated.'

'Heard from your brother yet?'

'I thought we had an agreement not to go there.'

'It was worth a shot,' she said, unabashed. 'So, any news for me?'

'You've kind of caught me on the hop,' I said. I really didn't want to talk to her. Not about Rob, nor the Saint, not even the weather.

'That's okay. Because I've been doing some digging, and I've found someone who'll speak to us about the night Tony Abbott died.'

Although I'd been about to make an excuse to hang up, curiosity got the better of me. 'Like who?'

'Like one of the cleaners. Klaudia Nowacki. She was a friend of Arun Choudhuri's. The caretaker on duty that night. You know he was murdered?'

'Yes.' I didn't say I'd seen his corpse. Too many questions would follow.

'She's very upset about it. She was on duty that night as well, or so she says. She's agreed to see us.'

'What does she know?'

'Put it this way, we can't do it by phone because how can we show our gratitude for her cooperation?'

'Ah,' I said. Klaudia wanted paying. 'How much?'

'If you want to make sure of getting something decent, bring five tons. But let's start at a bullseye and build up if we need to. No point in throwing it away.'

A bullseye was fifty quid, a ton one hundred.

'Okay,' I agreed.

'She can see us tonight. Can you get to Haringey by eight?'

I looked up Google maps to see exactly where Haringey was first, then did some swift calculations. 'Yes.'

'Let's meet outside her place at seven forty-five.' Fredericka rattled off the address.

'See you there.'

I hung up. I didn't want to go to the other side of London – Haringey was *miles* away – but the urge to get more information was paramount. Knowledge was power. I had to gather as many facts together as to what happened that night. I had to make sense of what was going on. Whether my wife was a snake or a serpent or something more cuddly like a squirrel. *But even squirrels bite*, a little voice whispered. Squirrels may look cute, but they have claws as sharp as needles and carry fleas, mites and lice.

Stop it, I told myself. Pull yourself together. Get yourself to a bank, then get your arse to Haringey and see what Klaudia has to say. You can face Susie later.

Chapter forty-seven

Another train ride to Victoria. A tube across town to King's Cross, where I changed onto the Piccadilly line. I stood for half the journey as there were no seats, but once we'd passed Holloway Road, the crowds thinned out. I exited at Manor House and headed down Green Lanes, past a pharmacy, a dry cleaners, a small well-stocked supermarket, all still open and doing a brisk business. Wind blew wet leaves through the air, and people walked hunched in coats, their collars turned up. Not many umbrellas because of the wind.

I walked past the Portland Rise Estate – Hackney Housing, according to the sign outside – and a few hundred yards later on the right I came to the block of flats I was looking for. Red brick, probably built in the seventies, four storeys. It was one of the nicer blocks on the street with balconies and some nice shrubs out the front, and the paintwork around the windows looked clean, unlike next door's which were peeling in great strips, the windows filthy.

A woman stood smoking by the brick wall. Fifties, stout, curly grey hair, short legs. She looked at me as I approached and she said, 'Nick.'

'Fredericka?'

'Glad you could make it.'

She had a grip like a man's and a direct gaze. 'You've got the cash?'

'Absolutely.'

'Let's go.'

Fredericka led the way. She buzzed the intercom and stated we were there. A voice said, 'fourth floor', and the door buzzed and Fredericka pushed it open. We walked up the stairs. Grey linoleum, pale blue walls. We came to a small landing. A woman stood in the doorway of one of the flats. She was in her late thirties, small and strong, with thin blonde hair tied back in a ponytail. I saw a faded tattoo on her wrist, a miniature butterfly, and another behind her ear. I think it was meant to be a seahorse but it had faded so much it was hard to tell. But the most striking thing about her, were her eyes, which were a sheer vivid blue ringed with darker blue, making you think you were gazing into a tropical sea.

No greeting. No handshake. Her serious expression didn't change as she nodded at us. Stood back and let us inside. Closed the door behind her. She moved ahead into a snug living room with a couple of colourful rugs, prints of mountains on the walls. Green plants lined the windowsill, some herbs.

'Where's the money?' she said.

'It depends what you have for us,' Fredericka said smoothly.

I brought out a fifty-pound note.

'Fuck that.' Klaudia's eyes watered in dismay.

I hurriedly added two more notes.

'No way,' she exclaimed. 'What I know is worth much more.'

'Give us a hint,' said Fredericka. 'Something to tempt us.'

Klaudia raised her chin. 'There was someone else there that night. Someone only me and Arun know about.'

I decided not to mess about any longer and brought out the remainder of the money, fanned the notes. I could sense Fredericka's annoyance but I didn't care. 'You tell us what happened that night,' I told Klaudia, 'you get the lot.'

Her hand reached out to take the money but Fredericka stopped her. 'You have to earn it first.'

Klaudia's eyes remained on the notes in my hand. 'Back then, I worked for My Fair Cleaning. We start at six o'clock as usual, when most people go home.'

'We?' I asked.

'Two of us. That day, it was Nicole and I.'

'Does Nicole have a surname?' Fredericka asked.

She frowned. 'I can't remember. We only really knew each other's first names anyway.'

'Who's Danya Benesch?' I asked. It was the only name on the reception list that hadn't been accounted for. However, I guessed it probably belonged to the middle-aged woman I'd seen on the CCTV tape.

'Who?' Klaudia looked blank.

I repeated the name. Klaudia shrugged. 'Never heard of them. Sorry.'

'So,' Fredericka prompted, 'you and Nicole started work, as usual…'

'We always start at the top and work down. Back then, they only had three floors. The rest were rented to other companies. Now, I think they have the whole building.'

Klaudia took a step back and folded her arms. Her eyes came away from the money briefly to rest on me.

'You started on the third floor?' I prompted.

'Yes. We always begin by cleaning the toilets. Then we go around emptying the bins. Removing all the junk people have left behind. Empty cups, lunch things. Then we dust. Polish. Our job is to clean without disturbance. To leave papers as they are, without moving them.' She rolled her eyes to let us know what she thought of *that*. 'Finally, we vacuum. Each floor.'

I nodded, trying to encourage her to continue.

'Nicola was next door, in Mr Carter's office, and I was in the big boss's office. Mr Abbott.'

'George or Tony?'

'Mr George.'

I gave another nod. I didn't know exactly where his office had been, but I didn't want to interrupt her too much before we got the gist of her story. I could nail down these details later.

'This is when he comes in.'

'Who?'

'I don't know him. But he is a nice-looking young man. Suntanned. Nice smile. He wants to check things in the office.

He says he's from a private security firm. It isn't my business, I let him do what he likes but I'm not worried. After six o'clock, Arun only lets in people who are authorised. This young man, he checks under Mr George's desk, around the office. He chats. He seems a nice person.'

I bet it was Rob, placing his bugs.

Chapter forty-eight

I looked at Klaudia expectantly. 'And?' I prompted her.

Fredericka was opening her mouth but I forestalled her with a repressive glance.

Klaudia's eyes kept flicking to the notes and away. We were coming to the meat of it, I was sure. This was the important thing.

'I heard voices,' she told me. 'I put my head around the corner in case it was Mr George, because if it was, I would have to get out quick. But it wasn't him, it was the young man. He was talking to someone.'

Klaudia closed her eyes for a moment and then they snapped open, as though she'd made a decision. 'He was talking to Rachel. I was surprised because she wasn't supposed to be working that night. Then he got in the lift, and she watched it close. She watched where it went. To the ground floor. And then she walked away.'

Silence.

'Who's Rachel?' I asked.

'Another cleaner. But it was her day off. She shouldn't have been there.'

'Did she know the young man, do you think?'

'They were talking.' Klaudia shrugged. 'I couldn't hear what about. Maybe they knew each other, maybe not.'

It was the first I'd heard of this Rachel. 'I don't suppose you know her surname.'

Klaudia shook her head.

'What time did you see them talking?'

'Mr Abbott, he asks me this also, but I don't know for sure. I hadn't been working for so long, so maybe six fifteen or so?'

'Didn't the police interview you too?'

'Yes.' Her gaze grew nervous. 'Mr George told me not to tell anything about the young man and Rachel. He made me swear. He was also…' Klaudia looked around her flat. 'Very generous.'

'You're not worried he'll be angry that you're talking now?' I asked.

'Yes,' she admitted. 'But Arun is dead. What if I die too? Nobody will know that Rachel was there. Except Mr Abbott.'

I couldn't see why it was such a big deal that an out-of-hours cleaner had been there and I had no doubt there was more to the story.

I took a wild stab in the dark. 'Did Mr Abbott know Rachel? Not just as a cleaner, I mean…'

Something moved in her eyes, and I knew I'd hit the nail on the head.

'Mr Abbott had a relationship with Rachel?'

She nodded.

'George Abbott?' I pressed. 'Or Tony?'

'Both.'

I felt more than saw Fredericka stiffen but I didn't look at her. My head was spinning. Both men had had relationships with Rachel? Perhaps it hadn't been Rob who'd killed Tony in a jealous rage, but George Abbott.

'They were both crazy for her,' she went on. 'She liked playing them against each other. I told her it would get her into trouble, but she said she didn't care. She got a kick out of it.'

A loud buzz ricocheted through the flat, making me flinch. The front doorbell. As Klaudia moved across the room to answer it, I put out a hand. 'You didn't see another woman that night?' I asked. 'Long dark hair, slim, around five foot seven?'

Klaudia shook her head. 'Just Rachel. And it was strange, because normally she is so proud of her looks, her–'

There came a loud crack and the sound of glass shattering and at the same time Klaudia was punched sideways as though someone had shoved her.

Crack!

Klaudia spun round. The look on her face was one of shock.

Her knees buckled and I dived for her, catching her, breaking her fall.

Snapshot images clicked across my vision.

Two spider webs of cracked glass in the window. Two rough-edged holes. Shards and splinters of glass on the floor.

Blood spreading across Klaudia's shirt. The look of terror in her eyes. She was whimpering.

Fredericka crouched beside me. She was shouting into her phone for police, ambulance, medics.

Klaudia was looking straight at me. She said, quite clearly, 'I'm frightened.' Then, 'Sorry.'

Her body trembled. 'No, no! Hang on, Klaudia.' My tone was fierce. 'Hang on. Fredericka's calling an ambulance, they won't be long…'

But her body continued to shudder and she kept looking at me with her huge blue eyes holding acres of ocean and then the light inside faded. It was like someone was turning the dimmer switch to low, then lower, and I was calling to her, 'Don't go. Stay with me.'

The light went out and her body gradually stilled.

'Fuck,' Fredericka said.

While she started CPR, I jerkily crawled across the carpet, through the broken glass to the window. Heart thumping, I inched to the sill and peered down, blinking into the shadows, then across the road to the block of flats opposite. I swept my gaze from side to side, searching for an open window with a gun barrel sticking out of it. Nothing. I looked up and down the street. Back to the block of flats. Something made me glance up. Right to the top of the building.

All my senses tightened into a shrieking screaming knot.

Someone was up there.

They were looking straight at me.

Chapter forty-nine

I ran like hell. I wanted to catch the person I'd seen on top of the roof. And if I couldn't catch them I wanted to see them, so I could identify them later, like in a police line-up.

I yelled at Fredericka, telling her where I was going as I flew across Klaudia's flat and hared down the stairs, along the hallway, and burst outside. Put my head down and charged over the street, narrowly missing a London bus and causing two cars to lean on their horns, but I didn't slow.

I pounded across the pavement, darting across the forecourt. Glanced up at the block of flats, to the roof and where I'd seen the figure… the sniper? The sharpshooter? The assassin? I didn't know what to call them, but I was buggered if I'd let them get away with it. I'd only had four storeys to run down, but they had twenty. They also had a gun. This thought slowed me up somewhat.

Breathing hard, I pressed my back against the wall, next to the front door. Would the killer come out this way? I wondered. Or was there a rear exit? How could I catch sight of them without them seeing me and shooting me dead?

The rear of the building, I thought. They wouldn't come out the front. I legged it around the back to find a car park, rows of industrial-sized wheelie bins along with a rusting fridge and a threadbare sofa tucked in one corner. I hovered for a minute or so before running to the front again. Which exit would they use?

I raced back where I'd come from and dithered briefly before I raced to hide behind the sofa. I hadn't had time to get out of sight when a figure exploded from the rear door and tore across the car park. Dressed head to toe in black, a balaclava over their head, they had a rucksack on their back but their hands appeared to be free. No gun that I could see. It had to be in the pack.

'Stop!' I shouted. 'You! Stop!'

The figure stumbled, making me think I'd startled them, but they quickly recovered and tore on. I gave chase. I didn't shout again. I wanted to save my breath. They were shorter, had a lighter build than me, and although I'd been a handy fly half at one point, I'd eventually become too heavy and moved to a hooker. The figure raced through the car park exit and swung left. I sprinted after them. Switched left, pushing my right foot hard, bracing myself for a tight turn and totally unprepared for the blow that met me.

The man's fist hit the side of my head. I went down like a stone.

'Sorry, mate,' he said. Astonishingly, he sounded as though he meant the apology.

The sound of running feet was drowned by the roar of a V8 revving. Headlights snapped on. I was scrambling up, disorientated, my feet not entirely attached to my body, trying to focus on the black Range Rover speeding into view. Doors opened and closed, swallowing the shooter and the man who'd bludgeoned me. The driver stepped on the gas. I knew it was futile but I ran after it. I ran as hard as I could. I ran until it was out of sight.

An ambulance passed me as I jogged shakily back to Fredericka, along with two cop cars. I saw one cop take me in from the back seat and then she was leaning forward and thumping the driver's shoulder, telling him to stop. She sprang out of the vehicle and came to me, hotly followed by three of her buddies.

'It's okay,' I gasped, still out of breath, my words coming in spurts. 'I'm with the woman… who reported the shooting. I was chasing… the car the shooter got away in. A Range Rover…'

'Sir. Please put your hands behind your back.'

The next minute I was handcuffed and stuck in the back of their patrol car with a burly cop on either side. I can't say I blamed them since I must have looked mightily suspicious jogging down the street, wild-eyed and covered in sweat and blood, but as I said, why would I be running *toward* the crime if I was guilty? Wouldn't I have been running away? They didn't answer that one.

It was only when Fredericka came outside and identified me, vouched for me, that they took off the handcuffs.

'Thanks,' I said. The police didn't acknowledge me, nor did they apologise. Cheers, I thought sourly. At least the bloke who'd clobbered me had said sorry. I didn't feel particularly enthused about sharing anything with them so I brought out my phone and called DI Barry Gilder. If Susie thought he was okay, then he ought to be okay, but then I remembered Susie was being a bit treacherous – to put it mildly – which made me hesitate, but only for a moment. If she was in touch with him, then I should I be too. Plus, he seemed to be heavily involved in all this, especially considering his shock when he discovered the hiatus between his father arriving at the Mayfair Group the night Tony died, and the police saying they'd arrived.

'It's like an Ashdown rush hour,' DI Gilder said when I announced myself. 'First your wife visits, and now you ring.'

'I was wondering what you're doing right now,' I said. 'As I'd rather like a sort of… second opinion.'

'Sure, why not. It's not like I'm doing anything else, like trying to relax after spending the day trying to stop the tide of criminality into the nation's capital.'

'I wouldn't ask if it wasn't important,' I snapped. I sounded exceptionally ratty, and although I knew my reasons he'd probably think I was just being bad-tempered, so I added, 'the police are with me.'

'Where are you?' His tone turned sharp.

'Haringey.'

'Haringey?' he repeated, sounding startled.

When I explained what had happened, there was a long silence. 'What are you, some kind of lure for this killer?'

'It seems that way.' I suddenly felt exhausted and moved to sit on the wall. It was damp with rain but getting a wet arse was the least of my problems. 'Look. I saw the shooter running away. I managed to get the number plate of the car they jumped in.'

'Fire away.'

I rattled it off.

'You told the officers there about it?'

'Not yet.'

'I suggest you do. I will be there in…' He paused and I pictured him studying his watch, gauging his travel time. 'Thirty minutes max.'

Chapter fifty

DI Gilder arrived at the same time as the forensic team. He raised a hand my way, then went to talk to one of the policemen. I watched them talk, occasionally sending glances my way, and then Barry Gilder went to the forensics van where he put on a pair of white overshoes and walked inside the building, no doubt to have a peek at the murder scene.

He was back within five minutes, putting the overshoes in a bag next to the forensic van, and then coming to stand next to me.

'Talk me through it,' he said.

Knowing a run-through with Gilder would make giving my statement to the Haringey Police much easier, I complied. He listened intently, a corkscrew of concentration between his brows, his head haloed by the streetlight behind him.

After I'd finished, the detective made me go over it all again, asking questions, probing. Finally, I ground to a halt. 'I think that's probably it,' I told him, bone weary. He stopped with the inquisition. Stood there looking up at the balcony, the windowpanes punctured with bullet holes. I passed a hand over my eyes. I couldn't believe I'd seen Klaudia shot. Held her in my arms while she died. Poor Klaudia. Poor, poor Klaudia. Did she live with anyone? I wondered. A husband, a lover? I hadn't seen any photographs of kids in her flat, which made me hope she didn't have children so they'd be spared her murder.

'Gilder,' the detective said. I hadn't realised he'd answered his phone. 'Unh huh. Right. Thanks for that. Really appreciate it.' He hung up.

'Got an owner for your number plate.'

His face was filled with tension.

'I don't think you're going to like it.'

Covered in Klaudia's blood, the side of my face still pounding, my hands and knees stinging from a multitude of glass cuts, I was almost past the point of caring. 'Who?'

'Mr Robert Ashdown.'

No way. Rob had been on the run, presumed dead, yet he'd registered a car? Through my confusion I realised Gilder was looking at me with an odd expression and for a moment I didn't recognise it, but then I did. It was pity.

Dear God, they thought Rob had killed Klaudia. Did I know my brother anymore? People didn't change that much, surely, even if they did work with MI5. And as far as Rob owning a Range Rover? You had to be joking. He hated them. Called them banker-wanker cars for nob heads. And where would he get the money to buy one? With a lurch, I remembered the missing million quid. Oh, shit. I took a couple of breaths to steady myself but it didn't seem to be helping. My mind was thundering ahead, thinking of Rob who knew where Mum kept our house keys – *so you got the CCTV then* – who knew how to bug an office block, who knew how to punch and disable an armed gunman.

'Sorry,' said Gilder. The pity didn't dissipate.

'You can't be serious.' I rose to my feet. My jeans were damp and clung to my thighs.

Gilder gave me a long look. 'It's as serious as it gets. It looks as though he had an accomplice, because someone rang the doorbell to get Klaudia to move for a clear shot.'

Unable to cope, I walked off. Presented myself to the woman cop who'd slapped me in handcuffs earlier. 'I'd like to make that statement,' I told her.

My third police station. More brick walls, more cream paint, more posters on the walls exhorting people not to drink, not hit one another, to report domestic abuse, rape, racial hate. It took less time than before, probably because I was getting good at coordinating and expressing my thoughts coherently. Not something I'd been longing to improve upon, I have to admit, and when I was released two hours later, it was to find I'd missed the last tube into town, and thus the last train home.

I stood on the pavement outside the station, drizzle dampening my hair and shoulders, wondering where to go. Part of me desperately wanted to ring Susie, have her come and collect me, tuck me up in her giant king-sized bed in her luxurious flat, but I knew it wouldn't happen like that. She'd want to know why my clothes were caked in blood, what had happened during every minute of every hour, and I simply wasn't strong enough to deflect her questions, let alone ask my own.

I looked up and down the street. Not a cab in sight. I wondered vaguely about calling Uber.

'Nick.'

I turned to see Fredericka stepping onto the pavement beside me.

'How'd it go?' I asked.

'Tiring.'

'Yes,' I agreed. I continued staring up the street.

'Have you got somewhere to stay the night?'

I realised it was time to get a grip and find a hotel or B&B. I needed sleep. Rest. I could worry about everything when I woke the next day.

'Not yet.'

I felt her studying me. 'Nobody coming to collect you?'

I looked at her. 'Nobody coming to collect you either?'

She smiled. 'My husband's on his way.'

Strange, I hadn't thought of her as being married. I'm not sure why. Perhaps it was her immense no-nonsense independent attitude that had led me to think she'd prefer living on her own, but how wrong could an idiot be?

'If you need a bed for the night, we have a spare room,' she told me.

I wasn't sure she was being entirely altruistic. She was a journalist. She wanted my story. The Saint's story. Rob's story. Klaudia's and Arun Choudhuri's too.

'No strings,' she added. 'I promise.'

'Like hell.'

That made her laugh. 'It's up to you.'

At that point, a green Skoda came into view and drew up beside us. A man climbed out, tall, much taller than Fredericka, with a pair of big Timberland boots and thick fisherman's sweater. He looked like an oil rigger. He hugged her close, kissed her on the lips, and although they didn't say anything, I knew they were a good couple together.

Fredericka looked at her husband then back at me. She said, 'This is Nick. He's coming to spend the night.'

Chapter fifty-one

Fredericka was as good as her word and, to my eternal gratitude, she didn't ask a single question. She gave me a double brandy in her kitchen, then gave me a glass of water and showed me upstairs.

'I hope you're not allergic to cats,' she said. 'Molly sleeps up here most days.'

'No allergies,' I said.

The bedroom was small and neat, with arty prints of London on the walls and books everywhere, on the wall shelves, on the bedside table, in towering stacks on the floor.

'Bed's already made,' Fredericka told me and fetched towels, a dressing gown, some soap and shampoo. 'If you chuck your clothes outside the bathroom, I'll stick them in the wash and get them dry for the morning.'

'You don't have to—'

'Nick, I can't have you walk out of here in blood-stained clothes.' She gave me a wry smile. 'What will the neighbours think?'

I showered and dried myself and went to bed. I had several missed calls from Susie, so I dashed off a quick text saying everything was fine – I could lie too, thank you – and that I'd ring her first thing. I didn't tell her where I was staying. Since I hadn't texted all day, she would assume I was in the cottage. Fine by me. I thought I'd fall asleep straight away I was so knackered, but it didn't happen for a while. Somewhere I heard a church clock chime once, and not long after that I nodded off and I went straight into a dream in which I was being chased down the street by two men but when I pounded around another corner it was to find the shooter, waiting, looking at me down the length of a barrel. They fired and as the bullet hit my chest, I woke up.

Sunlight streamed through the window. I struggled up, shrugged on the dressing gown and pulled back the curtains to see it was a beautiful day. My room overlooked a tiny garden, beautifully cared for, with a pond. Through a lower window in the building opposite, I saw a woman sipping from a cup, also looking over Fredericka's garden. It appeared as though she was having a thoughtful moment too, but her face was so serene I bet she wasn't thinking about murder. Or maybe she was? Things were so topsy-turvy I was beginning to wonder if anyone could be taken at face value anymore.

I texted Susie, who texted me back. *I've got to see you*, she said. *Like yesterday. I have stuff to share.*

Tonight, I told her. *Can you come home?*

She still occasionally referred to her London flat as home, but she knew what I meant. The cottage.

Of course. I'll bring dinner. Love you. She'd added some hearts but all they did was make me feel sad, rather than make me smile like they used to.

I opened the bedroom door to find my clothes piled neatly outside. I slipped them on. No bloodstains. Just a few small tears and rips in the knees of my jeans from crawling through glass. I trod downstairs to find Fredericka at the kitchen table, reading the news on her iPad.

'Coffee or tea?' she asked.

'Coffee, thanks.'

'Mike's already gone to work,' she told me.

'Please thank him for me.'

'Cereal? Eggs?'

I shook my head.

'I can't think of eating either,' she sighed. 'What a dreadful night.'

'I'm sorry. I had no idea…'

'That you were leading a killer to Klaudia's door.' Fredericka's gaze was bold, accusing.

I tried not to shrink back, but how could I not? Two people were dead because of me. Thanks to my floundering around like some kind of incompetent private eye, Arun and Klaudia had been murdered. I closed my eyes, feeling queasy.

'Talk to me, Nick.'

I opened my eyes to see the journalist leaning forward. 'Anything you say will stay here if you want it to. I won't tell anyone, not the police nor your brother or your loved ones unless you say so, and I certainly won't print a word until you give me the go ahead.' Her look was utterly open, sincere. Very intense. 'I've done this before, okay? I've nursed whistle-blowers, people heading for witness protection, people hiding from anything and everything. I'm an old hand. I know how things go. I know how to keep my mouth shut. And I know when to open it.'

I looked into her face, strong and resolute, and thought about telling her about Rob, Susie, DI Gilder, his father, the CCTV tape, the Saint, and the weariness I'd felt the previous night swept over me once more, like a tidal wave.

'You've got to tell someone, at some point,' she said. 'And I think you're bearing a big weight that needs unloading, preferably before it breaks you.'

I gave her a bit of a sardonic smile. 'And you'd be the best person to unload to, of course.'

'Of course.' She gave me a grin, her eyes gleaming with humour. 'How am I doing? On a scale of one to ten?'

Despite everything, I couldn't help but smile back. 'I'd give you an eight.'

'Not good enough.' She shook her head ruefully.

'Sorry.'

She pushed her coffee mug away. 'You've got a lot to contend with, so I can understand your caution. I applaud it, but be careful who you talk to, no matter how safe they appear. Promise?'

'I promise.'

I said it without really thinking, like I'd promise my mother I'd wear a waterproof to the shops because it was raining, and it was only a long time later when I remembered it, and regretted not heeding her advice.

Chapter fifty-two

The relief I felt when I arrived home was tempered by the fact I knew it was probably bugged. How else would the shooter have known about my meeting Klaudia? Unless they'd followed me, of course, but they would never have had the time to get on top of the roof and in position to kill Klaudia if that were the case. The cottage had to be bugged.

I sat in the car, phone in hand. A seagull flew above, kew-kewing, and I could hear an outboard somewhere, starting up. Familiar sounds of peace, of home. I opened my contacts list and called Seb. He installed alarms, wouldn't he know about other electrical devices, like bugs?

'I have a bit of an odd favour,' I told him.

'Fire away,' he said cheerfully.

'It's confidential. And I mean really, *really* confidential. Like if you tell anyone, I will hunt you down and stick needles into a puppy's eyes and make you watch.'

Seb had always been squeamish about anything to do with eyes. As kids, we'd tease him mercilessly. *Squeeze your eyeball till it pops. Puncture it and inject maggots inside. Stamp on it and watch it squirt.*

We were dreadful, no remorse, and poor old Seb would pale and sometimes even be sick, which of course just encouraged us.

'Crikey,' he said. 'You don't have to go that far.'

'I'm serious, Seb.'

'No more with the eyeball thing, okay?'

I agreed. 'I need your help, because I think our cottage is bugged. I want to know for sure if it is, or not. And what sort of bug. I don't want it or them removed. I don't think so, at the moment anyway. I just want it confirmed. Or not.'

Silence.

'This isn't a joke, is it.'

'No.'

I heard his breath gust down the phone. 'I'm no expert, man. I just install alarms.'

'But you're an electrician.'

'Yes, but this is a specialist field.'

I waited.

Eventually he said, 'Is this an I'm-watching-my-husband-to-make-sure-he's not bonking the gorgeous Ronja or does it go further? Like involving the er...' I heard him gulp. 'Anything to do with the boys in blue?'

'I honestly don't know.' Which was true. I had no idea how things were panning out, where they were heading. I felt like a boat without a captain, no tiller or rudder, left on a stormy sea to toss and turn where the tides and wind might take me.

'Blimey,' he said. I could tell he was reluctant, that deep down he wanted to say no but didn't feel able to do so to an old school buddy. 'Have you tried looking on the Internet?'

I didn't want strangers tramping around our cottage, finding listening devices, maybe even reporting them. I wanted people I knew and trusted on side.

'Please, Seb. I don't want to use anyone else. I need you. I need your help.'

Short pause, and then he said, 'I've got a job to finish, but I'll be with you by four. Let's see what I can do.'

'Four is great. Thank you.'

I spent the time in the cottage, doing some more thinking while I did some household chores – cleaning the fireplace, sorting and putting out the rubbish, chopping some kindling. My mind went round and round, trying to find answers but I knew I still didn't have enough information. I needed to know who Rachel was. What Susie had been doing at the Mayfair Group that night. Whether my brother was lying, or telling the truth.

At that point, a flash went off in my mind, a bit like a light bulb. Hadn't he said he'd met Sorcha in rehab? Where? Would it have been in London? I could check on his story, and if it were true, then everything else would be true, wouldn't it?

I called DI Gilder.

'Can you find something for me?' I asked.

'So long as it doesn't involve another dead body. Sorry. It's been a bit of a long night.'

'My brother told me he'd been in rehab, which is where he met his current partner, Sorcha. The woman on the boat I told you about.'

His tone immediately came alert. 'Any idea where? Which city?'

'He didn't say, but I'd assume London.'

'I'll try to find out, but I don't promise anything. It's been–'

'Twelve years,' I said wearily. 'I know.'

Chapter fifty-three

Seb arrived pretty much on time, bearing a toolbox and an anxious expression. 'I'm not an expert,' he reiterated.

'I know,' I tried to assure him. 'Let's have a look around. Quietly. I don't want them to know we know, if you know what I mean.'

Not wanting him to stumble on the photographs of Tony Abbott's murder scene, I tucked the envelope in the back of my jeans. Then I switched on our Sonos system, which played in each room, including the bathroom. Susie liked listening to Radio 4 in the morning, the news, the Sports Desk, Yesterday in Parliament, the weather, Thought for the Day. Lots of information, lots of comment. Me, I liked 6 Music. Much less stressful. Right now, a group called The Pirates was playing. I turned it up.

Seb moved around the cottage, peering and gently patting, probing beneath tables, sofas and chairs. It was a small cottage so it didn't take him long before he froze, hand beneath one of the kitchen stools. He bent over and had a look. He'd obviously found something because he reared back and made stabbing noises at the stool, beckoning at me, then stabbing again.

I took the stool and quietly upended it. A small, what looked like a ceramic device was clamped between the wood and one of the metal struts. At first glance, I thought it was part of the stool but knowing what I was looking for, it became obvious. Carefully, I replaced the stool. Turned to Seb and gave him the thumbs up.

His eyes glowed. Thereon, I couldn't stop him. Talk about a man with a mission. He found another bug in the living room, buried amongst the TV paraphernalia, and another upstairs. He'd just dismantled our phone handset on the top landing and was showing me another bug when a gust of air fanned through the cottage and Susie stepped inside.

She looked up and I knew straight away she knew what we were doing.

She said, 'Seb, thank you. You can go now.'

He shot me a slightly panicked look. The look of a guilty man, found with his hand in the cookie jar, or with his pants down.

'Thanks, mate,' I said.

He didn't need telling any further. He scooted down the stairs, scooped up his toolbox and was outside within ten seconds.

I stood at the top of the stairs, looking down.

She said, 'I put that there.'

I didn't say anything.

She walked up to the landing. Picked up the handset. Tapped the device, shiny black, like a beetle.

'Why aren't you at work?' I asked.

She sent me a level look. 'Because right now, you're more important to me.'

I felt the urge to apologise, and swallowed it.

'I've taken some "personal time". A couple of days, I told them. During which time I hope we might resolve some issues.'

She clipped the phone back together. 'Let's keep it there for the moment,' she said. 'Just in case.'

Just in case, *what*? I thought. Was she hoping to catch the Saint confessing to killing dozens of people on our tiny upstairs landing?

'And so you know, I put another one...' She showed me one hidden in the base of my bedside table light before trotting downstairs into the living room to the TV, where the wires and plugs hung out behind it. 'There.'

'Is that it?' My voice was stony.

A tiny frown marred her brow. 'Yes. They're top of the range. They can listen to conversations through thirty centimetres of solid concrete walls, windows and floors. This place is tiny. Why would I need more?'

'No reason.' I made sure my eyes didn't go to the kitchen stool. 'Why did you do it?'

'Why do you think, Rob?' Her tone was exasperated. 'You reckon having someone walk into our home and deposit an envelope in our living room while I'm in the shower is okay?'

'No, but why didn't you tell me that you'd bugged our home?'

'What, like me telling you about my asking your family to return our house keys?' She shook her head. 'Jesus, Nick. Don't you get it? I'm in security. I like being secure. There's also the small fact that I've had a bit of a personal and nasty experience that means I get a lot of value knowing that when my front door is locked, it's *locked*, and that nobody can just open the door and walk inside. Security–' she weighted the word with all the power of her voice 'means quite a lot to me.'

We stood, inches apart. I could smell her perfume – a spicy scent of some sort – and see the tiny lines radiating from the corners of her eyes. Laughter lines. Lines from squinting into the sun. Lines from narrowing her eyes at her adversaries, those poor saps in the Office. I hauled my mind back. I didn't like where it was going.

'So,' I said.

'So,' she echoed.

'You still haven't answered my question. Why did you put the bugs there?'

She put her head on one side. 'To listen. Why else?'

'To spy on me?'

'Why do you think?' Her eyes were hard and dark on mine, fierce.

'Er, I'm not you, so I don't–'

'You haven't been home for twenty-four hours. How do I know that? Oh, because I bugged our place because I've been so fucking scared of what's been going on and it was the only way I could get some sense of control and try to find out what was fucking happening in my life, in *our home*.'

It was so rarely she lost control, let alone swore, that I took a step back.

CJ Carver

'Sorry.' She passed a hand over her face. 'Shit. I can't believe this is happening. I've gone completely paranoid and you…' She looked at me. Her gaze softened. 'I have no idea what you're going through. I just want to protect you. Defend you. To the hilt.'

I swallowed.

'But I can't defend you if I don't know what's happening.' She shook her head again, softly, ruefully, but I couldn't help notice that she remained as tense as a bowstring. 'And I have no idea, do I? I've bugged our home, and I have no idea where you've been. Shagging Ronja, maybe? Hanging out with Etienne? Clara? What about the Saint? Seen him lately?'

Suddenly, I'd had enough. I walked into the kitchen and picked up the stool. Turned it over. Pointed at the tiny shiny ceramic device clinging to the metal struts.

She blinked twice. Then she took my arm and walked me through the cottage and out of the front door, only stopping when we were standing on the pavement. She looked at me, back at the cottage, then said, quite clearly, 'That one isn't mine.'

Chapter fifty-four

We ended up going to the pub. We couldn't talk at home, and since we needed somewhere neutral, somewhere that was homely but not home, The Anchor Bleu seemed to do nicely.

I had a beer, Susie a double vodka and tonic.

We sat in an alcove, looked at one another.

'I have a question,' I said. 'A fairly important one.'

I took a deep breath. I felt as though I was teetering on the edge of Niagara Falls, about to plunge into the immense crests of water without knowing if I'd live, or die.

'Why didn't you tell me you were there that night?'

'I'm sorry?' She looked perfectly blank.

'The night Tony Abbott died. You were there, right?'

She looked at me for a long time. It reminded me of Rob, the slightly wary assessing expression. Cool, calculating, no emotion. Perhaps it was a spook thing, but I didn't care for it at all.

'Who says I was?'

I affected a look of disbelief. 'The reception book. I was sent a copy.'

'Ah. Any idea who by?'

Rob, I thought, but instead I said, 'The same person who dropped off the CCTV tape.'

She nibbled her lip. 'If we could find who was sending us that stuff, I'm sure we'd find out who killed Tony.'

'What were you doing there?'

'Trying to protect my agent.'

'Your *agent*?'

'Yes.' Her gaze was clear, candid. 'Now this is to remain between us, okay? It's highly classified and normally I would never, *ever* give up an agent's name, but these are exceptional circumstances. Swear you won't tell anyone else.'

My mind was scrambling, trying to make sense of things but I managed to say, 'Okay. I swear.'

'Her name's Rachel Daisley. She was a cleaner there. She was my spy.'

I opened and closed my mouth, like a goldfish, before I felt my mind catch up. 'And Rob?'

She put her head on one side. 'He wasn't an agent of mine, if that's what you're asking.'

'But he was sent in to bug the place. Didn't you know?'

A spasm of annoyance crossed her face. 'Of course. Mark Felton and I were at cross-purposes here. He wanted intel, he was after *La Familia de Sangre.* But I was after the Saint. I wanted to nail the bastard, one hundred per cent. As far as I was concerned, we could go for the overseas criminals later.'

Atta girl, I thought, pride rising, and I had to haul my emotions back, stuff them in a box inside me, because not everything was adding up.

'But you said you weren't after the Saint. That you'd never worked with Rob. You said you met him at a couple of social events.'

Her gaze didn't stir from mine. 'There is something you have to understand about me, and my job.'

I gazed back. My heart was beating faster, and I was glad she couldn't see.

'The thing is, Nick, is that I have to lie. And I have to lie well. Extraordinarily well. Sometimes, the lie I'm telling will be the only thing between me and a bullet in my brain. I've got very good at lying. But one thing I will say in my defence and that is I lie only when I can see there's a benefit. Like protecting you, Clara, your family and mine. I will tell a thousand lies if it will protect us.'

I couldn't tear my gaze from hers. 'Rob?'

The single word dropped between us.

She didn't move her gaze from mine. Then she leaned back and closed her eyes. 'Shit.'

I sat and waited. Watched her look down and press her forefingers between her brows. Finally, she raised her head. Held my gaze once more.

Quietly, she said, 'I lied about him too.'

My pulse ticked faster but I didn't look away. 'Go on.'

She licked her lips. Glanced at the bar and back. It was the first time I'd seen her look nervous. 'You may not like what you hear,' she warned.

I'd heard her say this a couple of times before but this time, it didn't freak me out as much. I was obviously getting used to it.

'Go on.'

'In fact, I'm not sure if I want you to–'

'Susie,' I cut in. 'Get on with it, would you?'

She held up her hands. 'So. Here's the thing. I'm not sure how you're going to take it because I know you adore Rob. I know he drove you all nuts, but you thought he was okay deep down, didn't you.'

'Susie, just spit it out, would you.'

A quick jerk of a nod. 'Okay. Rob had a problem with drugs. He was a drug addict.'

She was looking at me as though waiting for me to act shocked, outraged or horrified, but of course she didn't know I'd met Rob, and that he'd already told me.

'Shit,' I said.

'Yes. Shit. You try having a colleague who is working undercover in *La Familia de Sangre* and flaking about with coke up his nose and MDMA up his backside. I was trying to keep him *safe*.' For a moment, I thought she was going to cry. Susie, tough nut and Superwoman, who rarely shed tears, looked as though she was on the edge.

'Suze.' My tone was gentle, filled with sympathy.

She stopped me with both hands held up, like a traffic cop's. 'Don't. Just fucking don't.'

I didn't.

'So,' she said. She was breathing in hard through her nose and exhaling through her mouth. A relaxing technique she'd told me about. 'Your brother, he was being a dick. He went into the Mayfair offices that night, coked up to the eyeballs, thinking he could do anything. Rachel tried to send him away, she watched him go down in the lifts, thought he'd left the building, but he fucking turned around and came back.'

'And?'

She closed her eyes. 'You may not believe me, but I still have no idea what happened after that.'

'What happened to your spy? Rachel?'

'She vanished. I never saw her again.'

I felt a moment's shock. 'What?'

'God, I hate reliving all this. It doesn't get any easier.'

Susie opened her eyes and I suddenly saw how tired she was. Her eye sockets were bruised and her skin tone had lost its healthy sheen and looked dry and lacklustre.

'Rachel disappeared,' she said. 'Before or after Tony was killed, we have no idea.'

I elected to ignore the fact she hadn't mentioned the dead woman yet and said, 'Did you know your spy was having a relationship with both George and Tony Abbott?'

'Yes.'

Long silence while Susie looked at me and I looked back. She said, 'Do you know who else she was sleeping with?'

My stomach turned to ice. 'No way.'

'She's a very attractive woman. Slightly feral. I think it was that mix of raw sexuality mixed with an aura of danger that made her so irresistible. She made the perfect agent. She could move anywhere in the building, gain access to all sorts of secrets.'

I stared at my wife, but I wasn't seeing her. I was looking at the Saint in his study, hearing his voice telling me that Rob had shot his girlfriend – *some bint with the morals of a cat* – and Tony in a jealous rage.

'Personally, I think someone found out she was working for us.' Susie looked at me with sad exhaustion. 'They killed her that night, and disposed of her body.'

I didn't respond. I was frozen. She obviously didn't know about the woman who'd been killed with Tony. Had Rob in some kind of drug-induced rage, murdered them? And what about the Saint? How did he fit into all this? He'd been sleeping with Rachel too.

'Nick?' Susie was looking at me askance. 'Are you okay?'

I managed to move my tongue, which seemed to have turned to board. 'Um… if Rachel was such a good spy, why didn't you get her to bug the offices? Why use Rob?'

'Things were more technical back then.' Susie glanced over my shoulder as the door banged behind me, letting in a blast of cold air. 'Hi, Paul.'

'Hi.'

I turned to see Paul Dookes, a neighbour of ours and Anchor Bleu regular, give us a wave before he headed to the bar.

Susie put her elbows on the table and leaned closer. 'Rachel's talent was sex. She was a good old-fashioned honey trap but she didn't have a technical bone in her body.'

My mind was having trouble computing everything. 'What happened to that middle-aged businesswoman?'

'She ran away.'

'With Rob chasing after her.'

'Yes.'

'Did she get away?'

'Yes.'

Susie's gaze held a challenge. For some reason, I felt my skin crawl.

'Isn't there a final question?' she said. 'You've done pretty well so far. I would have thought you could have put the last piece of the jigsaw into the puzzle with your eyes shut.'

'Who was the middle-aged woman?' I asked but I'd already worked it out because the woman hadn't been middle-aged. She'd been in disguise.

A look of satisfaction spread across Susie's face. 'Me.'

Chapter fifty-five

'Why didn't you tell me all this to start with?' I asked.

She gave me a look.

'Classified,' I sighed.

We'd moved to sit side by side by the fire, along with a bottle of Australian Shiraz I'd bought for us to share. The bar was busy, and most of the tables were taken up by people having supper. Not a bad night for a midwinter Wednesday and the good thing was that nobody was close enough to overhear us, especially since the conversational noise levels were up, and we kept our voices down.

'Not just classified,' she said, 'but we didn't want the Saint getting wind of the fact we had him in our sights. That we had not just one, but two agents in his organisation. And since you didn't know anything, he remains oblivious to the fact and I'd like it to stay that way now, and in the future.'

She shot me a meaningful look. Jesus. I wish she hadn't done that. My palms dampened at the mere thought of the Saint questioning me again. Unlike Susie, I hadn't had any training in how to withstand an interrogation, and if George Abbott got his hands on me again, I had no doubt I'd find it almost impossible not to spill every bean I had.

I cleared my throat, trying not to show my nerves. 'What about now?'

'After Tony's murder, Rachel and Rob both going missing, assumed dead, not many agents were willing to step up to the plate.'

'Right,' I said, moving along. 'Rob wasn't chasing you.'

'No,' she agreed. 'We were both running like hell.'

The story was that when she'd arrived that night, she'd gone up to the third floor. She hadn't seen Rachel or Rob, but she'd heard gunshots. She knew Rob had gone in armed and, pierced with horror, she ran down the corridor toward the sound. Rob erupted from the furthest office, wild-eyed and covered in blood, and she shouted at him, wanting to know what was going on, but he'd come at her, waving his gun and screaming like someone demented.

'Run!'

She had turned around, and ran for the stairwell with Rob right behind.

'He wasn't going to hurt me,' she said, but for some reason, she didn't sound too convinced. 'He'd just lost it. Gone nuts. He was terrified, and he terrified me.'

'You think he killed Tony?'

She put her head in her hands. 'Christ knows.'

I still hadn't shown her the photographs of the crime scene, and I wriggled on my chair, brought out the envelope. 'I received these in the mail,' I told her. 'They're pretty disturbing, sorry.'

'It's okay. I see a lot of pretty awful stuff in my job.' She gave a wan smile. 'Show me.'

I pulled them out and handed them over.

She looked at them for a long time.

'At least now I know what happened to Rachel.'

'But her face… You definitely know it's her?'

'I can't think who else it would be, dressed up like that.' Susie frowned, studied the pictures more closely. 'Yes, it has to be her. Same height, nice figure, great tits. Whoever did this to her was really, *really* angry. This wasn't someone in full control of their emotions. They went berserk. They wanted to obliterate her. Smash her to pieces. Literally.'

I turned away, feeling nauseous. 'I can't see Rob doing that. Even if he was on drugs, I just can't see it.'

'For what it's worth, neither can I.' Susie slipped the photos back inside the envelope. 'I know he looked like a madman chasing me across the foyer like that, but he wasn't going to hurt me. He was simply terrified. I can still hear him yelling at me, "Run!" He just wanted us to get out of there.'

'Where did you go?'

'I ran flat out for the tube station. I hurdled the barriers, can you believe it? I've never done that before, or since. When I looked back, he wasn't there. I don't think I lost him, I think he took a different route. I waited for him to ring me, contact me or the Office, but he never did. The next we knew, he'd drowned. We weren't sure whether to believe it or not. We considered the fact he might have staged the accident in order to give himself some time, but when he never surfaced, we had to face the fact he may well have drowned after all.

'And now he's back.' She gave a wry smile. 'I'd quite like to wring his neck.'

'Get in the queue.'

I stared through the darkened window, trying to think what else might have happened that night. I felt Susie take my hand, gently turn it over. 'How did you get these?'

She was looking at the cuts I'd sustained from crawling through the glass on the floor at Klaudia's flat.

'I went to see Klaudia Nowacki.'

'Good God.' Susie's eyes widened. 'She used to clean for the Mayfair Group. What did she have to say?'

I told Susie everything that had happened the previous night, except the fact Rob apparently owned the Range Rover which had whisked the shooter away. I wasn't sure why I kept that from her, but I think it was because I didn't want her totally biased against my brother.

I said, 'Klaudia was shot when she moved to answer the doorbell. When she came into clear view. The last thing she said was that she didn't see anyone else at the Mayfair offices except Rob and Rachel. The last words Klaudia spoke was that it was strange, because Rachel was normally so proud of her looks… and then Klaudia was shot.'

'Rachel was proud of a lot of things.' Susie sighed. 'Especially her figure, her talent for luring men into having sex with her and telling her things they normally wouldn't. She loved being a spy. She revelled in it, the power she thought it gave her.'

I reached over and picked up the bottle of wine. Topped up our glasses. Finally, I told her I'd met Rob. By the time she'd finished questioning me, we'd drunk the wine and were on coffee. I leaned back, stretching out my legs. 'Another thing,' I said. 'Is that Rob told me he didn't know who the middle-aged woman was.'

Susie arched her eyebrows. 'He knew it was me all right. Why would he lie about something like that?' She trailed off, frowning. 'I don't think he'd be protecting my MI5 status, not with you. So why say he didn't know me? I don't get it.'

'You weren't exactly looking like yourself. Flat shoes, tweedy skirt, grey hair. Even I didn't recognise you.' Which I have to say I found extremely disconcerting. Wouldn't I have recognised *something* about my wife, the woman I loved and had lived with for eleven years?

'No, no.' She was shaking her head, baffled. 'He *knew* it was me.' Her expression cleared. 'He would only lie to you if it was really important, say, to cause a smokescreen. I have no doubt he lied for all the right reasons, but it would be nice to know why.' She gave a groan. 'God, I wish we could just bloody see him together so we could sort all this out, once and for all. You could ask him everything you want, and I could clock him round the head for being such a pain in the bloody backside.'

It was at that point I decided to get us all three together. Something inside me knew that only by doing so would I get the absolute truth.

Chapter fifty-six

The next morning, I used the phone Rob had given me, and called him to set up a meeting. Susie was out. She'd decided to get some air and walk to the shops for some fresh bread, eggs and bacon. Having not had supper the previous night, just a bucket of wine and a mountain of conversation, we'd both woken starving hungry.

Rob's phone rang and rang. An automated message service cut in, and I told him I wanted the three of us to meet.

'Maybe we can do it on the water again,' I told him. 'It felt pretty safe.'

I didn't mention contacting Mum and Dad, or Clara and the kids. I wanted him and Susie to meet first, clear everything up, and then we could see the family together, with a coherent story. I wondered if he'd come up with any kind of plan to deal with the Saint yet. *Something clever, that doesn't get anyone killed.*

Although Susie and I were outwardly okay, being polite, going to bed together, her falling asleep as usual with her head in the crook of my arm and her thigh between mine, something had fractured and it wouldn't be fixed until I knew the truth. No matter that everything she'd told me made sense, she had still lied to me. And I wasn't sure how to deal with it.

I hid Rob's phone at the back of the kitchen drawer, behind the plastic organiser and out of sight. I didn't want Susie to find it and take things over. He was my brother, I'd contact him. A sudden clatter of metal on wood came from the hallway, making me practically jump out of my skin, but it was only the mail being pushed through the letterbox. My nerves were shredded. What I'd do to return things to normal, have my life back. My old, simple life, where I'd toddle into the office, work and chat and do some designing, have lunch and return home at the end of the day, felt so far from where I was now, it felt like someone else's life. Somehow, I had to get it back.

I put on the coffee machine. Checked my emails. Glanced through the BBC News online. When Susie still hadn't come back after forty minutes or so, I checked my phone to find a text from her.

Bumped into Mary. Going for coffee. Back soon.

Mary? Surely she didn't mean my mother. They may get along on the surface but deep down they couldn't stand each other. Not that I ever let on that I knew. Far better they thought I was unaware so family gatherings remained civil. My reasoning was that if their antagonism became general knowledge, they would have no reason to remain courteous to one another, so keeping a lid on it made sense. But Susie going for coffee with Mum? Something was up. Something was wrong.

I rang Sea Flax.

My father answered. 'Hello, son.'

'Hi, Dad. Sorry, I have to check something. Is Mum there?'

'Sure. I'll put her on.'

'Hi, Mum.'

'Gosh, what a surprise. To what do we owe this pleasure?' Her voice was cutting, making me realise how appallingly I'd been out of touch, especially at such a stressful time.

'Mum, I'm sorry. I've been trying to find Rob. It's been… let's just say it's been a bit crazy. I know it may sound odd, but have you seen Susie this morning?'

'Your wife?'

'Do you know any other Susie's?' My tone turned cutting in return.

'No, Nick. I haven't seen Susie. Why, is something wrong?'

'Everything's fine,' I lied smoothly. 'I just wanted to know, that's all. I'm sorry, I've got to go. I'll ring you later, I promise.'

I hung up quickly, before Mum could start asking questions. I texted Susie. *Let me know where you are, I'll come and join you. Starving. x*

I sat staring at my phone, waiting for her to respond. Nothing. I tried to concentrate on my emails, but my gaze kept going to my phone. I checked Rob's phone, just in case. Nothing there either. I began to pace.

Chapter fifty-seven

After another ten minutes, I grabbed a waterproof and put both Rob's phone and mine in my pockets. Left the house and walked the route Susie would have taken. I felt better now I was moving and I raised my head to the sky, feeling a faint heat from the sun despite the chill. Frost lay in the shade, white and prickly against lamp posts and shrubs.

I reached Bosham Walk in under five minutes. Nobody had seen Susie. Ted, in the tea room, asked if I'd heard from Rob, no doubt hoping to sell some sort of story, and I ignored him. Legged it along Bosham Lane and up Delling Lane to the Co-op. The checkout staff weren't sure if they'd seen her or not.

'She would have bought some bacon,' I said. 'And eggs. Some bread and milk. Maybe some baked beans. Everything for a cooked breakfast.'

One of the girls – eighteen or so, dyed hair the colour of copper – blinked. 'Yeah,' she said. 'I remember now. She said she was ravenous, could eat the hind leg off a galloping horse.'

'That sounds like her.' My relief was palpable. 'When was this?'

She looked at the clock behind her, on the wall. 'An hour ago or so.'

My ears started to ring. 'An hour?'

'Yeah. Is there a problem?'

'I'm not sure. It's just that she hasn't come home yet…' I didn't finish my sentence as I was jogging for the door. I stood outside, looking around, but I couldn't see anything to prompt me to take any particular direction. I ran to the car park at the back of the shop.

Three rows of cars. Some rubbish bins. Trees. A field at the back with a couple of grazing horses.

I had a fast scout around, knowing if I didn't check it out thoroughly it would nag me later. It was only as I began retracing my steps when I took in the shopping bag dumped on the ground. It looked full. Heart knocking, I went and had a look. Bacon, sausages, milk, bread, beans and eggs, and mushrooms because even though she didn't like them, Susie knew I loved fried mushrooms with my breakfast.

It's not her shopping, I told myself desperately. It's someone else's. *It's not hers*. I checked the receipt, shoved between the bacon and bread. My sweat turned to ice. She'd used her American Express card. The last four digits shown were the same as on her card.

Clutching the shopping, I spun in a circle, wild-eyed, frantic. Where was she? Why had she dumped the shopping? Oh, God, God God God. Something terrible had happened. I stood trembling, wondering what to do. Call the police? What would I say? I brought out my phone, trying to get my thoughts in order. I'd ring DI Barry Gilder, I decided. He'd know what to do, but when I rang, it went straight to voicemail. I left a slightly incoherent, panicky message, asking him to ring me. 'I need to know *what to do*.'

I hung up. Returned to the shop and asked questions. Had anyone seen Susie talking to anyone? Who else had been in the shop at the time? Did anything out of the ordinary happen? Had there been anyone suspicious?

I was talking to the manager of the store next to the flower stand, when my phone rang. I answered it immediately, hope spiralling.

'Susie?'

'Sorry, but she's currently unavailable.'

Fear flooded through me. 'No.'

'Oh, yes,' the Saint said. 'She's quite safe, artist. You don't need to worry. Unless you don't do as I say, that is, when her life will become intolerably unbearable.'

'Please don't hurt her,' I begged. 'Please don't.'

'Then you'll have to do as I say.'

'Where is she?'

'She's here, with me.'

'Let me speak to her.'

'You don't need to do that.' His voice was chiding. 'She's perfectly safe here.'

'Let. Me. Speak. To. Her.'

'No, I've already said, she's–'

I hung up.

My hands were shaking, my whole body quaking. Part of me couldn't believe I'd done that, but the other part of my mind had split away, knowing I had to show I wasn't going to be a pussy. I had to demonstrate a show of strength.

I suddenly realised the store manager was staring at me. 'Are you all right?' he asked.

I didn't answer. I stalked outside, clutching my phone in a hand that was pouring sweat. When it rang, I looked at the caller ID. *Unknown.* I let it ring seven times before I answered.

'Put her on,' I said and at the same time I heard her scream. It was a scream of real fear, of pain and terror.

'Stop!' I shouted. 'Stop it! I'll do what you–'

'Oh, good,' the Saint said, his voice oily. 'You get my drift.'

'Yes, yes,' I said.

Susie's scream had stopped. I felt my legs shudder, almost ready to collapse. What had I been thinking? I was an idiot. A stupid, incompetent, brainless idiot. How could I stand up to someone like the Saint? It was simple. I couldn't.

'Please,' I said.

'You know what I want.'

'Yes.'

'Bring him to Dennis's Boat Yard. By the northernmost shed. We'll pick him up there. In one hour. Don't be late.'

'Susie,' I said. 'You'll bring her. We'll do a–'

I was going to say "swap" but he cut over me.

'Don't call anyone, artist. Don't breathe a word, or your little wife will disappear. She will vanish, and there will be no body, no trace of her to be found, ever. Just like your brother's girlfriend. Understand?'

'Yes,' I said. 'And Susie will be there, won't–'

My word "she" fell into dead air.

Chapter fifty-eight

Susie could smell oil and salt, wood and plastic resin. The air had a dead cold about it, making her think she was in a warehouse or shed of some sort. The men had gone, and all was silent. She couldn't hear anything, no lapping of water or the crying of a seagull, let alone any sound of cars or traffic. Where had they brought her?

She could taste blood in her mouth from where she'd bitten the inside trying not to scream. She hadn't wanted to panic Nick but when she'd felt the cold blade of steel drawn lazily across her forearm, opening the skin as easily as slicing a ripe tomato, she hadn't been able to help it. The scream had come involuntarily, a mix of shock and pain and horror. She hadn't thought the Saint would do it.

More fool her.

She sucked air in and out of her mouth and nose, trying not to draw the cloth too close to her face and restrict the oxygen. She'd never been hooded before and when they'd jumped her near the supermarket – two men grabbing her arms from behind while a third pulled the hood over her head and drew the cord tight around her neck – she'd freaked out, gone berserk, lashing and kicking like a crazy woman until one of them had punched her in the side of the head.

Ears ringing, she'd been flung in the back of a car. Wedged between two thugs. Heart rocketing, pulse roaring, she'd spent the journey concentrating on her breath. On each inhale, she said the word *calm* in her mind, and on each exhale, *iron*. It didn't take long before her gasping slowed, her breathing returning to normal. She'd reined in her fear and held it wrapped in hands of steel. She wasn't going to let go, lose control again, howling like a deranged wolf, desperate for her mate, for Nick.

Nick. He was the reason she had to get out of here, to fight for him, defend him, to stop the bastards from destroying what she had. What *they* had.

How could she survive this? On the downside, she was at the mercy of her captors, but on the upside the Saint hadn't recognised her, thanks to the hood. Talk about small mercies. She had to hope luck would stay on her side and that he'd continue to see her as Nick Ashdown's wife, and not as the woman who'd been in the Saint's son's offices the night his son died.

Would she get away with it? She hadn't told Nick the whole story because she didn't want to lose him. But if she was forced, she might have to, and risk having him turn away from her. She knew he loved her, deeply and irrevocably, but when the truth came out, would his love remain firm? For better, for worse? She'd seen the distance in his eyes when she'd come home and found him with Seb, looking at the bug. She didn't want to see it again. She'd rather pack her bags and take the next flight to Australia than face the disappointment in his eyes.

She wriggled, trying to prevent her limbs from stiffening. She sat upright, arms behind her back, wrists in steel cuffs and manacled to something behind her. At the moment she had her legs crossed, but from time to time she'd release the pose to tuck them to the side, then the other side, shifting regularly, trying to keep the blood flowing so when something happened she was ready to use her legs and feet.

Her arm throbbed mercilessly from the knife wound. When she'd been cut, she'd felt the blood running in rivulets down her arm and over her wrist, dripping from her fingers. She'd been surprised when the Saint had ordered one of his goons to find something to stop the flow of blood. The goon had said, 'What?', sounding baffled, and Abbott had replied, 'For Chrissakes, find a handkerchief, a piece of cloth, anything. Bind it.'

She'd heard footsteps walking around the shed and then they approached. She couldn't help her flinch when the goon touched her, but she was glad he bound her wound tightly because it was deep and would eventually need stitches. No point in worrying about it. She had to concentrate on working this situation to her advantage. Make sure things went her way and that Nick didn't get hurt. She was smart, she just had to find the key to lead them through the door of safety.

Time trickled past.

Would Nick call the Office, she wondered. Mark Felton was out of the country, so it wouldn't matter if Nick pressed the great big Panic Button. She hoped he would. Otherwise it wouldn't be until Monday when she was missed. It was Thursday. Would the Saint keep her over the weekend? She doubted it. He may want Rob badly, but he wouldn't want to keep a hostage that long. Too risky. Please, Nick, she prayed. Call the Office. Speak to my boss. Set the dogs on this bastard. Have him for GBH and kidnapping, and lock him up, throw away the sodding key.

Time continued to dribble away. Wanting to see even a crack of light, she tried to shift the hood but it was tied too well. She guessed it was late morning. The Saint had wanted the changeover to be within the hour, but it hadn't happened. How had Nick managed to delay things so successfully? She'd been surprised at his tenacity in trying to find Rob. His bravery too. After twelve years of marriage, she honestly thought she knew him better than he knew himself, but he'd surprised the pants off her. He wasn't the conciliatory pacifist she'd once thought. He was a bit of a lion and she was, she realised, very proud of him.

The base of her spine tingled and she moved sideways, bracing her thighs together and raising her hips off the floor, holding herself firm before relaxing, trying to keep the blood moving. They wouldn't keep her here overnight, would they? Please God, no. She was already hungry and thirsty and didn't want to spend the night wriggling on the floor getting colder and colder. Hadn't the weather report predicted a cold snap? Frost overnight? She'd freeze in here.

She felt tears begin to form. Tears of self-pity. Tears borne from fear.

She opened her mouth, and focused on her breathing. She didn't want to cry. She didn't want to appear weak. She was as strong as iron, as steel. She would come out of this unscathed and return to her life as if nothing had happened.

Suddenly, the door opened with an aggressive crash. She turned her head to the sound, wishing she could get rid of the hood so she could fucking *see*.

'Fucking shit. Bastard.'

It was the Saint.

'Your fucking husband can't find your fucking brother-in-law.' She heard a clatter of metal and then the sound of things falling to the ground, as though he'd swept a table clear of objects. 'Jesus H Christ.'

The Saint was stoking himself into a fury. She had to hope it wouldn't be redirected at her but she couldn't help the flinch when she heard footsteps begin to approach. She could feel the sweat prickling over her body but she tried to hold herself strong and not cringe. Not to look like prey. It would only encourage him into violence.

'So, wifey. We're going to move you. Somewhere your husband won't know. Where I'm at home and he will be like a fish out of fucking water. What do you say to that?'

She was silent.

His steps stopped next to her.

'Hmm?' he pressed in a mocking tone. 'Cat got your tongue?'

Since whatever she said was likely to fan the flames of his anger, she remained silent.

'Oh, dear,' he said. 'Is wifey-wifey feeling fwightened?'

Fuck you, she thought.

'Poor little wifey,' he sang. 'Poor fwightened–'

'Not frightened,' she interrupted. Then, she added, 'Arsehole.'

It was as though someone had sucked the room of air. She'd expected him to kick her or slap her, but instead he went for her neck and she knew she'd made a monumental mistake. His fingers were on the hood cords and she was fighting him, regretting having baited him, wishing she'd kept her trap shut, and then the hood was whipped from her head.

Blissful cold air on her face, cooling her sweat-slicked skin. Clear oxygen in her lungs.

She saw she'd been right. She was in a shed. Opposite stood a workbench. There were saws and pliers, grinders and drills. Screw guns and hammers. She hurriedly averted her gaze. She didn't want to let her grip on the reins of her panic loosen.

'What did you say?' The Saint's voice was like ice.

She remained silent.

He stepped into view. Ducked down to look into her face. She didn't meet his eye but kept her gaze on his shoes. Wingtip Brogue Oxfords. Not something you'd expect an East End gangster to wear, but that was the Saint for you. He liked pretending he came from money instead of having to steal it.

'Look at me,' he said.

He leaned forward and gripped her chin in his hand. Tilted her head up. She could feel the muscles clench in her stomach as he leaned closer, close enough for her to see the enlarged pores in his pasty skin. His eyes crawled over her face and down her neck, over her breasts, to her feet and back.

He dropped her chin and leaned back, hands dangling between his knees.

'Bugger me,' he said.

And with those two words, she knew her world had come crashing down around her.

Chapter fifty-nine

How I managed to get the Saint to extend the deadline by two hours I'll never know. It was probably the raw panic in my voice that convinced him I wasn't lying and that I couldn't get hold of Rob. Since I couldn't stand still – waiting for DI Gilder to arrive was making me crazy – I went to Dennis's Boat Yard across the water from Bosham and south of Chidham. I wanted to do a recce, and maybe find a clue to lead me to Susie. I didn't think she'd be there. I expected the Saint to have stashed her safely elsewhere, but I had to go there, check the place out.

I drove past the sailing and activities centres, all quiet on a wet midweek school morning, and eventually pulled up on the roadside just beyond the dinghy storage site. Dennis's Boat Yard used to build boats as well as repair them, but thanks to its owner retiring, it was up for sale. I'd actually looked at it with half an eye when I'd first heard it was on offer – it was an attractive business proposition for a new owner with a ninety year lease and a peppercorn rent of under a thousand pounds a year – but the fact was that although I would have enjoyed the repair work, I wasn't a boat builder by any stretch of the imagination.

I approached the sheds cautiously. There were three, two of which faced the water. The third, the northernmost one, faced the road. This was the one where the Saint wanted me to bring Rob. I looked around but could see nobody, and no cars. Nerves hopping, I scouted the area. Empty. Totally and utterly, one hundred per cent empty.

I looked at the harbour on one side, the damp fields the other, the dead-end road ahead, and thought: why can't we lay a trap here? Why don't I ring MI5 and get them to ring the SAS, SBS and every specialist fighting force in the country and have them hide in the grass, on the boats in the harbour, before telling the Saint that Rob and I were here, and overwhelm him and his goons when they turn up?

I tried to think what Susie would be thinking, and all I could hear was her voice, yelling in my mind: *Ring the fucking Office, you idiot.*

Sorry, Rob, I thought, and before I could change my mind, I rang the number Susie had punched into my phone all those years earlier, which went to the department receptionist-cum-secretary, who apparently knew where everyone was, at any given time.

It rang once, before a woman answered. She simply said, 'Hi.'

'Hi,' I said. 'It's Nick Ashdown here.'

'Hi, Nick.' She sounded friendly. 'What can I do for you?'

'I, er… wondered if Mark Felton was around.'

'Oh, I'm not sure. He's been away, I'll check for you… Ah, you're in luck. He flew in this morning. Wait a moment.'

Two tiny clicks, then a man's voice. It sounded deeper and stronger than I remembered.

'Nick,' he said. 'How can I help?'

I stared at a seagull settling on a small sloop in the harbour. I suddenly felt ambushed and unable to put my thoughts into a coherent sentence.

'Nick?' he repeated. He sounded cautious, puzzled.

'Yes,' I managed. 'Sorry.'

A few seconds passed.

'Is everything all right?' he asked.

No, I thought. 'Yes,' I said. My voice was hoarse.

The seagull sent a stream of guano across the sloop's hatch and flew off. *Kew kew.*

'Where are you?' he asked.

My head was buzzing. If I told MI5 what was going on, I was risking Rob being hunted not as Superman, defending a restaurant filled with innocent people against a terrorist, but as a double murderer.

'Nick?'

Shit. I wished I hadn't rung him.

'Susie took some time off,' he said carefully. 'Personal time.'

'Yes, she did.'

Another pause.

'She's all right?'

I gulped. Began to sweat. What the fuck was I doing?

'Look,' I said. 'I'm sorry. I shouldn't have rung. I'm also sorry about last week. I hope you didn't think badly of Susie because of it.'

'I beg your pardon?' He sounded startled.

'I've wasted your time. Sorry.'

I hung up.

Shit, shit, *shit.* I grabbed my hair, kicking a grass tussock in frustration at my stupidity. What had I expected? For Mark Felton to confess he already knew the situation and was sending in the troops to fix everything? My naivety wasn't just derisible, it was downright embarrassing. I gazed out at the harbour, sludge grey beneath a leaden sky and felt like screaming. I was trapped between two people I loved and I didn't know how to save them both.

Chapter sixty

I was still kicking at tussocks, furious with myself when my phone rang. I checked the display.

Susie.

'Yes,' I said.

'You're early,' said the Saint.

I spun round, eyes frantically sweeping the area.

'You really think we'd stick to the original rendezvous?' He made a tsking sound. 'You must think we're amateurs.'

'Susie,' I said desperately. 'Let me speak to–'

'Stop pissing about, artist.' His voice switched, turning vicious. 'And go and find your fucking brother.'

He hung up.

I didn't bother hanging around any longer and drove into Chichester. I tried to see if I was being followed, but I was no expert and couldn't be sure. Had I seen the blue Nissan 4x4 before? And what about the Ford Focus, the Vauxhall and those transit vans? Nerves shredded, I parked opposite the Chichester PO box office service and checked out box number 2113 as Rob had instructed. I opened it without much expectation of finding anything, and just about fell over in shock when I saw what he'd left me.

A pistol.

Some ammunition.

And a note.

It's fully automatic. It's armed. Fifteen rounds. Just point and shoot.

I hastily closed the door. Put my hand against it as though to magic the contents inside away. My heart was thudding. I felt dizzy.

Where the hell had he got a gun? What did he expect me to do with it? I'd never handled a gun before. I was more likely to shoot my own foot than a barn door. Carefully, I locked the box door on it. Pocketed the key. Walked to my car. Sat inside sweating and trying to think.

Did Rob know Susie had been kidnapped? Was that why I couldn't get hold of him? But how would he know? Why did he want me to be armed? To shoot the Saint, probably. My pulse hopped. I didn't think I could kill a man, no matter how frightening. Or could I? I guessed I wouldn't know for sure until the time came. On the other hand, if I gave the gun to Susie or DI Gilder, or even Rob, they'd know how to use it.

My thoughts gradually levelled out. I returned to the post office box, and after a furtive look around, shoved the weapon into the waistband of my jeans and pulled my jacket down over it. Hell, it was uncomfortable. I walked back to my car feeling horribly conspicuous. It was with immense relief that I brought the gun out and shoved it in the glovebox.

I nearly jumped out of my skin when my phone rang.

DI Gilder.

'I'm at your cottage.' He spoke through gritted teeth, obviously furious I wasn't sitting around waiting for him.

'I'm on my way,' I told him. 'Five minutes max.'

'Jesus,' he muttered.

I drove home without bothering to look and see if I was being followed. Did it matter if everyone knew where I was? When I got to the cottage, DI Gilder was sitting in his car, a scowl on his face. The second I pulled up, he was outside and standing next to my door.

I said, 'Thanks for com–'

'Fucksake,' he interrupted. 'Your wife's been kidnapped and you're dicking me around?'

'Sorry. But I had to check a PO box in case Rob had left a message there for me.'

At that, his eyes widened. 'Has he?'

'No.' *But he left a Glock 19, stamped with* Austria *and* 9 x 19 *on its side.*

'So, what gives?' He walked to my front door. I followed.

Inside, I quietly showed him the bug beneath the kitchen stool before turning on the Sonos system and then walking him into the garden, where I brought him up to speed. I showed him the photographs I'd been sent, told him about the bugs my wife had planted. I told him everything, except the fact I had a pistol in my glovebox.

'Dear God,' he said when I finished. He was staring at the photographs, almost as though he'd seen a ghost. 'I had no idea.'

He looked across at me, expression penetrating. 'Your wife is sure the dead woman with Tony Abbott is Rachel Daisley?'

'As sure as she could be.'

'And Rachel was her spy in the Mayfair Group.' He sucked his teeth, looking pensive. 'Jesus. This case has twice as many heads as Medusa.'

'Tell me about it,' I said wearily.

'Where's Rachel Daisley's body?'

'I asked George Abbott, but he wouldn't say.'

'You did what?' He looked startled.

I'd forgotten to tell him about the Saint collecting me and taking me to his lair. I quickly filled Barry in.

'He showed you his *comics*?'

I nodded.

'Christ.'

Barry studied the photograph of the murdered woman, turning it from side to side as though he wanted to find another angle to the scene. 'I'll check all our Jane Does for that period. But I doubt we'll find a match. Abbott's probably buried her ten-foot deep in his back garden.'

I saw Barry flinch as his phone buzzed. He looked at the screen and frowned.

'Gilder,' he said.

When the person replied, he straightened up and looked straight at me, blinking in surprise.

'How did you get my number?' he demanded. His eyes remained on mine as he said, 'Yeah, yeah… okay.' He listened for a bit. Then he said, 'Okay,' again.

He held the phone out to me.

I raised my eyebrows. 'Who is it?'

'Your brother.'

Chapter sixty-one

'Hey, Nick,' said Rob. 'My man.'

'Christ,' I gritted into the phone. 'You have no idea. I've been going crazy trying to get hold of you…'

'I'm here now.' He sounded laid-back and relaxed. 'Fire away, big brother. See what I can do.'

A surge of hot rage tore through me.

'Okay, *little* brother.' My tone could have stripped paint. 'See if you can sort this: find Susie and rescue her from George Abbott, who happens to have kidnapped her and will kill her unless I deliver you to them. Oh, in case you've forgotten, Susie is my *wife*.'

Silence.

'Shit,' he said.

'Yes, *shit*.'

'Tell me what's happened.' He dropped all bonhomie and was brusque.

Having just run Gilder through everything, this second telling took much less time as I concentrated on the salient facts. When I finished, he said, 'I'm on my way.'

I was opening my mouth to ask how long he'd be, how he knew Barry Gilder's telephone number, but he'd hung up.

To my astonishment, Rob turned up barely ten minutes later. Not at the front door, but at the back, where he'd climbed over my neighbour's wall and crossed my garden.

'Where have you come from?' I asked.

'Mum and Dad's.'

'You're kidding me.'

'I haven't been staying there all the time.' He looked defensive. 'Just on and off a bit. They smuggle me in and out in the boot of their car.'

'Jesus.'

'Come on. Time's ticking. We need to rescue your wife, correct?'

I led the way into the kitchen area. I was moving to the stool to show him the bug but he got there first. He said, 'I put that there.' He snapped the device free and popped it in his pocket.

I could feel my eyes bulge.

'As a precaution,' he added, as though that was all the explanation I needed, and I was opening my mouth to demand *Why* and say *What the fuck*, but my mobile rang. I snatched it up.

Number unknown.

'Hello?'

'Hello, artist.'

My mouth was dry. Rob crowded close. I let him listen.

'Where's your brother?' the Saint asked.

'Close.'

'I need him, artist.'

'And I need Susie.'

'You agree to a swap,' he said.

I looked at Rob, heart clenched. He gave a nod.

'Okay,' I said.

'Here's what I want you to do. You're going to put your brother in your car and drive him to the coordinates I text to your phone. You will follow the directions without stopping, without deviating. I have put a real time tracker on your car so I will know straight away if you try to pull any tricks. If you remove the tracker, or if I get so much as a whiff you're trying to cross me, or even *thinking* about calling the police, sweet little Susie dies.'

Heart thumping, I said, 'I'm not sure if Rob will come with me.'

'Then you'll have to persuade him.' His voice was hard.

My legs felt weak. I put out a hand and gripped the kitchen worktop, trying to steady myself.

'Let me speak to Susie.'

'No.'

'I need proof of life or I won't contact Rob. I won't give him up unless I know for sure Susie's okay. Surely you can understand that.'

Small silence.

'Oh, all right.' He gave a sigh as though bored. 'I can see your point.'

There were some muffled sounds, men speaking. Then Susie said, 'Nick? Is that you?'

She sounded surprisingly strong, her voice clear.

'I'm coming to get you,' I told her.

'Have you rung the Office?'

'No, not…'

'Don't.'

'What?'

'If you do, Abbott will vanish me. There will be no evidence. Everything will be hearsay.'

I swallowed. 'Okay.'

'Don't be too long,' she said, and although I knew she meant it to be a dry remark, sarcastic, her voice wobbled.

I could hardly bear it.

'Hang tight, Susie,' I told her. 'We're coming. We'll get you out of there.'

'We've moved.' She spoke fast. 'Two-hour drive, now in a foresters' hut, four of them, seen three pistols, one shotgun – *No, stop! No!*'

Sounds of a scuffle came down the line. Susie kept shouting, *No, no!* Her voice was laced with rising panic.

'George!' I yelled. 'For God's sakes!'

'I can't trust her,' he snapped. 'She needs hobbling.'

I heard a soft thunking sound, like a log wrapped in cloth being dropped on the floor. Then the sound came again. I heard Susie scream, a sound that came from a place of terror and shock, and which drove a black spear in my heart.

'George!' I shouted. 'Stop!'

'Too late.' He sounded satisfied.

In the background, I could hear Susie whimpering, small involuntary sobs jerking from her throat. She was saying, *Oh God, oh God, oh God.*

'What have you done to her?'

'Made sure she's out of action.'

'What have you done?'

'Tommo used a piece of four by four he found behind a workbench.'

I was breathing so hard I thought I might hyperventilate. 'What?'

'He broke her arm. Ooooh, look at that. It's already swelling. There's quite a bit of blood too. And I can see some bone poking through the wound. It looks nasty, so you'd better hurry, artist, before it turns septic.'

Susie's whimpers turned to groans. Sick dirty groans that made my stomach loop and curl.

'Texting you now,' he said. 'You've got two hours.'

He ended the call.

I rang him back, but he didn't pick up and nor did it switch to any messaging service. It simply rang out. I was trembling and shuddering, nausea lodged against my ribs. A *ting* alerted me to a text. A Google map showed a bright blue pin in north London, just inside the M25. I expanded the map to see the pin was placed plum in the middle of a vast area of dense ancient woodland, grassland, heath, rivers and bogs.

My heart fluttered. 'Epping Forest.'

Chapter sixty-two

I knew why the Saint had chosen Epping Forest. He may have his posh house in the Home Counties, but he was an East End man, and the area was his spiritual turf. I had no doubt he was familiar with every track and trail, every remote meeting spot, every isolated and inaccessible area in which to bury dead bodies.

Epping Forest was synonymous with dead bodies. It was a dumping ground. A disposal site. Only the previous month a body had been found partially buried near a lake. A walker had seen dozens of rats scurrying around the trees and when he'd investigated further, found a decomposing body. Nobody knew how long it had been there.

Heart knocking, I said, 'They've hurt her. Really badly.'

'I heard,' Rob said, his face taut. 'I'm sorry.'

'I have to go to her.' I gave him a searching look. 'Will you come with me?'

'Of course.' He looked shocked I should ask.

'But what about when we get there? Are you actually willing to trade yourself for Susie?'

'I'd rather not.' He gave a twisted smile. 'I'm hoping we'll find another way.'

'He wants you, Rob.'

'I know.' He suddenly looked exhausted. 'He's relentless. I didn't kill Tony, but he won't ever believe me.'

I gave Rob a long, searching look. As he looked back, a light ignited at the back of his eyes. A light I remembered, which flared at whatever gauntlet that had been thrown down. It was the look of a fighter, a bit of a lunatic if I was honest, and quite scary once he got the bit between his teeth.

'Fuck him,' he said. His gaze became clear and strong, decisive. He grinned, showing twin rows of strong white teeth but his eyes were cold and hard. 'Let's do it. Get your wife back and kick George Abbott's arse into the stratosphere and beyond.'

He clapped a hand on my back and I felt a surge of energy and optimism flow through me. I moved, grabbing my car keys and striding for the front door.

'Wait.'

Barry Gilder forced me to a stop. I struggled not to push past him. Tried to get my brain to work but it was slow, moving through the sludge of wanting to do nothing but rescue my wife.

Barry said, 'Time to call reinforcements. It's gone too far.'

Panic filled me. 'But he'll kill her if he thinks the police are involved. She told me not to ring her work colleagues either, or he'll vanish her.'

'It's all about timing,' Barry went on. 'If I get it right, Abbott will arrive at the RV point and find it empty. Because it will *be* empty. He'll be in place, waiting for us and thinking he's all alone, but the police will be creeping up on him in the shadows.'

Susie said she trusted Barry Gilder, but I wasn't so sure.

'I won't ring them until we get close,' Barry said. 'But we need them, Nick. I don't want the Saint killing your brother, let alone anyone else.'

I stepped outside last. Set the alarm. I expected Rob to join us in the car, but he said, 'I have something to do first. Five minutes max.'

Disbelief warred with mistrust.

'I won't let you down.' He gripped my arm, gave it a shake. 'I'll follow you. We'll keep in touch by phone.'

My neck itched. I didn't like being separated.

'Did you get the gift I left you in the PO box?' He gave me a meaningful look.

'Er…' I glanced at Barry then back. 'Yes.'

'Bring it with you.'

'Is that where you're going?' I asked, eyebrows raised. *To get a gun?*

'Yup.'

I couldn't argue with that. Not when the Saint had three pistols and a shotgun. Nerves pinging, I watched Rob jog away.

True to his word he wasn't gone long, and he returned driving Dad's trusty old Discovery, filled to the brim as usual with sailing kit, everything covered in piles of dust sheets. Rob gave me the thumbs up and a tiny part of me breathed a sigh of relief.

I drove. Barry sat in the passenger seat. I took the A27 towards Arundel then picked up the A29 to head north-east for London and the M23, then the M25. I swept anti-clockwise along the London Orbital, trying not to speed, trying not to draw attention to myself, but I couldn't seem to keep my speed down. I'd drop to seventy mph and within minutes I'd be doing ninety. *Cool it*, I kept telling myself. *You don't want to get stopped by the police. You've got a gun in the glovebox, remember?*

I glanced in my rear view mirror to see Dad's bottle-green Discovery keeping tag not far behind me. We'd given Rob the coordinates the Saint had sent me and agreed I'd slow down if necessary, to make sure Rob was with us before we reached our destination, but he was no slouch behind the wheel and no matter what I did or how fast I went, he stayed with us.

'Twenty miles to go.'

Ahead, the motorway ran like a black ribbon through monochrome countryside. On either side were damp fields of mud and acres of standing water. Handfuls of wet looking farm animals slumped together in miserable groups. The sky was looming grey, and threatening rain. Barry sat quietly next to me.

I counted the junctions down. Thirty. Twenty-nine. Twenty-eight.

'Exit's in ten miles,' I told them.

I heard a snicking sound from beside me. I turned to see Barry Gilder priming a handgun. Where the hell had that come from?

'Is that thing legal?' I asked. Unlike other forces around the world, British police weren't armed unless they were part of a firearms unit, and I was pretty sure Barry was just a plain old detective, and not allowed a gun.

He sent me a flat gaze. 'Do you care?'

My gut said, *sod it*. Things were out of my control. Why quibble about guns when I had one too? My gaze went to the glovebox. What had Susie said? *Four of them, seen three pistols, one shotgun…*

There were four of us too. Five, if we included Susie. We also had two pistols. Almost even-stevens at the Gunfight at the OK Corral.

I felt a hysterical urge to laugh. Clamped it down. Concentrated on the traffic around me.

We crested a long hill, the motorway carving through a long valley. The dashboard clock told me the temperature had dropped from eight to six degrees outside and that it was just after two o'clock. Two hours until sunset.

And then it happened. Overhead gantries flashed white. *Accident. Slow Down.*

'No,' I said.

'Shit,' muttered Barry.

Please God it had already been cleared away. The motorway police and accident response service were usually incredibly swift to remove cars and debris to the hard shoulder, their priority to keep traffic moving, prevent any build up that might cause further accidents, but if you caught an accident when it had just happened, you could be stuck for an hour or more.

The traffic slowed down. Sixty mph. Fifty.

'Please,' I groaned.

As we cruised around a long corner, the car ahead jammed on its brakes. Thirty.

I was gripping the steering wheel so hard my knuckles bled white.

Please, I prayed.

We came to the end of the bend and my heart plummeted. Ahead was a river of red tail lights, stationary traffic all the way to the horizon.

Chapter sixty-three

Slowly, we cruised to a halt. The next exit wasn't for another four miles.

'Switch on the radio,' said Barry. 'I'll check traffic news.'

In the distance, I heard a siren. Looking in my rear view mirror, I saw a blue flashing light approaching.

'Shit,' I said as an ambulance raced past on the hard shoulder, hotly followed by two motorway patrol cars. If the emergency services hadn't got to the accident yet, we could be here for *hours.*

'Follow them,' said Barry.

'What?'

'I've got my warrant card.'

'What about Rob?'

'I'll think of something.'

I put on my indicator and inched my way across. The second my tyres gripped the hard shoulder, I punched the big red triangle on my dashboard to switch on the hazard warning lights. Trickled past the traffic queues. Behind me I saw Dad's Discovery follow, hazards also flashing.

It didn't take long to get to the crash site. Maybe three minutes. A Citroen lay upside down across the hard shoulder and slow lane. A second vehicle was crushed against the central reservation, the third just behind it with a crumpled bonnet. Glass and bits of metal lay everywhere. The ambulance service team was already at work. Five people appeared to be involved. Two were standing but the rest were on the ground in disarrayed and shocked heaps.

As soon as we appeared, an officer strode across.

Barry leaped outside. 'Sorry, pal. We're in a bit of a hurry.'

The cop gestured angrily behind us, obviously telling Barry to sod off and get back in the queue, but Barry persisted.

It didn't work. Things grew heated.

I heard the traffic cop snarl something sarcastic along the lines of he was sorry Barry would get home late for his tea, and just as I was wondering if I should get out and fall to my knees and beg, my phone rang.

'Why have you stopped?' asked the Saint.

'Traffic accident.' I was curt.

'Like I believe you.'

'It's true,' I hissed. 'Check the Internet. Three car smash.'

'You've got your brother?'

'Of course.'

'Let me speak to him. I want to make sure you're keeping your end of the bargain.'

'He's in the car behind us.'

'Are you sure about that?'

'Yes!' The word was a shout of frustration and fear.

I could hear him breathing. Finally, he said, 'How long until you get here?'

'I don't know. Twenty minutes? Thirty?'

'Twenty minutes. Not a second more.'

He hung up.

I twisted in my seat to see Barry Gilder on the phone, talking urgently. He passed his phone to the officer who spoke for a while, looking between Barry and me, and Dad's Discovery. Then he handed Barry's phone back. Things happened fast after that. The cop leaned down to look at me.

'Follow me,' he said.

Walking ahead of us, he guided us between the wreckages and around the worst of the broken glass. As soon as we were clear, Barry jumped inside and said, 'Go.'

I floored it.

The BMW rose smoothly to the challenge of an empty motorway and a heavy foot on the accelerator. By the time I eased off, the needle rested on 140 mph, and I only slowed because Dad's old Discovery was struggling to keep up. Even so, we made junction twenty-six in under five minutes.

'How did you persuade the cop to let us through?' I asked.

'I rang your wife's office.'

I was opening my mouth to protest that she'd told me specifically *not* to do that, but he overrode me.

'I know what you said,' Barry snapped. 'But we need all the help we can get. I spoke to Mark Felton. Told him the situation, and not to go in until my boss gives him the go-ahead. She's one of theirs. He doesn't want her vanished any more than we do.'

I had to hope to God that Barry was right, and that MI5 wouldn't blunder in and cock everything up.

Taking the dual carriageway to the roundabout, I swung left and ducked east to join the A104, a road that ran directly through the forest. Trees lined the road, rough grass verges on either side opening up into stretches of brown bracken and gorse. A mile on, I slowed down, looking for a track on the right which would, according to the coordinates the Saint had left, lead us straight to him.

I steadily rounded a sweeping bend and there it was. A rough track of stone and gravel, rutted with potholes filled with rainwater. I turned onto it. Crawled along, leafy low-hanging branches brushing against the windows. Although the Discovery had made the same turn, Rob had slowed right down, following us at a distance.

Barry's phone rang. He looked at the display. Answered it. 'Boss, thanks for clearing me. I'm sorry I couldn't say much with Plod listening in, but I'm on a—'

I could hear a woman's voice, sharp and angry, trying to override him, but he kept going.

'Kidnapping case. We're going to the rendezvous now. I need backup.'

There was a pause, and then came more angry noises.

'No,' he said, 'this isn't a joke. We're meeting George Abbott, who's kidnapped an MI5 officer.'

I half-listened to him giving a DCI Ann Harris the lowdown. From what I could gather, she was shorthanded and was going to struggle to put a team together. She was also spitting fire at the short notice and let Barry know in no uncertain terms she didn't appreciate it and nor did she approve of anything he was doing or had done or would do in the future.

Finally, he clicked off the call. 'Christ almighty. Facing George Abbott's going to be nothing compared to her.'

My stomach was rolling in a sea of oil, making me feel sick. I had a sheen of sweat all over my body and more sweat seeped down my spine to soak into my waistband.

I crossed the bump of a small bridge. Checked my phone and the blue destination push pin.

'Nearly there,' I said.

We passed a massive boggy pond with silvery bronze plants at one end and giant rhubarb plants with umbrella-shaped leaves at the other. Birds flitted in and out of bushes. A squirrel darted across the track ahead. It felt as though we were in another world.

We came upon a clearing. An area of rough grass and ferns. I stopped. We were on top of the push pin on the map.

'We're here.'

I saw Rob pull up behind me. I kept the engine running. I didn't want to switch it off straight away in case we needed to get out of there quickly. That said, I couldn't see anyone. No cars, no people. Nothing except dripping oak trees, beech, some silver birch. A blackbird darted from one bush to another but otherwise all was still and silent.

The phone in my hand rang.

'Who the fuck is that with your brother?' the Saint asked.

I twisted violently in my seat.

My blood pressure spiked off the chart.

Rob stood stock still next to Dad's car. Behind him stood a man.

I blinked rapidly, wondering if I was imagining things.

Twelve years may have passed but he had the same strong body I'd seen on the CCTV tape. His hair had gone grey and his jowls sagged, pulling his skin down and making him look like a saddened Basset Hound, but it was the same man all right.

David Gilder, Barry's father.

He was holding a gun to my brother's head.

Chapter sixty-four

'And who the fuck's in the car with you?' the Saint demanded.

I had to work my mouth to answer. It had turned to cotton wool. 'Barry Gilder.'

'Put him on.'

But Barry was yanking open the door and striding furiously to his father.

For Chrissakes... I flung my door open and hastened after him, clutching the phone, my feet squelching in wet ground, my heart belting away like an industrial piston on overdrive.

'Dad.' Barry Gilder stopped in front of the men. 'What the hell are you doing?'

His father looked at him. His expression was flat. 'What do you think?'

'But Mum said you were in Finland. Fishing with Michael Wujek.'

'That's what I told everyone, yes.'

David Gilder glanced at my phone, which was squawking furiously. We could all hear the Saint going nuts and I was going to speak to him, try to calm him down, but David Gilder shook his head sharply, shoving his gun harder into the side of Rob's head.

'Don't move,' he said.

I stilled and at the same time, the Saint's voice went quiet.

'Look,' said David Gilder reasonably. 'It's simple. I spotted an opportunity.'

I saw his son's skin pale. 'No, Dad. Please, no.'

'There's a reward for this piece of scum. You really believe he didn't kill those people? That he wasn't screwing that woman,

Rachel, or that he wasn't so high on crack that he didn't go insane and cause that bloodbath?'

Rob held my eyes. His hands were bound in front of him. He had a gun against his head, but he was unnaturally calm. Where I was sweating, my pulse racing, he looked totally composed. It was weird. Was he in some sort of fearful fugue? Or had his old security training kicked in?

Barry was practically hopping from foot to foot, infuriated. 'But taking money from George Abbott, it's–'

'He tells me you're on his payroll too.' His father's eyes held a cold challenge. 'So don't tell me you're whiter than white.'

'But I didn't have a choice. He told me that if I didn't find Robert Ashdown, one day Hayley would go to collect Noah from school and he wouldn't be there. We'd never see him again, and–'

'Enough,' his father snapped. 'Let's do this thing. Get this man's wife back. You do want that, don't you?' He flicked a look at me.

'Yes, yes,' I said. 'But not if Rob–'

'Good.'

David Gilder reached over and grabbed my phone. Clicked it off. Passed it back to me.

He eased the gun from Rob's head, but not too far. He said to Rob in a conversational tone, 'How was that, do you think?'

'Stirling,' he said, giving me a wink. 'You should be on the stage. I nearly fell for it and I already knew the plan.'

Silence. There came the cawing of a crow. The swirl and rustle of a breeze lifting leaves. All these things were at the edge of my consciousness as I tried to make sense of things.

Barry said slowly, 'You did that for George Abbott's benefit?'

'I still am,' replied his father. His eyes were clicking around the clearing, sensing, evaluating. An old warhorse returning to the battleground. Then he looked at me. 'I'd shake your hand, except it would give the game away.'

'Game?' I repeated. My voice was dusty.

'You got everything I left for you?' he asked me. 'The CCTV tape? The photographs?'

I stared. 'It was you?'

'Rob couldn't do it,' he told me reasonably. 'He might have been spotted.'

I remembered what my neighbour had said when I'd asked her if she'd seen anyone entering our cottage. *He was an older man… I thought it was your father.*

'I don't understand,' I said.

'It's simple.' Rob turned his head slightly to look at David Gilder. 'This man saved my life.'

But he's on the Saint's payroll, I thought. *He lied about when the police turned up.*

'No,' I said. I'd decided I didn't trust his father even if he had given me the CCTV tape and the photographs.

'Think about it, Nick.' Rob's mouth went tight. 'But don't take too much time over it. David saved my life. He helped set up my fake drowning. He hid me from the Saint. I consider him my *friend*. Get with the programme, will you?'

He's your friend until he gets the reward. And he still has a gun against your head, remember?

'You think I don't want to bring Abbott down?' David Gilder's gaze was like a pair of iced lasers on mine. 'He's had my balls in a vice nearly all my life. I've been unable to move, to live freely, and now he's got my son caught in the same trap. You think I don't want to end that?'

I stood there, desperately unsure. I didn't know what to say. Didn't know what to do.

Rob asked, 'Do you trust me?'

He held my eyes. They shone with sincerity and warmth.

I nodded jerkily.

'Then trust him.'

I swallowed. I didn't see I had much choice. There were at least four of the Saint's men waiting for us. If Barry and David Gilder came along, it would make it even. Four each side. Was I making a mistake? I couldn't tell. I was in such a state of alert I was having trouble identifying any instincts or emotions. I had to trust Rob with this. Trust my brother.

'Okay,' I said.

My phone rang.

'Put Barry Gilder on,' the Saint demanded.

I passed Barry the phone.

Chapter sixty-five

Barry put the phone on loudspeaker so we could all hear.

'What the fuck are you doing there?' the Saint asked. 'Having a fucking tea party?'

'Delivering Robert Ashdown to you.' He kept his voice level. 'As you wanted.'

'But what the hell is your father... No matter. You're here now.'

'Yes. We needed the two of us. Ashdown kicked up a bit of a fuss when we went to get him. I had to taser him.'

Barry's father gave Barry a small approving smile at the embellishment.

'Did you?' The Saint sounded impressed. 'Thank you, Barry. I'll make sure you won't come to regret it.' His voice then changed. Became cold. Oily. 'But if I come to doubt your loyalty, you know which little boy will have his legs amputated tomorrow.'

Barry's entire body spasmed. For a moment I thought he might retch but he took a noisy gulp of air, then another.

Dear God, I thought. This crazy plan had to work. David and Barry Gilder had to destroy the Saint, because if they didn't, neither of them could live with the damage the Saint would wreak.

'Now,' said the Saint. 'I'm sending someone over. I want you to do as he says.'

I turned to see a big white guy appear through the trees. He had mouse-coloured hair that was longer at the front and buzz-cut up his neck and over his ears. He wore a windcheater and jeans, army surplus boots. The windcheater had NIMETU in red on it.

'*The Nameless*,' Barry murmured. 'It's the name of a street gang. Eastern European.'

As NIMETU stepped into view, at the same time, half a dozen men also appeared. Each held a weapon. Each weapon was trained on the car. I saw semi-automatics, shotguns. A couple of Uzis.

My adrenaline went into free fall.

The Saint had brought an army.

'Oh, God,' Rob said. 'Oh, no.'

Barry gulped audibly. 'It'll be all right. I've called the troops, remember. They're on their way.'

Please God they get here soon.

The man in the NIMETU windcheater held a sawn-off shotgun in both hands. He was flanked by two men. One held an Uzi, the other a Glock. They approached slowly. NIMETU jerked the end of his sawn-off shotgun at us.

'Phones,' he said. 'Throw them.'

His voice was accented. Definitely Eastern European. Maybe Estonian, or Albanian. I found it hard to differentiate between them.

'Where's my wife?' I asked.

'Phones,' the man snapped.

I threw my phone to one side. Heard a clatter then a splash as it hit a puddle.

The black eye of the shotgun's barrel swivelled to Barry. 'And you.'

I hoped Barry had left the line open as he threw his phone onto the ground.

'And you.' NIMETU jerked the barrel of his shotgun at Barry's father.

'Back left pocket,' he told NIMETU.

NIMETU looked at Barry. Said, 'Get it.'

Barry lifted his father's phone from his pocket, chucked it on the ground. I saw that Rob also had a phone in his rear pocket, but nobody checked him. He was the prisoner, after all.

NIMETU swooped and picked up all three phones. He walked a few paces away and threw them, hard. I heard the splash as they hit water. A pond, a lake. Whatever. They wouldn't be working anymore.

NIMETU returned. 'Weapons,' he demanded.

'None,' said Barry. 'We're civvies, okay?'

'We'll see about that.' He backed up a little. Waved the shotgun at them. 'You two.' He meant Barry and me. 'Turn round.'

We turned.

I saw NIMETU pull out a pistol from Barry's waistband. 'Some civvy,' he said, spitting on the ground.

'Where is she?' I asked.

'Arms up.'

I did as instructed. Watched the man with the Uzi sling his weapon with its strap across his back. He came and patted me down. Shoulders, arms, legs, ankles. Then he went to Barry, did the same. Swift, professional. But they didn't pat Rob down. Not so professional after all.

'Walk.' NIMETU waved the gun at a pollarded tree which had a massive crown of thick, trunk-like branches. 'Over there.'

I shivered as the temperature dropped and my breath misted before me. The ground was sodden, and I'd barely walked ten paces and my shoes were soaked through. I leaned close to Rob. 'Is your phone on?' I whispered.

He gave a tiny nod.

Barry had given his boss, DCI Ann Harris, everyone's phone numbers earlier. When his and mine didn't work, she'd track Rob's phone. The troops would find us. I had to hope it was soon, but what would happen when they arrived, God alone knew. I prayed we'd survive that long.

As we walked through the forest, the cold bit harder. I could hear the wind playing in the high branches of the trees, causing them to creak and whisper. The light weakened.

'Is my wife okay?' I asked NIMETU.

'Shut up.'

We came to what looked like an animal trail. Followed it, snaking through the trees. Our footsteps rustled and squelched through carpets of wet leaves. To my disbelief, we kept walking.

'Where the hell are you taking–?'

The butt of a gun hit the back of my head. A sharp clip, above my ear. It hurt like hell and was expertly placed not to knock me out as much as to shock me. Make me compliant. I was trembling, my heart hollow. Christ. The Saint had hired real pros. My dread increased.

We walked for over forty minutes. I lost all sense of direction and had no idea where we were. Dread sat on my shoulder and fear in my stomach. If I got out of there alive, I was going to take Susie sailing in the Caribbean. Sod the money.

'Stop there.'

The voice came from ahead.

The Saint.

Chapter sixty-six

Nick. The name came into Susie's mind. He was coming. Rob too. And David Gilder. Barry Gilder. Father and son. She didn't trust either of them. She needed to see what was happening, to know Nick was all right. That her future was going to be safe.

She levered herself onto her knees and leaned against a tree trunk. Waves of pain emanated up her arm, into her shoulder and neck and into her brain. She'd already vomited from the pain, but it had settled to a mind-numbing shriek.

Her guard raised the pistol as she made to get to her feet. Shook his head. She lifted her good arm in a pleading gesture.

He hesitated.

She struggled up.

The pain in her other arm intensified at the movement. Her vision blurred. She waited for it to pass. It was only a broken arm, she told herself. It would heal. And it wasn't as bad as the Saint had made out to Nick. He hadn't broken the skin. There was no bone showing, no blood. It was a closed break. Her forearm was shattered, and although the pain was pretty bad, along with the swelling, she could at least function.

Not that the Saint knew that. He thought she was debilitated. He thought he'd won. How little he knew her, knew how tough a woman could be.

Her thoughts blurred. Grey clouds seeping at the edges, threatening to envelope her in a thick blanket of fog. She pushed it back. She had come so far, she mustn't give up.

'It's time.'

The Saint was there. Tall, in a dark winter coat and fedora, his chisel-like face grim, he looked like a character out of one of his comic books.

Her mind cleared as though a gust of wind had pushed the fog away. She was focused, alert. But she kept her shoulders stooped, her gaze on the ground. Defeated. Beaten.

He took her good elbow in his hand. 'Walk.'

He was taking her to do the swap himself? She had to stop herself from laughing out loud. How stupid could one man be? She thought he'd be more savvy, but obviously he was blinded by revenge, not wanting his men to kill Rob, but to do it himself, make himself look big and all powerful. He was sending a message. *If you mess with my family, no matter how long it takes, I will make you pay by my own hand.*

Little did he know she had the same intention. She surreptitiously eyed his other hand which held a Walther P99, a semi-automatic. All ready to go.

She would have to be fast, *superhuman* fast, to grab it.

Would it be possible?

She'd have to ignore the pain when it came. Pretend she didn't have a broken arm. Mind over matter. Adrenaline would help.

He led her slowly to a small footbridge that spanned a narrow stream. It was a simple construction, three feet wide, no handrail. The Saint forced her ahead of him. The wind had dropped and an ethereal mist had settled on the ground, making it seem as though they were walking through gauze. She could hear their footsteps, soft in the mulch. The brush of their clothes.

And then something else. A soft sucking shuffling sound. A wet sweeping. She realised it was several pairs of feet brushing through leaves.

The Saint brought her to a halt.

And there they were.

Nick, Rob and David Gilder, Barry Gilder, surrounded by a bunch of tooled-up thugs. For a moment she couldn't believe it. The Saint had brought a goddamned army.

Her gaze adhered to Nick. He was her priority. He was ashen, but he looked okay. He stepped forward. He said 'Susie' in a desperate tone but the man behind him grabbed him and pulled him back.

And then Rob stepped forward. Nobody pushed him. Nobody forced him. He moved as though sleepwalking, staring at her as though he couldn't believe what he was seeing.

He said, 'What are you doing here?'

Rob kept coming. She tensed her muscles in readiness.

'I don't understand,' he said.

As she uncoiled, beginning to twist so she could kick the Saint's knees from under him, swoop her hand and grab his gun, she heard Rob say, bewildered, appalled, 'I thought you were dead.'

Chapter sixty-seven

I heard Rob say, 'I thought you were dead,' but I didn't take it in.

I was absorbed with Susie, her eyes darkened pits of pain in a face of sheet white. She had what looked to be a makeshift bandage on one arm, and the other, which was broken, she held close to her waist.

And then to my shock, she was twisting, snapping round so fast I barely saw what she was doing, and the Saint was surprised, overbalancing, and the next thing he was staggering to the side, toppling into the mush. Susie swarmed over him and when he raised his head, she head-butted him smack in the middle of his face. I heard gristle crunch and saw the Saint's men racing for her – they couldn't risk shooting her without shooting their boss – but she had his gun and she was holding it against his head and they were too far away.

She fired.

The shot cracked in the dead air of the forest. At point-blank range, the bullet hit him in the side of the head, just above his right ear. He was dead before his body slumped to the ground.

Susie ducked behind Abbott's body but before anyone fired a single shot, a man yelled, 'It's a trap! The police are here!'

Everything went crazy.

The Saint's men began running. They ran as fast as they could. Anywhere, everywhere. A blur of jeans and boots and weapons as they pelted through the trees for cover. Running like rabbits who knew a pack of greyhounds had been released on their tails.

I moved for Susie but I was slow, still shocked, and suddenly Gilder Senior moved past me, breaking into a run. To my confusion I saw he was running for Rob.

Suddenly Rob swung round. His eyes were on me.

'Run!' he screamed. 'RUN!'

I stood frozen, uncomprehending as Rob moved.

I saw Susie swing the Saint's gun round and train it on my brother's fleeing form.

David Gilder was still racing for Rob. Head down as if he was in a rugby charge, he was running full pelt.

Susie's aim was steady. Aimed straight at Rob.

She pulled the trigger.

Her first shot caught him high, the bullet passing through the soft flesh of his neck. His head snapped back. He didn't fall straight away but the impact made him stumble, right into David Gilder's path. The two men collided and at the same time she fired again, hitting the retired detective above the cheekbone. The bullet drilled through his eye and into his head, bursting on the other side of his skull.

Both men plummeted to the ground. Lay utterly still.

Then Barry Gilder was grabbing my wrist and pulling me away.

'Run!' he yelled at me.

I hesitated, but only for a moment.

Susie was raising her gun. She was bringing it round, aiming it for us, seeking Barry or me I didn't know.

I ran.

Chapter sixty-eight

I raced through the forest, trying to protect myself from the tree limbs that reached into my path, whipping and snatching at me. Barry Gilder crashed alongside, both of us throwing up muddy water and leaves as we careened among the wet trunks.

We separated at times, forced apart by twisted thickets, shrubs and bushes, but we'd soon come together again, running neck and neck.

Once we came to a stream. We splashed through it and up the other side, slipping and sliding until we ended up on all fours, hands grabbing ferns and rushes, our feet scrambling in the mulch until we reached the top. Then we straightened and ran some more.

I had no idea how long we ran for. It felt like hours, days, and when Barry Gilder slowed, my breath was like fire in my throat, my lungs heaving. I wanted to stop, catch my breath, but Barry Gilder shook his head.

'Keep going,' he told me.

We went on, heads down, trying to peer through the mist, trying not to trip on tree roots. With poor visibility, we were forced to slow further, sometimes flanked by oak, then beech. My mind was numb, shocked. I couldn't stop replaying the moment Susie had shot Rob. The way she'd been focused, intent. Her hand steady. Her eyes as calm as if she was meditating.

My wife just killed the Saint.
My wife just killed my brother.
My wife just killed a retired detective.
My wife wants to kill a DI and possibly me.

'What's going on?' I hadn't realised I'd spoken out loud until Barry Gilder answered.

'I'm still trying to work it out,' he panted. 'But it's my guess your wife has something to hide.'

'She's an MI5 officer,' I responded. 'She has loads to hide.'

'I mean something personal.' He glanced at the side of my face.

I watched the mist drifting among the trees and tried to still the panic in my heart. 'Like what?'

But something inside me was already crawling, as though I had dozens of wasps in my veins, buzzing, desperate to get out. Something I already knew deep down, but didn't want to face.

Chapter sixty-nine

We kept walking. I felt the hand of grief grip my heart as I pictured David Gilder running for Rob, trying to tackle him, bring him to the ground and present a smaller, more difficult, target. Protecting his witness to the end. And what about Rob? My throat thickened and I swallowed, pushing my anguish away. It would have to wait until later. When we were safe, and when I had the time and privacy to break down, and weep, and regret not telling Rob how much I loved him, was proud of him.

In the distance, I heard a faint clatter and as it grew louder, I realised it was a helicopter. It passed closely above, coming to hover perhaps half a mile away, above the murder scene, I supposed.

We crossed another stream, having to paddle through it, our shoes sodden and muddy, my feet frozen, each step squelching. I heard Barry's heavy breathing, occasionally smell the man's acrid scent of adrenaline and fear.

And then I heard something. A small regular disturbance of leaves behind us. I snapped around in an instant, fear clawing at my throat.

Barry gestured for me to move behind the sturdy trunk of a mature beech tree. When I was in place, he went to slip behind another tree.

I was cold and wet, my nerves shredded, but I gritted my teeth. Tried to listen.

Nothing.

Then it came again. The small sound of leaves being disturbed in the undergrowth. A deer? A dog?

I looked across at Barry, eyes wide.

Barry put his finger to his mouth and shook his head. I shivered, trying to still my breathing but it was hard when my heart was thumping so hard.

Suddenly I saw a branch flicker. Heard the sucking sound of mud.

Whatever it was, it was close.

And then there she was, stepping out from behind an oak tree, her shoulders back, confident and strong even with her broken arm held close to her waist. She held a gun in her right hand.

I thought we'd be hard to see in the gloaming of the forest but we could have been lit in neon for the amount of time it took her to spot us. A fracture of a millisecond fell before her eyes went straight to mine then swept to Barry.

They stared at each other. He didn't look away. It was as though it was just the two of them.

'Hello, Rachel,' he said.

Chapter seventy

'Why, DI Barry Gilder.' She widened her eyes coquettishly. 'You've gone and worked it out all on your own. Aren't you a clever clogs.'

Rachel? My mind became a whirl. I thought Rachel was Susie's agent. The woman who'd been killed with Tony Abbott.

'How long have you known?' She sounded curious.

'Not long enough.'

'You've just put it together?' Her face brightened. 'Just now?'

'I have to say...' Barry cleared his throat. 'It's one of the best impersonations I've ever witnessed. Not that I knew the real Susie Fleming, of course... but I'd bet my last breath that the real Susie and you – her impersonator – are now so entwined, nobody could tell them apart.'

She stepped forward. Stood barely two yards from him. 'Am I prettier, do you think?' She turned her head slightly, to show off her profile.

I watched Barry put his head on one side as though considering.

'I've had the kink in my nose taken out,' Susie said. 'My teeth have been straightened too. It's amazing what a good cosmetic surgeon can do. I've duped so many people, you wouldn't believe it.'

'Even your family.'

'Ha.' She looked amused. 'They were probably the easiest to manipulate. They fell for the whole mugging story like you wouldn't believe.'

My soul was shivering, unable to comprehend what I was hearing. Susie wasn't Susie? She'd taken on another woman's identity?

Behind her, my eyes went to a faint flicker and then a blaze of lights erupted, turning the sky from black to brown.

Susie turned to see what I was looking at. I saw the raw flick of annoyance on her face.

'All terrain scene lights. Never mind.' She was nodding, obviously working things through. 'We can still contain this.'

She brought up her weapon.

She was going to shoot Barry.

Trembling, petrified, I stepped out from behind the tree. I spread my hands.

'Susie,' I said.

Distracted for a second, Susie turned her head to me.

I walked towards her.

She was watching me, her attention no longer on her gun, or Barry.

And in that moment, Barry went for her.

Chapter seventy-one

I saw Barry push his head down and charge for Susie.

'Susie!' I yelled, wanting to keep her diverted, keep her attention on me.

And then Barry was on her. She fired but it went wide. The sound of the shot punched through my shock. I started forward, wanting to stop Susie, stop Barry, but Susie fell backwards, reeling from the force of his weight, clutching his arm and bringing him down with her.

I tried to grab Susie's hand, the one that held the gun but she belted it against Barry's head. She hit him again, and again. She was grunting with the effort.

Barry pushed his weight on top of Susie. Put his hands to her throat and squeezed.

I went for Susie's gun again but she was faster than me. Much faster.She twisted like a snake and pressed the barrel against his head and pulled the trigger.

Her first shot hit him in the jaw, drilling through his mouth and out the back of his head. The second tore through his forehead. Soft brain tissue and blood sprayed everywhere. He slumped on top of her, his weight pinning her to the ground.

I wanted to go for her gun again, but she was already sweeping it round, the barrel coming my way, so I did the only thing I could think to do.

Run.

Chapter seventy-two

I charged through the forest like a wounded buffalo, bewildered and terrified, making enough noise to deafen the dead, but adrenaline can only last so long, and soon it had faded from my blood and my legs softened, exhausted and leaden.

I nearly fell to my knees at one point, and the temptation to stop and rest was almost overpowering, but I forced myself to keep walking. I didn't know in which direction, or where I was going, I was just walking to get away, to try to think and somehow, survive.

My wife wasn't Susie Fleming. She was a woman called Rachel Daisley. Susie had said Rachel Daisley was her agent in the Mayfair Group. That Rachel was a cleaner. Undercover. But Rachel had been my Susie all along.

Had killing Tony Abbott been an MI5 operation?

I couldn't understand how Rachel had joined MI5. They had personnel checks and security verifications, records, DNA…

'No,' I said out loud. I couldn't believe it. I *wouldn't*. But then I remembered her raising the gun and shooting the Saint, shooting Rob and Barry Gilder. I'd seen how her eyes had been empty pools of black. As emotionless as ink.

I kept walking, remembering things that had been lurking at the corner of my senses, things that had disturbed me only a little at the time, that I had talked myself out of. Things that now took on a different light.

Susie's father. The pain in his eyes as he spoke honestly to me. *I tried my best, hoping the little girl I loved was going to get better and come back to me. But that's not how it works with traumatic brain injuries. It's like they have a complete personality change. It's not their fault. They think they're the same person, but they're not. I couldn't cope with it. I felt awful, but when the doctor said we should return home, I was relieved.*

Susie's mother.

She looks the same, but different. It's like everything's just a bit off, you know? I know she had to have her face rebuilt, along with her jaw and teeth, but she's still not the same. She can't remember anything about when she was young. She used to love playing dress up with my clothes. All that's gone.

Dear God, how were they going to handle knowing their daughter wasn't their daughter? The next thought came crashing through like a freight train.

If my Susie was Rachel, then where was the real Susie Fleming? I stumbled to a stop.

I was picturing the woman who'd been shot with Tony Abbott, her face bludgeoned into pulp. I could hear Susie's response when I showed her the photograph, her decisiveness that it was Rachel.

Yes, it has to be her. Same height, nice figure, great tits. Whoever did this to her was really, really *angry. This wasn't someone in full control of their emotions. They went berserk. They wanted to obliterate her. Smash her to pieces. Literally.*

Had my Susie obliterated the other Susie's features so she wouldn't be recognised? So she could take on her identity? Rachel's body had never been found. The Saint had taken it, in order to protect his family, and disposed of it, God alone knew where.

Rachel, I guessed, then slipped into her role as the real Susie as smoothly as milk being poured into a glass. She'd made up the mugging to explain away her cosmetic surgery bruises, and invented her brain injury to cover her memory loss and personality change.

My muscles and joints had begun to stiffen in the cold and as I shifted slightly to walk again, hearing my shoes suck in the mud, the squish of liquid, another squelch came from close by.

'Nick,' she said.

Chapter seventy-three

'I won't hurt you. I promise.'

My thoughts and emotions became a twisted blur. I was exhausted and cold and my brain seemed to have ceased functioning. Right now, it was screaming *run!* but I didn't think I'd get far. She'd tracked me all this way, and would continue to track me. She had a broken arm but that hadn't stopped her. She was indefatigable, my wife.

My wife?

'If you're Rachel Daisley,' I said, 'does that mean our marriage isn't legal?'

She gave a long sigh. One of those that meant I was being irritating.

I went on. 'If you gave false details on our marriage certificate, which is a legal document, then it's invalidated. Isn't it?'

'Dearest, darling Nick.'

She stepped into view. For a moment, I had trouble recognising her. Head to toe, she was covered in mud. It was in her hair, across her face, all over her clothes. She looked down as though seeing herself through my eyes. 'A bit of a mess, eh.' She gave a rueful smile. 'But nothing a hot bath and a whisky won't fix.'

For the first time, I noticed she wasn't holding the pistol.

'Where's your gun?' I asked.

She tilted her chin behind her. 'Back there. Safe. I wanted to talk to you without it. To show you I trust you. That I love you, my gorgeous wonderful sexy husband. And to tell you that we are married in the eyes of the law. Always have been and always will be, if you just hang on tight, and let me explain.'

I opened and closed my mouth. I felt dizzy, close to losing any mental faculty I had. She'd killed my brother, and she wanted me to *hang on tight?*

'See it from my point of view,' she said. Her tone was reasonable, as though we were discussing something we'd just watched on TV. 'I was thirteen years old when I was diagnosed officially as a sociopath – which is the same as a psychopath except it sounds more socially acceptable – and my life ended. Can you understand how awful it was? One minute I'm a normal girl, the next I'm tarred with a psychological brush that blackens me from head to foot and nobody, and I mean *nobody*, wants a bar of me.'

'You killed Susie,' I said. 'The real Susie.'

'Having a label like that stopped me from doing what I wanted, don't you see? And when the label wasn't there anymore, I could be anything I wanted and nobody could stop me.'

'Rob saw you kill Susie,' I said. 'He witnessed it.'

'She was nothing.' My Susie made a dismissive gesture. 'She wasn't half as good as me, you know. We met at an induction interview. It was actually one of the other interviewees who noticed how alike we were. Same build, same hair, eye colouring. He said our likeness could be incredibly useful as spies. It made us laugh, me and Susie. We became friends until she was accepted into MI5 and I was rejected. They'd found my psychological profile, you see. Said I wasn't the right stuff.'

'So you killed her. Took over her life.'

'I made a far better officer than she would have in a million years. I would never have been lured to the Mayfair offices that night, for example. Talk about stupid. Both of them, actually. Susie and Tony. God, it was so easy to set up it was like taking candy from babies. I'd told Susie to meet me outside the lifts on the third floor – I'd spun her a story that it was to do with an MI5 exercise in role play – and bingo. There she was, bright-eyed and expectant… all I had to do was show her my gun, George Abbott's gun, and march her into Tony's office.

'They really thought I was threatening to shoot them in order to take pictures of them dressed up in that S&M gear, and sell it to the papers. Laughable, really.'

'You set it up so nobody knew Susie was the target,' I said.

'Nobody missed Rachel when she vanished,' she agreed. 'And nobody missed Susie because, ta da. She was there, albeit beaten up after her "mugging".'

It had almost been the perfect crime, I realised, until Rob had arrived and messed things up.

She stepped forward until she was close. Really close. Looked up at me. Into my eyes.

Chapter seventy-four

'We have a great life together, don't we.' Susie's voice was soft. 'We do stuff together, we laugh, have fun. Holidays, movies, sailing, living together. I know I have to go away sometimes, because I struggle occasionally being that person who's so nice, but I'm always back because we're a team. You're my husband. You are my life.' She raised her hand as if to touch my face but when I reared back, dropped it.

'Without you…' She swallowed. 'My life won't be the same. People won't like me anymore. They won't trust me. I like my life with you, Nick. It's really good. I love you and I love my job. I'm going to be DG one day. Guaranteed. Boss of MI5. Just think. You'll be married to one of the most powerful women in the land.'

Was she sane, or insane? I couldn't work it out.

Better say nothing.

'So,' she said. She reached out as if to take my hand but I took a step back. I couldn't help it.

She shrugged. 'I guess it'll take you a little time to adjust.'

I stood there. Dumb, paralysed.

'But it's for the best because, finally, I can now relax. Everyone who knows the truth has been silenced.'

Except me, I thought.

'Don't worry.' She smiled, a bright smile that used to light up my day, but now sent my skin crawling. 'I'm not going to kill you, my love. We shall walk out of the forest together, and continue our lives as we've done the past twelve years. In harmony.'

I wanted to ask what story she was going to come up with as to why she'd shot two police officers as well as my brother and the

Saint, but decided she was so adept at lying, setting smoke screens, there seemed no point.

She put out her hand again, wanting me to take it. 'Shall we?'

I stood silently, ice flowing through my veins.

'Nick?' Her voice held a tentative question but I heard the quiet warning beneath it.

I was opening my mouth, I wasn't sure what I was going to say, when a man said, very quietly, 'Susie.'

She didn't move, didn't flicker an eye, but I saw that cloak of stillness drop over her.

The man had spoken from the forest behind her. I couldn't see him but he was close. *Really* close.

'I'm armed,' he went on in the same soft tone. 'And I'm not alone. I want you to remain calm and not do anything stupid that might force me to shoot you.'

'I don't believe you've got a gun. The Office doesn't–'

'I found it in your husband's glovebox.'

At that, her jaw softened. She stared at me. 'Nick?'

I unstuck my tongue from the roof of my mouth. 'Rob gave it to me.'

'Fucksake.'

The man said, 'Turn round, Susie. Slowly.'

'Oh, come on.' She affected an exasperated tone. 'I'm one of the bad guys now? Look, the Saint shot those two men, Robert Ashdown and David Gilder, and I took him out. George Abbott, dead as a fucking doornail. I'd call that a good day's work.'

'Raise your hands above your head.' His voice was hard.

'You're serious?'

'One hundred per cent.'

'Ah, shit.'

Small silence.

'Raise them, Susie.'

'I can't,' she said. 'I have a broken arm.'

'Put the good one up.'

When she didn't move, he screamed, 'Put it above your head or I will shoot you!'

She flung her good arm in the air, but instead of turning round, took a step toward me.

He fired.

Chapter seventy-five

Susie didn't fall. She didn't move. Her arm was still raised, her gaze on mine. An icy incredulous stare.

She was shocked, I realised. She hadn't thought he'd shoot. 'You make another move and I won't miss the second time,' the man warned. He stepped into view. Early forties. Fit-looking. Smart suit, spattered with mud. White shirt. Tie. His arms and wrists were held straight, his head cocked to one side, looking straight down the barrel.

'This has to be a joke,' Susie said, but she didn't move.

There came a scamper of leaves and a uniformed police officer appeared with a German Shepherd at his side, pulling on its harness.

'Nick,' the officer said. 'I want you to move towards me, please. Away from Susie.'

'Don't,' she hissed. Her eyes flashed at me.

My knees were soft, my body trembling.

'Nick.' The officer was firm. 'Do as I say.'

I edged to the side. Susie watched me go. Her face was expressionless. The officer moved to meet me, gripping my upper arm and swiftly advancing me to the side but I stopped and pulled free. Turned round.

I saw the man in the suit approach Susie. He was less than a yard from her, eyes still sighted down the barrel of his gun, when she made her move.

For a moment, I couldn't believe it. She had a broken arm, a makeshift bandage on the other, and she was dropping down, ducking onto her right knee, levering herself into a spin with her left leg, diving her left hand down, going for the base of her spine, lifting her shirt and bringing out her pistol.

She'd lied about being unarmed.

And then she was bringing up her weapon, her eyes trained on the man in the suit.

She was fast, but he was no slouch either.

The second her gun was visible, he fired.

I heard the sharp *chink* as his bullet hit her gun.

He fired again.

Her gun flew to the ground. She made to go for it but he said, 'Don't.'

He didn't shout the word but he didn't have to. It was laced with meaning. *Don't make me*, he said. *I don't want to shoot you. But if you force the issue I will kill you.*

Susie's gaze was on her gun, but she didn't move.

'Face down,' he told her.

'I can't,' she said.

'You can and you will because if you don't, I will shoot you.'

Achingly slowly, never leaving her eyes from her weapon, she lowered herself to the mulchy ground.

The man stepped across fast and kicked her gun away. Then he came to her and brought out a pair of handcuffs. He crimped one cuff around her good wrist, and then he brought it to the small of her back where he locked the other cuff to the rear belt hook of her jeans. He went to her gun and unloaded it. Shoved it in his waistband. Then he put his hand beneath her good elbow and pulled her upright. Walked her to where I stood with the dog handler.

As he approached, I said, 'Who are you?' My voice was hoarse.

He looked at me as if for the first time.

'Mark Felton,' he said. 'I'm Susie's boss.'

I looked at Susie. She looked away.

'Susie?' I said.

She shrugged. 'I'm not saying anything until I get a lawyer.'

Chapter seventy-six

I watched as Susie was put in the back of a police car. Her expression was as dense and cold as stone. She didn't look at me as she was driven away. She didn't look at anyone. She looked straight ahead, chin up, as though she wasn't bathed in mud with a shattered forearm resting on her knee.

'What was that back there?' Mark Felton nudged his chin behind us, at the forest. 'Over who I was?'

'I thought I'd met you,' I said. 'But I hadn't. It was someone impersonating you.'

There was a flare of curiosity in his eyes but I didn't explain. I was thinking of the coils of lies lying on top of one another, the schemes and intrigues Susie had created, all the smoke and mirrors she'd used. I realised nothing she'd told me could be believed.

Nothing.

Not a single word.

I said, 'My brother never worked for MI5, did he?'

'I'm sorry?' He looked startled.

I watched as the patrol car, with Susie inside, vanished out of view. Swallowed into misty darkness.

'She told me Rob worked with you,' I told him. 'But it was a lie.'

Mark Felton was staring at me.

'Susie and I met at Rob's memorial, you see. She came and spoke to me. She wore a long summer dress. She told me she was there because she used to work with Rob. And then when we got together…'

'You believed her?' His eyebrows rose.

'I believed everything.'

I continued to stare at the space where the patrol car had been for a long time.

Chapter seventy-seven

I left London while Susie was being charged with multiple murders, along with a host of other indictments, and only returned when the Old Bailey turned her down for bail and I knew she was firmly incarcerated. I hadn't wanted her to find me and possibly follow me to St Margaret's Hospital and finish off what she'd started.

Rob was sitting up in bed when I arrived, holding hands with Sorcha, who'd shed her Norwegian sweater and was wearing a figure-hugging corduroy dress that stopped just above her knees. Dad sat in a chair in the corner with the newspaper and Mum was fussing around Rob's room rearranging the cards and well-wishing gifts that had flooded in ever since the story broke.

Not only was my brother Superman for bringing down the terrorist in the restaurant, but he'd solved a cold case that had troubled people for years.

Everyone loved a hero.

'Darling.' Mum came and gave me a kiss. Love and compassion shone in her eyes. 'How are you bearing up?'

I didn't know how to answer. I'd loved Susie so much, allowing my most vulnerable self to be deeply seen and known by her, that I wasn't sure who I was anymore. I'd cultivated love with her for over a decade and I was twisting on the rope of betrayal. It burned and ate at me like an animal that couldn't satiate its hunger.

Susie had slipped under my skin, infected my blood and conquered my heart, and now she was gone, I was a mess. I was living with what my doctor called PTSD symptoms – hypervigilance, flashbacks and confusion – and although he'd given me some pills, I hadn't yet taken them. I'd seen the therapist he recommended once, but I'd been so overwhelmed by the complexity of the story and my part in it that I'd quickly fallen silent and spent the remaining forty-five minutes staring out of the window, mind logjammed.

'I'm surviving,' I said.

Dad pushed back his chair. Came over and gripped my arm and gave it a shake. 'You'll be all right,' he told me. 'You're like your brother. Strong as an ox.'

Rob gave me a smile with his eyes. He'd only started speaking a couple of days earlier. A gunshot to the neck was, the surgeon told us, diagnostically and therapeutically challenging. The high density of vital structures in the neck made it virtually impossible for him to escape without permanent damage of some sort, but looking on the bright side, the bullet had missed his spinal cord. He'd had surgery to reconstruct hard tissues and started rehabilitation of the oral vestibule, but we'd been told he might need another couple of operations to correct residual deformities before he could think about coming home.

It was going to be a long haul, but at least he was here, and he was alive.

I crossed the room to kiss Sorcha on the cheek. It was thanks to Sorcha that we knew Rob's story. How he'd always been the happy wastrel we'd loved. How he'd come into money through drug running between George Abbott and *La Familia de Sangre*. How he'd become addicted to crack cocaine. Started making mistakes.

It had been David Gilder who'd stopped Rob's car on the M25 and found a suitcase of drugs containing fourteen packets of MDMA. A search of Rob's hotel room uncovered just under a million pounds cash. He'd already sold most of the drugs to George Abbott and was due to sail the money back to the Spanish gang, but David Gilder had other plans. Instead of arresting Rob, he made him a deal. Rob would work undercover for him, starting with bugging the Mayfair offices, and David Gilder would keep him out of jail.

'You didn't work for MI5?' I asked Rob.

'Never.'

The night Tony died, Rob had gone to the Mayfair offices. He'd followed a young pretty woman through the foyer – the real Susie – before going to bug George Abbott's office, half chatting to the cleaner, Klaudia Nowacki. Back in the corridor, he was going to bug Tony Abbott's office, except another woman stopped him.

'Rachel,' I said.

'Yes,' Rob confirmed. 'She was dressed as though she was middle-aged with flat shoes, a dumpy skirt and a grey wig, but she was young, around the same age as me, early twenties.'

I remembered what Klaudia had said, just before she was shot that it was strange, because *normally she is so proud of her looks.* Klaudia had been puzzled as to why sexy Rachel had dressed so dowdily. Now we knew why. To disguise herself so nobody, least of all anyone watching the CCTV tape, would recognise her.

'I thought I could charm my way around her but she sent me packing. Scary woman actually. I took the lift back to the ground floor to fool her, then I came back. I didn't want to leave without bugging Tony Abbott's office.'

His gaze turned distant as he remembered the rest of that catastrophic evening.

'I interrupted Rachel as she was bashing in another woman's head.'

'The real Susie,' I said.

He nodded. 'I recognised her from earlier, in the foyer.'

'And?'

'She was still alive. The real Susie. I could see her breathing. I didn't think, you know. I just went for Rachel. She tried to pull out a gun but I was much stronger. I got hold of it. She ran. I ran after her, down the stairwell and across the foyer and outside.'

He closed his eyes. 'Christ, she was fast. Like a bloody whippet. I lost her in the tube station.'

Rob went on to tell me how things unravelled when he called David Gilder. Apparently an anonymous caller, who we guessed to be Rachel, had rung the Saint on his personal line and told him hat Rob had killed Rachel and Tony in a jealous rage, and the Saint had fallen for it.

'Rachel would have seen me delivering drugs,' Rob told me. 'She knew who I was. I didn't know her though. It was the perfect set up to discredit me, the only witness to the murders, as well as frame me.'

'So you never had an affair with Rachel. My Susie, I mean.' Above all the smoke and mirrors, I had to make this clear in my mind.

'No.' His voice was firm. 'I'd never met her before that night.'

David Gilder warned Rob not to go to any police station, that the Saint was on the lookout for him and it was likely a cop on his payroll would hand him in.

With a bounty of a million pounds on his head, every criminal in the country looking for him, Rob had no choice but to disappear.

'David helped me,' Rob told me. 'When I sailed my skiff into the storm, he was out at sea, waiting to pick me up. He stuck me in rehab, which is where I met Sorcha. Together, we started a new life in Ireland.'

His eyes went to Sorcha, who gave him a wry smile and said, 'Where we would have lived happily ever after if we hadn't gone to London.'

I said, 'Why didn't you tell us you were alive?'

'David told me not to. George Abbott was watching Mum and Dad, Clara and you. He was never convinced I drowned. He'd send someone to check out Bosham from time to time, just in case. I couldn't risk it.'

'But you went to London.'

'I thought we'd be safe,' Rob said. 'It had been twelve years… and I wanted to propose somewhere really special. But things didn't plan out that way.'

Talk about an understatement.

'Why didn't you deny you worked for MI5? When I mentioned it on the water?'

He plucked at his hospital blanket. 'I'm sorry about that. But David and I knew there was more going on than just the Saint wanting my blood – we wanted to find out what it was. It was like the more we knew, the more we didn't, so he told me to find out what you knew and not give anything away. He was adamant. When David put it together, he didn't want to tell you because he was worried about what she might do to you, to keep her secret safe.'

Like kill me, I thought.

'I spoke to Etienne,' Rob said. 'He's off the hook now *La Familia* know the cops confiscated their money. They've written off their boat too, thank God, but even though it looks like they've cleared me off their slate, I won't be holidaying in Spain again.'

I picked up the newspaper. It was the first time we hadn't been headline news. I flipped the pages to see we'd been relegated to page three. Byline Fredericka Covington.

DNA test shows MI5 officer was imposter.

They'd found Rachel's DNA on the rooftop opposite Klaudia's flat as well as inside Arun Choudhuri's kitchen.

Seven people dead.

All murdered by my wife.

Chapter seventy-eight

'I've missed you,' she said.

I'd missed her too. I'd missed her body in my bed, the sound of her showering in the morning, brushing her teeth, the kiss she used to give me before she left for work. I missed the light sound of her footsteps on the path when she came home each Friday, the sound of her voice, excited and happy, how she'd come to me and wrap herself in my embrace. I missed the smell of her so badly I'd gone to bed with a bunch of her clothes one night, and bawled like a baby.

'How have you been?' I asked. I couldn't think of anything else to say.

'Bored.' She looked around. 'No matter what they try to make you believe, criminals are not intelligent.'

We were in the jail's Visits Centre. Pale yellow walls, tables and chairs bolted to the floor. The room echoed with voices. Husbands, brothers and sisters, parents. There had to be over fifty people, all trying to make themselves heard. I hadn't wanted to come, but my therapist had encouraged me to apply for a visit last month, and when the time came, I decided I may as well go. I still had questions that needed answering.

But now I was here, I couldn't seem to form any words. My wife sat opposite, slim and strong, her skin glowing with good health, her eyes bright, her hair gleaming. She looked as though she'd just come back from an active holiday abroad, kayaking or skiing. I, on the other hand, looked as though I'd been on a two-month bender. Which I guessed I had since I was using alcohol to dull the pain, to help me pass out each night. Not great, but it was the only way I was managing to cope.

'You look well,' I managed.

She pulled a face. 'There's nothing to do except go to the gym. I've started a course in Spanish though. *Te amo.*' She held my eyes. 'It means I love you. It was the first thing I learned, in case you came and visited.'

I felt a bite of guilt and glanced away.

'It's okay. You're here now.' She ran her fingers through her hair, fluffing it up. 'So, what's new? Is everyone going mad to interview you? Have you sold your story for a million? You should, you know. It would make a great movie. I'd like Keira Knightley to play me. She'd be good. Fragile but tough.'

'You're not exactly fragile,' I remarked, suddenly finding my voice.

She beamed as if I'd said something clever. 'No. You're right. Never fragile. Tough as old boots, me.'

Tough. That's what her psychiatrist had called her. I'd seen him the week before I came. My therapist had arranged the meeting in the hope he might help me understand Susie – I couldn't think of her as Rachel – and how things went wrong, but he didn't do that.

He said, 'She didn't "go wrong". She's the same person before she was arrested as she is now.'

I thought that over. Couldn't get to grips with it. I said, 'She didn't want to kill me.'

'She most certainly didn't. You were the supplier of her "normal life". Why would she want to start again? She'd have to seduce another man, build up the relationship she wanted. It would be a lot of hard work that she didn't want to afford. She was ambitious, am I right?'

'She wanted to be the head of MI5.'

'And she could well have done a good job. If she'd come into it legitimately. She has less of a moral conscience than the rest of us, which isn't a bad thing when the chips are down and tough decisions have to be made.'

I stared at him. 'She killed seven people.'

I could have said she'd picked seven flowers from the garden for all the effect my words had.

'In her mind,' he went on, 'it was perfectly legitimate. She'd tried to control things as efficiently as she could, trying to lead things in the direction she wanted them to go, and when it didn't work, she decided to eliminate the threats to her and her lifestyle the only way she could think of. Yes, she was ruthless, but to her she had no option.'

'You're saying she was cornered?'

'That's one way of putting it.'

He folded his hands on his lap, expression sombre.

'Every society,' he said, 'needs particular individuals to do their dirty work. People who are fearless. People who aren't afraid to make tough decisions, who aren't scared to put themselves on the line. To be cool under fire. To stand alone, and not be distracted by an emotional conscience. If your wife hadn't been an MI5 officer, she would have been drawn to something similar, like a soldier, or a bomb disposal expert. Even a surgeon or barrister, if she'd had the education. She has a sharp intellect that could have been incredibly useful to, say, the banking industry. Some of the most remarkable traders are sociopaths.'

I looked at Susie and said, 'Your psychiatrist says you slept with George and Tony Abbott because it amused you. And satisfied some kind of power play.'

Her eyes flared. 'One thing you have to understand is that was Rachel. Rachel slept with those men. Susie, that is me right now, today, slept with nobody, *nobody* else once she came out of hospital after the supposed mugging. Since then, the only person she's slept with is you.'

Long silence.

Did I believe her?

She leaned forward again, expression intent. 'You could say I'm two different people. Rachel was back then, doing things because they brought her pleasure, but now I'm Susie, who tries not to hurt anyone anymore. I was secretly in therapy for ages, learning what was expected of me as a normal person. I've done all right, haven't I? I mean, we were happy? Had a good marriage?'

I couldn't get any strength into my voice. It was an effort to keep talking, fighting to understand. 'He also says you… struggle with empathy.'

A flutter of what might have been distress – irritation? – crossed her face, but it was quickly gone.

'I know I'm not quite right,' she said, frowning. 'But it never bothered you before.'

I nodded in agreement. My voice was sad when I said, 'No, it didn't.'

Chapter seventy-nine

Susie watched Nick shrink on himself. He looked dreadful. His skin was ashen and his normally thick shiny hair had turned lacklustre and dull. She didn't know how to lift him out of this hideous black mood. She wanted to take him by the hand and make his spirit glow, see him laugh again. She didn't like him like this, all miserable and grey, and although she knew it was her fault, she couldn't feel what others called guilt, or remorse.

What was the point?

She'd done her best to stop the truth from coming out, and she'd failed. She'd tried her hardest to do it without bloodshed, but in the end, that's what it took. And it had nearly worked. So very nearly had she got away with it, and then Mark bloody Felton turned up with a gun he'd found in Nick's glovebox, of all places. Given to him by his shit of a brother.

What she'd like to do to Rob when she got her hands on him. She couldn't believe he was still alive. She'd shot him through the neck, normally a fatal blow, and although she'd wanted to stop and shoot both David Gilder and Rob through the head to make sure they were dead, Barry Gilder and Nick had nearly reached the tree line and she knew if she didn't go after them straight away, she'd never find them. She'd told herself she would come back and finish the two men off. Once she'd dealt with DI Gilder and got her husband back.

She'd never wanted to hurt Nick. She knew she was different, but she'd softened her edges for him. She knew she could hurt him easily, so she was super careful, watching her words. She behaved as sensitively as she could to his feelings. She comforted him when he was hurt instead of telling him not to be a baby. She stroked his male ego until he purred. She mirrored him whenever she could.

Her first psychologist had taught her how to integrate into the world, how to hide among empaths without drawing attention to herself, and she'd done pretty well, learning to hold her tongue when people were being unbelievably stupid and swallowing any scathing comments before they erupted.

It was hard work, which was why she'd spend four nights a week in London, where she could be herself and snap and snarl at anyone she liked. But now everything had come crashing down and she was here, and he was there.

He said, 'You threatened Helen Flynn. She was only an HR flunky at the Mayfair Group. You terrified her.'

'Not personally,' Susie told him. 'I sent Ryan and Theo, two junior officers. They thought it was official because it involved the Saint. Same goes when they snatched your briefcase, and later when they picked me up in the Range Rover.'

She gave him a look of respect here, because she never thought in a million years he'd run after someone with a gun. Admiration plus, as far as she was concerned.

He said, 'Barry Gilder said the Range Rover belonged to Rob.'

'Yes,' she agreed. 'It's all about timing, you see. I knew you'd report the number plate. So I rang good old Barry when I thought he'd be expecting a call from the PNC – Police National Computer – and all I said was, "PNC here," and he said, "Great. The Range Rover." If he'd said anything else I could have made an excuse about ringing the wrong cop.'

'You bugged my car.'

'Yes.' She leaned forward, wanting, *willing* him to understand. 'It wasn't that I didn't trust you, my love, I was trying to *protect* us.'

'You lied about Rob working for MI5.' His voice was tight.

She tried not to roll her eyes. She knew he wanted answers but did he have to pick at every scab?

Chapter eighty

'It was a mistake,' Susie sighed. 'Boy, did it come back to haunt me. I have to be honest, I never thought I'd see anyone from the funeral again, and at the time, when you asked how I knew Rob, it seemed like a good excuse for my being there. Besides, it was fun too, to see you think of your brother in another light. Doing something you were proud of.' *I did you a favour* she wanted to say but she'd learned this wasn't the right remark to make to an empath so she kept quiet.

'And Mark Felton?' he asked. 'The older man I met in the café? Who was he?'

'An actor.'

Nick gave her one of his looks that meant, *go on*.

'I've used him a few times over the years,' she admitted. 'Kevin Parsons. He's reliable and believable–'

'He's played an MI5 officer before?' Nick looked appalled. 'He could go to jail.'

'He does it because he thinks it's a bit of fun.' She shook off Nick's concern, thinking about Kevin, how useful he'd been. He'd played her father a couple of times, an older brother. He'd also joined her at Rob's memorial as one of Rob's work colleagues – people would have thought it strange if she'd come on her own for someone she didn't know particularly well – and although Nick had barely glanced at Kevin back then, she'd still been relieved that he hadn't recognised him when she'd presented him as Mark Felton. Kevin had also pretended to be her doctor in the hospital, when her parents had flown over from New Zealand after her supposed mugging. She'd paid him extremely well and as far as she was concerned, neither of them had broken any law.

She leaned back, breathing deeply, hating the stale acrid air and longing for a cold salty breeze against her face, wetting her hair, the sound of the curlews coming from the mud flats. She may never get back to Bosham, but there were other seaside places to live in the world, like Australia. Her mind drifted a bit, wondering how hard it would be to learn to surf now she was in her thirties, but she brought it back with a snap when Nick asked her about her childhood. Just as she knew he would.

She tried to lay it out honestly, because she knew if she didn't do that and he caught her out again, it would definitely be the end of their relationship, but it was hard not to distort her story because telling lies came so naturally.

At one point, tears filled Nick's eyes but she couldn't think why. She'd told him about her father beating her before locking her in the cupboard beneath the stairs because she'd accidentally broken the pepper mill, a present from his grandmother, but it could have been any misdemeanour because he beat her a lot.

'I didn't mean to upset you,' she said sincerely.

'No, I don't suppose you did.'

He studied her for a long time. Her eyes drifted to the wall clock to see that they only had five more minutes. Time behaved differently in prison. Either it sped along at a great pace, or it dragged interminably, making her want to weep at the tedium, the monotony of it all.

'I've been reading up on sociopathy,' he said, surprising her.

'Oh?' She raised her eyebrows.

'Apparently you have a natural talent for duplicity.'

'Why do you think I became a spy?'

'You like money, power and control.'

Her eyes twinkled. 'Why do you think I chose little rich girl Susie?'

'You're charming, witty and charismatic, and–'

'Great in the sack.'

His mouth twitched and her spirit soared. He had almost smiled. It was the greatest gift he could have given her. She could build on that twitch of a smile, she thought. She could start making plans, forming strategies, tactics. Already her mind darted ahead, excitement igniting her nerve endings as brightly as fireworks.

'I've signed up to be studied,' she told him. 'It was the prison doctor's idea. Dr Verne knows how bored I get, so he's lining up loads of professionals to prod and poke me. We don't know enough about sociopathy yet but with so many of us around, it's time to tackle the issue. We're not all murderers and predators, you know, and now sociopaths can be identified with a brain scan, we need to understand the issue.

'Personally, I don't want to be tested one day and packed in a train the next, to be sent to a concentration camp and "cleansed". We're going to be the next witches if we're not careful. Hunted down and put away. I'd like to help prevent that.'

She leaned forward, wanting to take his hand but not daring to in case he withdrew it. She didn't want to take one step back, two steps forward. She wanted to be stepping forward *all the time.*

She said, 'Dr Verne's thinking I might have damage to my orbitofrontal cortex, and that maybe my front temporal lobe isn't working very well. So lots of scans, which will get me out of here from time to time. Give me a break.'

She glanced at the uniformed guard standing nearby, back against the wall. He caught her eye and she gave him her death stare. The one which scared the crap out of people. He immediately looked away.

'What will the tests do?' Nick asked.

She heard the subtext. She wasn't stupid. 'There's no treatment, if that's what you're asking. I can't be cured.'

The bell rang to signal the end of visiting time.

They both got to their feet.

'I'm sorry you're in here,' Nick said. He looked miserable.

'My own fault.' She shrugged. 'But it was a good ride while it lasted. It beat cleaning offices, I can tell you.'

His expression altered, indicating he'd just remembered something.

'What is it?' she asked.

'How did you get an induction interview? I would have thought the security services…' He trailed off. Gave a sigh. 'You lied.'

'Of course.' She gave him a cheerful smile.

For a second, the warmth in his eyes nearly flickered out, but then it steadied.

He smiled back.

'I should have guessed,' he said wryly. The smile remained. 'Because what else would a sociopath do?'

Chapter eighty-one

Fifteen months later

It was a beautiful May day when I went to see Hayley and Noah, Barry Gilder's family. Since it was so sunny, the May blossom hanging like great pink and white pom-poms from every tree, we agreed to meet in Hyde Park, at the Diana, Princess of Wales Memorial Fountain. I hadn't seen them since Christmas, and in that time Barry's son seemed to have grown at least six inches and taken on more of his father's looks. He had the same slate grey eyes and steady composure I remembered in his father, the same caution before he spoke.

'You get more like your dad every day,' I told him, which made him and his mum smile.

Kids of all ages had shucked off their shoes and were playing in the water fountain, chasing the water as it cascaded along the Cornish granite. Hayley held Noah's shoes as he went and played, quickly teaming up with a couple of boys who were playing tag over the bridges.

'How are you doing?' I asked her.

She considered my question, and then said, 'We're okay,' sounding surprised. I hadn't appreciated before how pretty she was, but the bruises of grief were fading, with the sun behind her, turning her auburn hair into bright copper and her eyes jewel green, I saw she was more than pretty. She was beautiful.

I wondered what she saw in return. I couldn't be termed beautiful in any sense of the word, but at least I'd stopped drinking. It had taken nearly a year until I'd finally started to get to grips with myself, my shock and grief, and although I wasn't the handsomest man in the world, I hoped I wasn't too embarrassing to look at. I'd showered, remembered to shave, and I was wearing a pair of faded jeans and the same sunglasses and shirt that Susie used to chuckle at, saying they made me look like a Mediterranean yachtsman.

Hayley said, 'The money came through not long ago. It's helped a lot. We might even go away on holiday next year. To Disneyland, if we can.'

She was talking about the money her father-in-law had tucked away. David Gilder hadn't spent a single penny the Saint had paid him, but put it in a savings account where it stayed untouched until he died. Being under the police radar, it was now Hayley's and Noah's. After what they'd been through, I thought they deserved every penny.

We fell into step along the Serpentine. Mothers and strollers, babies, a couple of picnic blankets on the grass with smooching young couples. Summer was on its way and for the first time since I could remember, my spirits lifted into a kind of optimism.

'What about you?' Hayley asked.

I'd tried going back to work for Ronja, but instead of being comforting, the old routine just seemed to intensify my anguish. It was Rob who suggested going into business together, something different until I got back on my feet again, and with some of Mum and Dad's money, some of mine, we bought Dennis's Boat Yard.

Rob had spent the last twelve years working in a boat builder's yard and with my experience in repairing the odd yacht, along with Dad's more extensive knowledge of the trade we made a pretty good team. Mum answered the phone and did the books, and as word got around, we got really busy.

I still hadn't given up my dream of being a comic book artist though, and had got back in touch with Top Dog Comics, who were reviewing the artwork I'd sent them. I wasn't holding my breath for a full-time artist's job, but as Rob kept telling me, you had to be in it, to win it.

'I'm pretty good, actually,' I said, hearing the same note of surprise I'd noticed in hers.

'And Susie?'

I knew she was talking about my Susie, and not the real Susie. The real Susie's family had held a memorial for their murdered daughter and although they'd invited me, genuinely sorry for me for what had happened, I hadn't been able to bear going. It would have been too weird. I'd seen Susie's parents Victor and Marjory when they'd flown over, and had found it disturbing, unsettling and extremely upsetting. I hadn't seen them again.

'I wouldn't know.'

Hayley gave me a sideways look. 'Well done you.'

It had taken a supreme amount of courage and fortitude, but twelve months earlier, and with the help of my therapist, I'd ended all contact between me and Susie. I never said a formal goodbye. It simply came to me one day, as I walked out of the visits centre, that I didn't have to go again. That I didn't have to talk to her again if I didn't want to.

I stopped all contact. Returned letters from her unopened. Changed my phone and email numbers. Moved house.

Going cold turkey felt the right thing to do. That way there was no confusion. I had to start learning how to live without her. Find myself again.

The first month was horrendous. I felt as though I was living at the bottom of a treacle jar, everything was such an effort, but gradually my mind cleared and for the first time, I saw our relationship with a more detached eye.

I saw how I'd become a fly in her web. How I'd lost my self-identity. How I'd swallow anything she told me thanks to her seasoning her words with endless praise about how understanding I was, how proud she was of me, how much she adored me. It took a while, but eventually I was able to stand back and see her for what she was: a charming, charismatic, fiercely intelligent woman whose motives were to manipulate and coerce, ruthlessly and without remorse.

When I started divorce proceedings, I expected Susie to do everything to try to reel me back in. I was ready for her to refuse to sign documents, to question everything, to beg, plead and threaten, demand to see me, but instead there was a deafening silence. Every document that needed signing was signed promptly and sent back by return. She didn't contest a single point.

'The decree nisi came through last week,' I told Hayley, lifting my face to the sun. 'I'm a single man again.'

Hayley gave my arm a squeeze. A couple of horses and riders trotted past, bits and stirrups jingling. The sun was warm on my shoulders and in my hair. We chatted about Noah's school, Hayley's working at the local surgery, and after we'd eaten an ice cream each, sitting on the grass, Hayley said it was time to go. 'See you anon,' I said. I kissed her on the cheek. Shook Noah by the hand.

I watched them walk away, glad they were doing okay. Glad I was doing okay too, and blissfully unaware of what waited for me just around the corner.

Chapter eighty-two

My new home, still in Bosham, was a detached period cottage built out of Sussex flint and brick, with roses climbing the walls and a view of the water. It had a conservatory, a garden shed and a swing seat, and best of all, a jetty at the bottom of the garden, where *Talisman* was moored. Normally I wouldn't have been able to afford such a stunning property, but with Susie not contesting my solicitor's bold request for half the value of her London apartment, I hadn't hesitated. I'd practically bolted away from my old cottage and all those memories of us, and the instant I walked into my new home, I felt something fundamental inside me unwind, and relax.

I was approaching my cottage and thinking about whether I'd join Rob for a pint in The Anchor Bleu later, when I took in the car sitting in my driveway. As I approached, a man climbed out, hefting something bulky, and walked to my front door. I was frowning, trying to recall what I might have ordered, when the man returned to his car and I saw him properly.

Fifties, spectacles, soft grey hair, paunchy jowls. Skin as pale as the underbelly of a fish.

A torrent of icy alarm ran down my spine.

It was Kevin Parsons. The actor who Susie had used to impersonate her father, her brother, whoever might be useful to her, culminating in his pretending to be Mark Felton, MI5 officer.

For a second I couldn't believe it. The police had tried to find Kevin Parsons without success, but here he was. On my fucking doorstep.

I rammed the throttle to the floor. My ancient BMW sprang forward but it was no match for his vehicle, which tore off with a throaty roar. When I caught a glimpse of the number plate, I knew I didn't stand a chance. It was Susie's super-beefed-up turbocharged Audi, but even though I knew it was fruitless, I gave chase. It didn't take long before he dwindled away from me into the distance but I kept going, only giving up when I came to the main road to Chichester and the Audi was nowhere to be seen.

I called the police, who made a report, and finally I turned for home, apprehension in my belly and fear in my heart. I considered calling Rob to meet me there, but I didn't want to endanger him. I parked on the road, not in my driveway, and walked cautiously to the bulky package on my doorstep.

Which wasn't a package at all.

It was a carry cot.

Inside which lay a sleeping baby.

A note was tucked in the edge of the blanket. *Nick.* Written in Susie's bold slanted handwriting.

My knees gave way. I sprawled on the ground. Mouth dry, pulse leaping, I reached for the note.

He's yours, she'd written. *One hundred per cent. But if you want to do a DNA test, just say the word. He's cute, but I'm afraid I make a crap mother. You'll be a brilliant dad. You'll teach him how to sail and how to be a good man. Just like you. x*

My fingers were tingling as I brought out my phone and dialled.

'Mum?' I had to clear my throat a couple of times after she answered. 'I've got some news for you and Dad. Are you sitting down?'

Lightning Source UK Ltd.
Milton Keynes UK
UKHW011238311220
376133UK00001B/128